One moment she _____ **peaceful and sce** _____ **Mountains and b** _____ **Brody was yanking her into the dirt and covering her body with his as a bullet hit the ground inches from where they were sitting. The dissonance was hard to compute.**

"Is it...a hunter?" she asked, hearing the tremble in her voice.

Brody shook his head. "Not unless they're hunting humans. They have a clear view that they're shooting at people, not animals."

"But why—" More shots rang out, cutting her off.

She flinched, and Brody hugged her tighter against him.

"Good question," he said when things grew quiet again. "If this were still Prohibition, I'd say we were close to stumbling across someone's moonshine."

Anya scoffed a humorless laugh. "Maybe it's something similar. An illegal crop?"

Brody puffed out a breath. "Who knows." He stretched to look out from their hiding place. "Look, we have to move," he said, his tone urgent. "We don't have enough cover here."

As if to prove his point, another bullet pocked the earth near her feet.

Dear Reader,

Summer is here! One of my favorite things to do on sunbaked days is to find a shady (or air-conditioned) spot to curl up with a good story with a happily-ever-after. If that is on your list of summer favorites, may I offer you this tale of adventure, danger and unexpected romance?

Return with me to idyllic Cameron Glen, the vacation retreat owned by the Cameron family, in the heart of the Western North Carolina mountains. When Brody Cameron lands in the emergency room after a freak accident, he meets beautiful ER nurse Anya Patel. Brody and Anya feel an immediate attraction, but Anya is already in a relationship. Their ships pass in the night...only to come crashing together again months later when they are both part of a search and rescue operation that goes horribly sideways. As Brody and Anya fight for their lives, they discover evidence of murder—and a deep love that promises a happy future together...if they can survive a serial killer.

Please enjoy Brody and Anya's story and have a wonderful summer!

Happy reading!

Beth Cornelison

CAMERON MOUNTAIN RESCUE

Beth Cornelison

HARLEQUIN
ROMANTIC
SUSPENSE

Recycling programs
for this product may
not exist in your area.

ISBN-13: 978-1-335-73839-4

Cameron Mountain Rescue

Copyright © 2023 by Beth Cornelison

For questions and comments about the quality of this book, please contact us at CustomerService@Harlequin.com.

Harlequin Enterprises ULC
22 Adelaide St. West, 41st Floor
Toronto, Ontario M5H 4E3, Canada
www.Harlequin.com

Printed in U.S.A.

Beth Cornelison began working in public relations before pursuing her love of writing romance. She has won numerous honors for her work, including a nomination for the RWA RITA® Award for *The Christmas Stranger*. She enjoys featuring her cats (or friends' pets) in her stories and always has another book in the pipeline! She currently lives in Louisiana with her husband, one son and three spoiled cats. Contact her via her website, bethcornelison.com.

Visit the Author Profile page at Harlequin.com for more titles.

For Jeffery and Kelly—I'm so glad you found each other!

Prologue

Sophie Bane stumbled through the weeds and encumbering scrub brush and licked her dry lips. Oh, Lord, she was thirsty. She'd kill for even a small sip of water.

Why hadn't she brought water with her? Why hadn't…

But she had. Hadn't she?

She reached in her knapsack and fumbled until she found her water bottle. She uncapped it and tipped it up. Nothing came out.

Her heart sank, and she sighed tiredly.

So tired…

So thirsty…

So confused.

She turned, glancing around her at the mountain scenery. It all seemed familiar. Was she walking in circles? Could she tell anything by the sun?

She squinted as she peered up at the bright sun. So

bright. She'd lost her sunglasses this morning when she had lost her footing and tumbled down that slope. Or was that yesterday?

Dehydrated. She'd heard people became confused when they got dehydrated. She should have brought water. She glanced down at the bottle in her hand and tipped it up to her mouth. Nothing. Right. Empty. She stashed it back in her shoulder sack and kept walking.

How far had she come? She'd intended to hike ten miles. The trail was easy enough, her sister had said. Good prep for the half marathon next month. If Gina could do a half marathon, she could too.

But this was no trail. She'd gotten lost. Then more lost. Was that a thing? More lost?

She should have brought more water. Who knew the sun could be so harsh in the mountains? That hiking was such thirsty work? It had been cold on the morning she'd set out. She'd worn a jacket. She shouldn't have needed more than one canteen. Until she got lost. Until everything got so confused.

Trees. She saw trees ahead of her and headed toward them, out of the sun. Maybe in the shade she could rest, get her thoughts straight and figure out which way to go.

In the blessed cool of the shade, she slumped to the ground, savoring the dampness of the moss. Moss…

Moss grew on the north side of trees. Hadn't she heard that once? That you could tell direction by…or was it west? Or…east? Tears pricked her eyes. God, she didn't know! Couldn't remember. She was so confused…

She dozed for a moment, then heard a noise that seemed out of place. Sitting up, she plucked leaves from her hair and glanced around her. Had she heard an animal? A bird or—

Her breath caught. Across a wide grassy field, she spotted a cabin of some sort. Inhabited by the look of it. She could make out a garden growing in the back and clothes drying on a line.

Water. Food. Directions. Maybe even transportation back to town!

"Thank you, thank you, thank you," she whispered to the sky. Shoving weakly to her feet, she hurried across the meadow and struggled up the step to the front door.

Her knock was answered by a middle-aged man whose graying hair made him look older than she guessed he was. And he stank of being unwashed. But she didn't care. She smiled at him and gasped, "Hi."

He glowered and in a gruff tone asked, "Who the hell are you? What do you want?"

"I…my name's Sophie, and I'm lost. I…could I please have some water?"

He pushed past her to step onto his porch and scan the meadow.."You alone?"

She nodded. "Yeah. My first mistake, huh?"

He eyed her up and down and grunted. "Yeah."

As she met his dark eyes, ice tripped up her spine, and the hair rose on her arms. Some primal internal voice in her brain shouted, *Run!*

She took a stumbling step backward, but the man's hand clamped around her wrist. He jerked hard, dragging her inside his cabin, and Sophie screamed.

"Go ahead," he said with a sneer. "Scream all you want. Nobody's around to hear."

Chapter 1

Seven months earlier

"I got one!"

Brody Cameron glanced toward his five-year-old niece, whose fishing pole was indeed bowed as she tugged on it. "Good girl! Reel it in nice and easy."

He set his own pole down on the massive trunk of a tree that had fallen into the river some years ago. While the oak's trunk was wide enough to walk on, sit on, fish from, the network of branches now extending into the water created a honey hole where fish could hide. "Need any help?"

"I can do it," Lexi assured him, still tugging hard.

When the silver flash of a fish breeched the water, revealing its size, Brody shifted his gaze further down the trunk to his brother Daryl. The splash of the fish had actually drawn the sixteen-year-old's attention away from his cell phone. How Daryl was texting his friends and fishing at the same time, Brody couldn't say.

"Hey, D, get the net. Looks like a decent-sized trout," Brody called as he moved closer to Lexi, despite the pixie's insistence she could land the fish alone.

Daryl, who'd been adopted by the Camerons when he was orphaned as a toddler, tucked his phone in his back pocket and retrieved the small fishing net as asked. Brody took the net and eased up beside Lexi, who was clearly struggling.

"Munchkin, you're doing a great job, but I don't want you to fall in the river." He set the net aside and put his arms around his niece, then his hands over her hands on the reel. "Give him some slack. Let him get tired."

"That's it, Lexi! Bring that bad boy in," Daryl said, taking his phone out again to record the event.

Brody and Lexi wrangled the trout closer, patiently reeling the fish in a little at a time. When their catch was close enough to haul in, Brody called to Daryl. "Net him, D."

Daryl moved toward the fishing net, but Lexi squawked, "No! I want to! It's my fish!"

Before he could stop her, Lexi ducked out from his arms, grabbed the net and lunged toward the fish flopping near the surface of the water. With five-year-old enthusiasm, Lexi flailed the long handle of the net toward the water…and lost her balance on the sloped tree trunk.

She squeaked as she plunged into the murky river. And went under.

"Lexi!" Brody shoved the fishing pole into Daryl's

hands and dropped to his haunches to grab his niece. But she didn't resurface.

The water was too muddy for him to see anything but the vague outline of Lexi's white shirt.

In a matter of seconds, his mood went from mild concern, irritation and amusement over his niece's tumble to full-out alarm.

"Where is she?" Daryl asked, his own curious tone edged with worry.

Wasting no time, Brody ripped off his shoes and jumped in the muddy water next to the spot where the five-year-old had disappeared.

As the cold water enveloped him, Brody searched the wavering brown depths and swam quickly to his niece. His pulse shot higher when he found her limp and unresponsive. He tried to lift her, push her to the surface, but her shorts were snagged on something. Groping semiblindly, he found the piece of wire that had snared Lexi, a loose piece of submerged hurricane fencing. Working quickly, he ripped the fabric free of the rusted wire and kicked hard to propel them both to the surface.

Daryl was lying on his stomach, hands outstretched, and grasped Lexi under her arms.

"Get her…on her side!" Brody called as he gasped for a breath. "She has to…cough up water."

After Daryl had Lexi stretched out on the tree trunk, he offered Brody a hand.

He waved off his brother's help and pointed at his niece. "Help her! Call 911."

Battling tree limbs, Brody attempted to hoist himself from the water before deciding he'd swim to the bank and climb out there.

As he swam, he could hear Lexi cough, retch and

whimper. Thank God! Daryl muttered encouragement to Lexi before Brody heard, "Yeah, um, my niece fell in the river. I think she's okay, but...uh, can't say exactly. Around the big bend by Hillier Farms."

Brody's feet found the squishy mud of the bank, and he dragged himself, weighed down by his sodden clothes, toward the steep bank. As he navigated the weeds, mud and trash along the edge of the water, he began to wish he still had his shoes. The submerged fence that had troubled Lexi extended all the way to the bank, twisted and torn, sharp ends poking everywhere. A tetanus nightmare waiting to happen. Not to mention the snakes that could be lurking in the tall grass.

Shoving those concerns aside, he cut a look over his shoulder to his brother and niece, who'd begun crying. "How is she? Is she bleeding anywhere?" He slogged his way through the mud, calling, "I'm coming, Lex! Don't cry, Munchkin!"

What happened next, Brody couldn't really say. It happened fast. In a blur. He lost traction in the mud and went down.

And the ragged-fencing nightmare caught him.

He even didn't feel it...at first. Then the shock of his fall morphed into assessment. In shallow water. A tangle of fencing. A stinging hand, sore wrist and...a thin metal rod piercing his upper thigh. Brody's gut swooped. His heart did a slow roll.

And the pain of that rod through his leg found him.

He loosed a roar of anguish, grabbing at his thigh. "Daryl, I—"

The fiery throbbing choked him, stole his breath.

"Brody?" Daryl called to him. "Are you all right?"

He gathered enough air in his lungs to rasp. "No."

He used one hand to assess his situation, feeling the protruding metal in his leg. *Hellfire.* He was skewered. Stuck like an insect pinned in a science exhibit.

Sloshing through the foot-deep water to him, Daryl appeared beside him, phone still to his ear. "My brother's hurt, too. I don't—"

Brody saw the moment Daryl noticed the rod through his leg, the blood coloring the water. His younger brother paled beneath his dark complexion. *"Holy..."* Daryl's throat worked as he swallowed, then he shouted in the phone. "Just send an ambulance! Hurry!"

Tossing the phone on the dry ground, Daryl waded into the water, quickly running into the problem of the submerged fence. He spewed a few bad words and looked for another way to reach Brody.

Teeth clenched, Brody struggled to control his breathing, stay conscious. Over the pounding beat of blood in his ears, he could still hear Lexi crying. He angled his head, looking for her.

The drenched girl was sitting on the tree trunk, watching. Clearly weak and wobbling. Terrified. She rose to unsteady knees and inched toward the shore.

Damn. He really didn't want his young niece to see the gruesome condition of his leg. The whole situation would scare her. "D," he said, fighting for the breath that pain squeezed from his lung, "get Lexi. Put her... in my truck."

"But you're—"

"Get Lexi!" he said, his tone sharper than he intended, but he was in no mood to argue with his brother. The arm he was braced on to keep his head above water slipped in the muddy riverbed. The sudden shift in his position jerked his leg and sent fresh paroxysms of pain shooting through him. Mindful of his niece watching, Brody bit his bottom lip to muffle the cry of pain. Swallowed the invectives he wanted to scream.

What to do? He drew a few deep breaths, hoping to calm his mind enough to focus on the problem at hand. As a volunteer fireman, he knew enough first aid to realize removing the thin metal spike was a bad idea. Especially in his thigh. Some rather important blood vessels were found in the upper leg. The fact that he was still alive now and hadn't bled out told him he hadn't severed his femoral artery. That was the good news. The bad news was he and Daryl had to find a way to get him out of the water and to the hospital without removing the fence debris that had turned him into a shish kebab.

Another angled glance showed him that his brother was carrying Lexi up the hill toward the truck on his back. "Daryl!"

His brother stopped, turned.

"I have…wire cutters in my…toolbox. Bring them back…with you." He prayed his teenaged brother, whose life outside of school revolved around video games and texting girls, knew the difference between wire cutters and hedge clippers.

Daryl nodded and continued up the wooded hill.

Brody closed his eyes, ground his back teeth so hard his jaw ached. He tried not to think of the bacteria and other filth seeping into the open wound on his leg or how this injury would set him back at work. He was the main workman in his landscaping business, and they were in the peak summer season. And the volunteer fire department had been hopping lately with brush fires, thanks to dry conditions and summer lightning.

When he clenched his fists, smelly mud and rotten

vegetation from the river oozed through his fingers. Blood loss and pain were dragging at him. Minutes passed—or seconds—he couldn't be sure, but the fire in his leg, the heat of the sun became living things chewing him, crushing him, weakening him…

"Brody!"

The panic in Daryl's voice was clear, and Brody struggled to open his eyes again. He wanted to give in to the oblivion.

He opened his eyes, his lids fluttering as he blinked against the bright sun.

His brother's face appeared above him, frowning. "Geez, you scared me. I thought you were dead!"

"Lexi—" Brody said, or at least he thought he did.

Apparently, it was more of a moan, because Daryl said, "Easy, Brod. I'm gonna get you out."

Daryl started tugging on him, and Brody could soon tell his brother was trying to lift him off the metal rod. He found Daryl's wrist, closed his fingers around it. "Stop. Gotta cut. Below. Wire stays in…til hospital…" He squinted at his brother, searching his face for understanding. "Got wire cutters?"

His brother held up the tool he'd retrieved.

Brody twitched a pained smile. "Bingo."

As Daryl set to work, fumbling under Brody's leg to find and snip the offending fence scrap, the jostling shot stinging bolts up every nerve. Even his hair follicles hurt. Brody groaned, cursed a blue streak, gritted his teeth.

And passed out.

Brody roused again as he was jostled on a stretcher and loaded into the back of an ambulance. He fought off the mental cobwebs, an internal sense of urgency nudging him. When he tried to sit up, he found his chest strapped to the gurney. "No..."

What was nagging him?

A gentle hand came down on his shoulder. "Easy, friend. We're taking you to the hospital now."

He angled his head to look up at the familiar face. Mark what's-his-name. He'd met the EMT a few times both through calls for the Valley Haven VFD and through mutual friends. Mark turned his attention to ripping open sterile packets of needles and swabs.

The nagging urgency prodded Brody again—hard—even as his movement caused excruciating pain to streak from his leg up his back. "I...have to..."

He heard voices at the open end of the ambulance bay. Daryl. An EMT. A small whimper.

"Lexi!" Brody rasped as the urgency gelled. He struggled again to sit up.

Mark's hand returned. "The girl is fine. Mostly. A little shock, but she's coming with us."

Suiting Mark's claim to action, Daryl climbed in the ambulance with Lexi, who had a blanket around her shoulders.

"Sorry, dude. No room for you. You'll have to meet us at the ER," Mark told Daryl.

"But—" his brother started.

"D, drive my...truck."

His brother's eyes widened with excitement. "Really?"

"And call Emma...to meet us."

Daryl nodded. "I did. Jake too."

"Mommy..." Lexi cried, hearing her mother's name.

His brother's face disappeared as the patient bay door was closed, and Brody sank back into the pain.

The next face he saw, as he roused again in the hospital, was far more appealing to him than his brother's. The swarthy, fine-boned face smiled at him as he blinked the room into focus.

"Ah, blue eyes," the South Asian nurse with a thick black braid said. "I had been betting on hazel eyes." She stared straight into his eyes now, a slight pucker between her sculpted black brows as she shone a bright penlight at him. "Pupil reaction is normal. That's good. Can you tell me your name?"

"Brody Cameron."

"Birth date?"

He gave her the information she needed and swallowed a bout of nausea as the pain in his leg throbbed. He reached for his leg. The rod was still there. But his muddy jeans were gone. He had a sheet over him, but... He shifted a self-conscious glance to the attractive nurse again. Had she been the one to cut away his jeans? Clean the river mud from his thigh?

"We'll get that thing out soon. I promise," she said. "But we need images first to see what damage was done internally."

Brody grunted his understanding. Closed his eyes and clenched his teeth against the stinging of the wound.

"From one low to ten high, how would you rate your pain level?"

Brody took a moment to assess. "Eleven. Where's Lexi? Is she...okay?"

"The little girl that came in with you is fine, with her parents and enjoying a milkshake. We're keeping her a little while for observation, just to be sure."

"Thank God." Relief surged through him, followed

by guilt. He'd promised Emma he'd take care of Lexi…
"Ow!" He flinched as the attractive nurse lifted his hand
to examine the cuts and a bolt of pain shot from his wrist.

She stilled. "What ow? Where ow?"

"Think I sprained my wrist when I landed."

"Hmm." She made a note on a clipboard. "Guess
that'll need to be x-rayed." She set the clipboard aside
and took a small vial from the tray at his bedside. "This
will make you feel much better. Okay?"

As she injected the pain medication into his IV shunt,
he narrowed his gaze on her hospital ID, clipped to the
chest pocket of her scrubs. *Anya Patel.*

"Anya," he said aloud as a warm fuzziness washed
through him. He could feel the tension in his body melt,
the pain subside.

"Yeah, Blue Eyes?"

"Hmm?"

"You said my name. Did you need to tell me something?"

Brody swam through the fog now settling over him.
Bliss. The relief from the pain was bliss. "Your name's
Anya."

She flashed a crooked smile. "Yeah."

"It's pretty. Like you."

Her smile brightened as she began cleaning the cuts
on his hand. "Thank you."

Someone entered the room. "Radiology is ready for
him."

Brody's bed was adjusted and rolled toward the hallway.

"Anya Patel…" he said, his head swimming muzz-
ily. "Will you marry me?"

She chuckled and squeezed the toes of his good leg.
"Sorry, Blue Eyes. I have a boyfriend."

* * *

Anya chuckled to herself as the handsome, sandy-blond patient was rolled away for his CT scan. She'd heard all kinds of things muttered under the influence of morphine, but this was her first marriage proposal. If not for Mark, she might have followed up on Blue Eyes' flirting. He was devilishly good-looking. Despite his obvious pain, he'd been charming…and concerned for his niece. Both won him points in her book.

She headed back into the room next door, where a pretty brunette glanced up from her daughter's bedside. "How is Brody? Can I see him?"

"He just went back for a CT scan and X-rays. The doctor needs to know exactly what damage the wire caused before we can remove it. He should be in surgery within the hour, though." She stepped over to the little girl and cocked her head to the side as she made a general assessment of the little girl's condition and checked the monitor showing her vital signs. Everything looked good. Her pulse and blood pressure much improved from when she came in. "Miss Lexi, I think you're almost ready to go home. I'll have the doctor sign off and get your discharge in the works. Sound good?"

Lexi slurped the last of her milkshake and nodded. With a frown she added, "My fish got away."

Anya frowned her confusion. "What fish?"

"She says she was trying to net a big fish she'd caught when she fell in the river. Brody saved her," Lexi's mother said. "According to Daryl, my other brother who was there, Brody was wading out of the water when his…" She glanced at Lexi and hesitated, clearly choosing her words carefully, "*accident* happened."

Anya nodded. "I see."

"Uncle Brody's my hero!" Lexi said with a grin. Then her expression dimmed. "Is he gonna be okay?"

Anya winked. "I'll make sure of it. I promise!"

So her proposal came from a man of incredible blue-eyes, a sense of humor *and* heroic deeds? Brody Cameron really would make *someone* a good fiancé. Just not her.

"Sprained wrist, puncture wound through your leg, weeks of physical therapy… So what does this mean for work? For the Christmas trees?" Brody's middle sister, Cait, asked that evening in his hospital room.

"The Christmas trees should be fine until I'm back on my feet," Brody said, referring to the Fraser and Douglas firs his family raised under his supervision. "I've showed Eric what to do for the trees in the coming months and the other landscaping needs around Cameron Glen, and I can hire someone to help him."

"And I thank you for giving my son gainful employment this summer before he starts college," Cait's husband, Matt, said. "So how long will you be out of commission?"

Brody shrugged. "You know doctors don't like to be pinned down to specific time frames. When I asked, I got, 'Everyone heals at their own pace' and 'if we manage to avoid infection, it will depend on how your physical therapy progresses.'"

Matt gave a knowing grunt. "I heard that one."

Brody gave his brother-in-law an awkward grin. Matt had lost his leg from the knee down in a military career-ending bombing overseas. "I guess I sound kinda whiny to you, considering what you dealt with, huh?"

Matt shook his head. "Not at all. It's not a contest where the most serious injury wins. You've had a legit setback with this." He waved his hand toward Brody's now-bandaged leg. "You're allowed to gripe…for a day or two. Then you put it in perspective. You focus on healing, keeping a positive attitude and getting your life back on track."

"Well said!" a female voice said from the door.

Brody craned his neck to see who was coming in. He couldn't deny the buzz of pleasure when the attractive nurse from the ER stepped into view.

"Am I interrupting?" Anya asked.

Brody hit the button that raised the head of the bed so he could sit up straighter. "Not at all. What brings you by?"

"My shift just ended, and I wanted to check in on my could-have-been fiancé before I went home." She flashed a smile, her teeth white against her mocha-toned skin and her dark eyes bright with teasing.

"Fiancé?" Cait asked, confusion knitting her brow. "What?"

Brody felt the heat of embarrassment prickle his scalp. "So I didn't dream that? I really proposed to you?"

Matt laughed. "Oh, I want to hear this story!"

Anya chuckled and waved them off. "He hadn't had the painkiller in him for two minutes before he asked me to marry him. I knew it was the morphine talking, but I was still flattered."

Brody met his sister's crooked grin with a scowl. He'd never hear the end of this. His doped-up proposal would be rehashed at family gatherings from now until the end of time.

"I didn't mean it…of course," he fumbled.

Anya clapped a hand to her chest. "What? You don't mean that! Don't take this from me!"

She seemed so truly disappointed that Brody back-pedaled. "What I mean is, I wanted to ask you out." He realized that even asking someone on a date after knowing them for so few minutes, under such unusual circumstances could still be deemed odd and rash. "It's just… I thought you were pretty."

"Thought?" Cait asked, clearly amused by his awkward explanation.

"Think. I…you are very attractive…and—"

Matt folded his arms over his chest and settled back in the chair by Brody's bedside. "Aw, he's tongue-tied. This is entertaining."

"Y'all shut up. I'm still on painkillers. I…" He scowled, feeling himself flush.

Anya chuckled quietly and stepped closer to his bedside. "All I'm saying is a girl doesn't get marriage proposals from charming heroes every day. I thought it was sweet."

"Hero?" The term made him itchy.

"Absolutely. You saved your niece from drowning at your own peril." Anya tipped her head and lifted her eyebrows as if her description of events said everything.

Brody knew better. If he'd kept Lexi safer, if he'd not slipped in the mud, if he'd done any number of things differently…

He shrugged. "Whatever."

"Well, just the same, if I weren't five months into a relationship already, I probably would have accepted…" She paused dramatically and lifted the corner of her mouth. "A date." Her mood shifted as she examined his

IV stand to read the labels of the bags hanging there. "So they're keeping you to administer IV antibiotics, huh?"

"Yep. God knows what was in that river water or on that rusty wire. I got the feeling my doctor was excited to see what his cultures might grow."

"Please tell me they gave you a tetanus shot," Cait said.

Anya glanced at her. "Oh, yes. Did it myself in the ER." A jangling tone sounded from Anya's pocket, and she pulled out her phone to check the screen. "Oops. Sorry, but I should take this call. Feel better fast, Blue Eyes. Okay?"

"Yeah." Brody watched Anya leave, and a strange feeling tripped through him that the one person who could make him feel better had just stepped out of his room. And his life.

Chapter 2

Seven months later

In the months following his release from the hospital, Brody's leg healed fully and grew strong again with physical therapy and exercise. How could it not heal? With three sisters, his mother and grandmother all doting on him and overseeing his recovery, his leg had no choice but to heal. The Cameron females were a force to be reckoned with. Even Daryl added his voice to the encouragement and nagging to keep up with his physical therapy exercises. And his brothers-in-law, Matt and Jake, were more than willing to push and encourage him at the gym and on therapeutic evening runs to rehabilitate the leg muscles.

Not that Brody would have had it any other way. A full and fast recovery was the only acceptable option for him. His landscaping business, the Christmas tree farm, his volunteer work with the local fire department and search and rescue team all required him to be in top physical form. So as winter melted into spring in Valley Haven, Brody was ready to get bedding plants in the ground for his clients, remove dead shrubs at the local bank and replace them with sod and young crape myrtles, and return to the roster for the Valley Haven VFD.

"You're willing to take a test of your physical capabilities to prove you're all healed?" Jerry Romano, his commander with the volunteer fire department, asked on a Monday morning in late March. Jerry eyed him from behind his desk at the local high school where he was principal.

"What kind of test?" Brody asked.

"The training course at the firehouse. The ropes course at the park. You pick. I just need a demonstration that you're up to speed."

Brody gave a nod. "Name the time. I'm eager to get back at it."

"Good. How about tomorrow at six p.m.? Firehouse," Jerry asked.

"How about tonight at six?"

Jerry chuckled as he stood to shake Brody's hand. "You are ready to get back. Fine. Tonight it is."

Brody left Jerry's office with a spring in his step. As he passed through the front office, he heard a familiar voice say, "It's just awful. She's the third to disappear in the last two years."

He spotted his older sister, Emma, at the counter, bent over a copy of the morning newspaper.

When the principal's office door closed with a loud clunk, the receptionist, the school nurse and the office administrator all glanced his way and greeted Brody with a chorus of "Hello, handsome."

He flashed the women, none younger than fifty, a charming grin. "Hello, lovely ladies. Emma."

Emma sent him a puzzled glance. "What are you doing here?"

"I could ask the same of you," he countered, giving her a side hug as he turned his attention to the newspaper that held Emma's attention.

"At the end of this class period, I'm meeting with Ms. Busby ahead of the assembly on Friday about personal safety for teens and sex trafficking awareness."

Brody nodded. Emma and Jake had been the founders and key facilitators of the safety program at the high school in the wake of their older daughter Fenn's kidnapping last spring. Thankfully, Fenn had been recovered safely, and Emma's mission was to ensure that no other teenaged girls in their town were kidnapped.

"I was just checking in with Jerry. I'm starting back with the fire department." He motioned to the headline that read "Searchers find no sign of missing hiker." "How long has this hiker been missing?"

"Three days now. She just vanished. She and her boyfriend were camping near one of the popular trails north of town. Her boyfriend says she went for a morning walk while he slept in, and she never came back."

Brody grunted. "Is he a suspect?"

"He hasn't been held by the police, so I don't think so." Emma exhaled heavily, and Brody gave her another hug. Having gone through the trauma of a missing and endangered daughter, Emma was especially sensitive to similar cases in the area.

"They'll find her, Em," he said, trying to boost her morale.

"Will they?" Emma gave him a worried look. "They never found the two that went missing last year in the same area."

Brody opened his mouth. Closed it. He had no answer. Instead, he gave his sister a warm embrace and whispered, "We can pray they will."

The loud clang of the school bell reverberated through the office and halls, sending a swarm of students flowing into the corridors from every classroom door. Brody spotted Daryl at his locker with a couple of his friends and backed out of his hug with Emma. "There's D. I'm gonna catch him and say hi before I head back to Cameron Glen. I'm planting Fraser seedlings today. Good luck with your assembly."

"Thanks. Love you, Brod," Emma said. In the last year, his sister never missed the chance to tell her family she loved them. Another change since the trauma of Fenn's kidnapping. Emma—his whole family, really—had learned not to take any moment, any person for granted.

He winked at Emma. "Back atcha, sis."

Stepping out to the hall and winding his way upstream in the flow of young bodies rushing to their next class, Brody approached Daryl from behind, unseen. Grabbed him in a bear hug with a loud, "Aurgh!"

Daryl jumped. His friends laughed.

Shooting a glower over his shoulder, Daryl shook Brody off. "Hey, don't do that. Not cool."

"What? I can't even hug my own brother?"

"Not in public. And especially not at school. Why

are you even here?" Daryl closed his locker and hiked his backpack higher on his shoulder.

"What? I need a reason beyond embarrassing you?"

His brother rolled his eyes. "Whatever. I gotta go. See ya."

Rather than say the words and embarrass Daryl further, Brody formed the "love you" hand sign and nodded to D.

Daryl arched an eyebrow in acknowledgment, and as he turned to walk away, made the same hand sign behind his back, out of his friends' line of sight. Brody chuckled as he headed out to his truck. He remembered being a teenager, wanting to impress his friends and girls, and being easily humiliated by adults in his family.

Okay, he still liked to impress his friends and women, but at least he had a better, more mature perspective.

Later that day, Brody wrapped up his seedling work after several hours on a sunny hillside at Cameron Glen, his family's one-hundred-and-fifty-acre property that included several Cameron family homes, the Christmas tree farm and ten rental cabins. He left one of his employees to prepare the remaining seedlings for planting tomorrow and headed home for a quick shower, even though he knew he'd be getting sweaty again for his test with Jerry. While at home, he grabbed a protein bar and bottle of water and made it to the firehouse with ten minutes to spare. When he passed all the physical challenges with flying colors, Jerry whistled his admiration and shook Brody's hands in admiration. "I can have you back in the rotation this weekend. Work for you?"

"Sounds good."

Jerry hitched his head toward the street. "Come on. I'll buy dinner at Eddie's."

Brody rubbed his stomach, his mouth watering at the thought of a thick hamburger and cold beer at the local bar and grill. "You're on. I'm famished."

He followed Jerry to Eddie's Grill, and as they stepped inside the dimly lit restaurant, the men scanned the tables looking for an open seat.

"Back there, by the window?" Jerry said, casually pointing out an empty booth.

"Lead on." Brody motioned for his boss to precede him.

"Harris and Baughman are on their way to join us."

Brody almost missed Jerry's comment. His gaze had snagged on a table of women in scrubs, laughing and toasting boisterously. One woman in particular made his pulse stumble and his memory hiccup. He slowed, searching his brain for the reason this woman, a beautiful Indian woman with long, thick hair past her shoulders and a heart-stopping smile, triggered this sense of déjà vu.

As if feeling his attention, the woman raised her mocha gaze, and her eyes locked with his. Her expression shifted from the jubilance she'd been sharing with her friends, to intrigue then recognition. Her smile bloomed again. For him. And it clicked. The ER nurse who'd been on duty last summer when he'd skewered his leg at the river.

Warmth and gratitude flowed through him, and he stepped over to the table with a smile of his own for the dark-eyed beauty. "Well, hey there."

He racked his brain for her name but drew a blank.

He glanced at her name badge, but it was flipped backward, her name hidden—dang it!

"Blue Eyes! How are you? How's the leg?" she asked.

He patted it. "Good as new. Been back at work for a few months, and I'm even returning to the rotation with the volunteer fire department this weekend."

"Excellent! I'm so glad."

"Listen, I'm glad I ran into you. I wanted to thank you for everything you did that day I came in the ER. You were the epitome of professionalism and skill but more than that. Your kindness and warmth really made a difference when I was at my worst."

The nurses sitting with her exchanged knowing glances, and she—geez, he wished he could remember her name!—flashed an embarrassed grin. "Thanks. Just doing my job."

"Maybe. But I wanted you to know how much I appreciated your care that day. You were…great." He turned his focus to the other scrubs-clad women at her table and motioned to them, as well. "In fact, thank you *all* for the work you do. I know recent years have been exceptionally trying and stressful for healthcare providers, and as one who received such meaningful attention and care when I needed it, I want you to know you're appreciated."

A chorus of grateful responses answered him as he returned his gaze to the ER nurse. "In fact, what are you drinking? I'm buying the next round for your table." He glanced at the table to try to determine what the women had been toasting with. He saw a beer, a margarita, a highball glass…

"Oh, that's kind of you, but we're about to leave, and

we're probably at our limit to safely drive," his lovely ER nurse said.

Disappointment stabbed him until he spied the table's bill lying next to one of the empty plates. He grabbed it. "Then I'm picking up your tab. As a thank you to all of you ladies."

His offer brought a round of demurrals, thank yous and flattery, all of which he dismissed with, "My pleasure. Y'all have a nice night."

His nurse stood and leaned toward him to give him a chaste kiss on his cheek. "That's kind of you."

The sweet scent of coconut enveloped him over the odors of grilled meat and beer that perfumed the restaurant. The brush of her long hair on his arm sent a tantalizing skittering sensation through him. A flash of desire flowed through Brody, and his breath caught.

As she bent to take her seat again, her name badge dangled, turned. *Anya Patel.*

Bingo.

He gave her a final smile and nod as he left the table. "Have a good evening, ladies. Anya."

"No fair!" Christy complained as Mr. Tall, Blond and Handsome strode away from their table. "You get gorgeous young guys with hearts of gold, and I get warty old men with diarrhea and groping hands."

Anya laughed. "I've had my share of warty old men, diarrhea and groping hands. Trust me. Blue Eyes there was just a lucky break in a blur of gore and grief."

"So…what do you know about your good-looking patient, besides that he's a charmer and gorgeous and generous?" Holly asked.

Anya furrowed her brow trying to remember. She

couldn't even come up with his name. Not surprising, considering how many patients came and went through the ER every day. But Blue Eyes had stuck in her memory…sort of. Because of his handsome face, his heroics saving his niece…and his drug-induced proposal. Blue Eyes would likely never know what that throwaway line, spoken under the influence of painkillers meant to her. Especially now, in light of how things ended with Mark.

Anya cut a glance to the corner booth where Blue Eyes had joined another man, and her heart gave a little patter. As with most of her patients, she'd likely never see Blue Eyes again. But she'd cherish the memory of the day he'd come through her ER and unwittingly given her a gift that she'd treasure for years to come.

Being a volunteer department, the Valley Haven firemen didn't spend the hours they were on duty at the firehouse. The volunteers kept up with training, maintained the trucks and other equipment and checked in regularly with the chief, but they were free to go about their lives as usual until called. They were required to stay in town while on duty, keep their schedules clear of conflicting activities and wear their pagers at all times.

Brody was at his parents' house having Sunday lunch with the whole Cameron clan when his pager vibrated on his hip. A mix of eager anticipation for the thrill of firefighting and disappointment for the interruption to his family meal hit him at the same time.

"Uh, I've gotta go," he said, removing the device in order to shut off the buzzing alarm.

His mother met his gaze across the table, spread with more food than one family could eat at one time. "A fire call?"

"Maybe. Could be any number of things. We'll see." He wiped his mouth and scooted his chair back.

"Do be careful, *a bhobain*," his grandmother said, using the Scots Gaelic endearment for "my darling" but also "rascal," which he'd heard frequently from her in both contexts growing up.

"Always am, Nanna."

"I'll save a plate for you that you can have tonight," his mother promised, her eyes saying, *So please come home safely!*

He blew the worried women a kiss and patted Daryl on the shoulder as he exited the dining room. "Save me a piece of that cake, dude."

"Maybe," Daryl said, his tone droll.

Climbing into his truck, Brody took a cleansing breath, mentally shifting into work mode. He drove quickly to the firehouse where the other volunteers were already piling into four-wheel drive vehicles and the fire department's Jeep. The volunteers didn't seem to be in a big hurry, and no one was in bunker gear.

"So…not a fire?" he said to Jerry as he greeted him.

"Search and rescue. Someone found the missing hiker's backpack a few miles from where she disappeared. We're supporting local SAR teams for a full-scale search of the area." Jerry tilted his head and gave Brody a measuring look. "That leg of yours up to a hike in the mountains? There'll be a good bit of climbing, rough terrain."

Brody returned a nod. "I'm good to go."

"Let's load up then. We're meeting the rest of the search team at the foot of the nearest trail to where she was spotted and initiating the grid search from there."

Brody piled into the Jeep with his fellow volunteer

firefighters, who'd also been trained in search and rescue. The other men greeted him with handshakes, fist bumps and jokes about being a rotisserie chicken as they welcomed him back into the fold. Thirty minutes later, they'd reached the meeting place where a dozen or so other men and women, decked out in hiking gear, two-way radios and area maps awaited them.

As Brody climbed out of the Jeep and scanned the faces around him, smiling at old acquaintances from previous searches, a newly familiar voice reached him from behind. "Blue Eyes?"

He turned and spotted Anya grinning at him from a cluster of searchers unloading medical supplies. Her thick black hair was hung in a single braid down her back, the way it had the day they first met in the ER, and she was garbed in khaki cargo pants, hiking boots and a long-sleeved plaid shirt over a T-shirt. His spirits lifted at the sight of her, his pulse ticking faster, but he didn't stop to analyze why he was so pleased to see her. He grinned widely as he crossed the distance to her. "Why if it isn't my favorite ER nurse. You're going out on the search today?"

She lifted her arms from her sides and gave a little shrug. "I am. My first one." She aimed her thumb behind her. "My friend Jenny has done this for years and asked me if I wanted to be part of the team. She said having people with medical training on the searches is always helpful."

Brody nodded. "It is. First search, huh?"

Her eyes widened as if intimidated by the thought. "Yeah. As in, I only completed the training a couple weeks ago."

"Stick with me. I'll help you out," he said, then realized how it sounded and added, "I mean, I'm sure you'll be fine. And…anyone out here will be glad to help you if—"

Anya laughed and touched his shoulder. "I feel like you should be beeping now, with the way you're backing off your offer. You don't want to partner with me on the search?"

"No! I mean, sure! I'd love to partner with you. Although…we don't so much partner as walk a grid—" Brody stopped himself, embarrassed at how rattled he sounded. He took a deep breath and squared his shoulders. "But you knew that."

She chuckled. "I did."

"Everyone circle up! Let's get started!" Jerry called through a bullhorn.

As Brody and Anya made their way closer to the rest of the searcher group for instructions, she gave him an apologetic look. "I'm afraid if you don't want me to call you Blue Eyes all day, you're going to have to remind me of your name. I've seen a lot of patients come through my exam room since last summer and name retention is not my strong point."

He nodded. "Of course. Brody Cameron. And you're Anya?"

"Wow! Very good. How'd you—"

He flashed a crooked smile. "I cheated. I read it off your name tag at Eddie's earlier this week."

"Ah." She wagged a finger at him. "Right."

From the bullhorn, Jerry began giving general greetings and directions. "It's already almost two o'clock, so we only have about five and half hours of daylight. We'll need to be back here by sunset. I don't want anyone out on the mountain after dark. One lost hiker is quite enough. We don't need lost searchers, too."

Jerry then directed the assignment of two-way radios. "Thanks to budget constraints, we only have ten radios. That should be enough for every other person on the line to have one. Command will be on channel three. Everyone else on channel one. The missing woman's name is Sophie Bane. If you find anything, report to your squad leader. All right, let's head out."

As the searchers formed a single file line, spaced about six feet apart, Brody received a radio, shifted his backpack of supplies to his back and took his place. Anya joined the formation next to him.

Conversation was frowned upon as a distraction. Not only were searchers expected to pay full attention to the ground they were covering for signs of the missing hiker, but volunteers needed to be able to hear each other and their radios should anything be found. Just the same, Brody and Anya found ways through hand signals and facial expressions to communicate brief messages.

Thumbs-up—You're doing a great job.

Tongue out panting—I'm getting hot.

Canteen held up—Want some of my water?

A wave and head shake—No, thanks.

Raising her canteen—I have plenty.

Tapping his wrist with furrowed brow—How long have we been at this?

Lifting two fingers—Two hours.

Brody rubbed his leg, and Anya noticed. Frowned. Pointed at his thigh—You okay?

He shrugged. Nodded—I'm fine.

Mid-afternoon, a whistle blew and radios crackled with Jerry's voice. "Let's take a break, folks. Rest.

Drink up. Stay hydrated. Have a snack, and we'll get started again in about ten minutes."

Brody stuck a small flag in the ground to mark where he'd left off and strolled over to the large rock Anya had found to sit on. He joined her and dug in the pocket of his backpack for an energy bar. He broke off half and offered it to her. "Wanna share?"

"Thanks, but I brought—" she dug in her cargo pants leg pocket and extracted a granola bar, "—this."

He tapped his energy bar to her granola snack. "Cheers."

"Couldn't ask for a prettier day to do this," Anya said, casting her gaze to the cloudless sky. A light breeze ruffled a few loose strands of her hair near her ears, and Brody was struck again by how beautiful she was. Her thin, straight nose; oval face; fine bone structure.

She caught him staring. "What?"

He shook his head. "Nothing. Sorry." He glanced at the sky. "Yeah. Beautiful day."

"If I remember correctly, you have a big family. I recall several siblings in the ER and later in your room. Right?" Anya said.

"Yep. Three sisters and one broth—"

A strange cracking sound interrupted Brody. He frowned as he glanced in the direction the sound had come, just as another loud pop rent the air. Brody tensed, sitting taller and looking around for the source of the noise. Tree branch breaking? Fireworks?

"What the hell?" another searcher shouted. "That sounds like—"

Another crack. The ground near Brody's feet exploded, sending dirt and pebbles flying.

Without pausing to overthink the oddity of what

was happening, Brody grabbed Anya and yanked her to the dirt behind the rock where they'd been sitting, hip to hip.

"What's happening?" Anya asked, her voice vibrating with fear and confusion.

From behind the cover of the granite boulder, he glanced at the grass where the dirt had erupted. Something metallic reflected the sunlight. Brody blinked and his gut swooped.

A rifle bullet.

Jerry shouted through the radios, "Gunfire! Take cover!"

Chapter 3

*G*unfire?

Anya struggled to process the truth as the other searchers screamed and scattered in different directions.

One moment she was enjoying the peaceful and scenic view of the Smoky Mountains and blue sky, the next, Brody was yanking her into the dirt and covering her body with his as a bullet hit the ground inches from where they were sitting. The dissonance was hard to compute.

"Is it…a hunter?" she asked, hearing the tremble in her voice.

Brody shook his head. "Not unless they're hunting humans. They have a clear view that they're shooting at people, not animals."

"But why…?" More shots rang out, cutting her off.

She flinched, and Brody hugged her tighter against him.

"Good question," he said when things grew quiet

again. "If this were still Prohibition, I'd say we were close to stumbling across someone's moonshine."

Anya scoffed a humorless laugh. "Maybe it's something similar. An illegal crop?"

Brody puffed out a breath. "Who knows." He stretched to look out from their hiding place. "Look, we have to move," he said, his tone urgent. "We don't have enough cover here."

As if to prove his point, another bullet pocked the earth near her feet. She yelped and drew her knees closer to her chest, which only meant her tush was sticking farther out from the protection of the barrel-size rock the two of them huddled behind.

Brody levered up to cast his gaze around the meadow where they'd been resting. "It'd be nice to know where the shooter is first."

Anya peeked around the side of the granite lump. The hill they'd been climbing slowly as they searched crested in about one hundred yards. From the top of that crest, she thought she saw movement. Something dark. Then a flash.

Crack!

One of the searchers, running for cover behind a large evergreen tree stumbled, fell. The man beside him turned, grabbed him under the arms and dragged him out of sight, behind the evergreen.

"Oh, my God," she muttered on a quavering exhale. "That man was hit." Training kicked in, needling her. "Brody, I have to go help him. He's hurt."

When she tried to rise, Brody put a hand around her wrist, stopping her. "Hang on. You won't do him any good if you get shot getting to him."

"But I—"

"Let me think." He pressed his mouth in a firm line, his heavenly blue eyes growing hard and determined. "We have to time this right."

As she studied the set of his square jaw, felt the heat of his body close to hers, Anya acknowledged how grateful she was that Brody was with her. She felt safer—safe being relative at the moment—with him beside her.

More shots rang out as the other searchers bolted hither and thither. Brody moved to a crouch. "Get ready."

With his hand under her elbow to help her change positions, Anya rose to a squat, her heart thumped like a wild rabbit in her chest, the beat loud in her ears. Brody laced his fingers with hers.

"When I say 'go,' run like hell for that spruce tree where the downed man is. Okay?"

She bobbed her head. "Right."

Anya held her breath while Brody sized up the situation, waiting for the right moment. When shots rang out again, sending up a spray of dirt, grass and stones farther down the hillside, Brody jerked her hand and barked, "Go!"

He hauled her along behind him, his own pace surprisingly fast on the uneven and steep terrain. She stumbled a couple times but stayed upright until they collapsed together behind the spruce where three other searchers, including the injured man, were already huddled.

A man Anya knew as Tim, another searcher with her team, held his hands over the man's wound, trying to stem the bleeding. Tim was whey-faced and wide-eyed. "You're a nurse, aren't you?"

She gasped for air, still winded from her sprint, and fought her shirt from her shoulders. "Yes."

"Please, do something for him! He's my brother!" Tim said, his voice cracking.

Anya crawled closer to the man with the wound in his chest. She checked for a pulse and found one. It was thready. Weak.

She balled her outer-layer shirt and pressed it hard on the wound, avoiding Tim's panicked gaze. The outlook for her patient was grim, and she hated to think of his brother's loss and grief. Tears filled her eyes as she continued applying pressure.

Brody moved into position across from her. "What can I do to help?"

"Got a medevac handy?" she asked, casting him a quick worried glance.

"Will he be all right?" Tim asked, his tone saying he knew the bleakness of the situation but was desperate for some grain of hope.

"Cameron!" a man shouted behind her from some distance. "This way! Into the trees!"

Brody raised his head. Waved to the man who'd been on the bullhorn earlier, then shouted, "We have a man down!"

Even from their distance, she heard the curse word the other man bit out.

"You go," Anya said to Brody, then turned toward the other two men. "All of you. There's…" She took a breath. "There's not much we can do for him. But I'll stay and keep pressure on the wound, just in case."

Tim gave a raw moan that crawled down Anya's spine and made her soul hurt. She was no stranger to heartache and loss, and Tim's grief reverberated inside her.

She stared down at the red stains on her shirt as she held it to her patient's wound and fought back her own tears.

Brody reached over and wrapped his hand around her wrist. Squeezed gently. When she glanced up at him, his eyes were warm, kind…resolved. "I'm not leaving without you."

Something in her chest kicked. His willingness to risk his own safety to stay with her touched her deeply. "I…no, Brody. You should—"

"I'm staying." He glanced at the other men, aimed a finger toward the man who'd beckoned them. "When there's a break in the shooting, head for those trees where Jerry is. The woods will provide some cover. Better than here."

Anya dared to glance up then, to meet Tim's bereft eyes. His throat worked as he swallowed hard. Nodded. "His name is Donnie."

Anya's heart squeezed, and she nodded, moving aside as Tim bent to kiss his brother's forehead and whisper private words to his loved one.

The second man put a hand on Tim's back, muttering condolences as they both readied themselves to sprint to the line of trees.

Anya touched Donnie's neck again, searching for the faint thump that would tell her he was still with fight, still clinging to life. But the thin pulse was gone.

"Now!" Brody said, sending the other two men off.

As Tim and his companion raced away, Anya raised her chin and met Brody's gaze again.

"What?" he asked.

She wet her lips and sighed. "He's dead."

Brody stared at her as if he didn't understand for a moment before shifting a pained gaze to Donnie. He mumbled a cuss word, then laid a hand on the dead man's shoulder. "Rest in peace, friend."

Anya rocked back from Donnie's side, landing on her bottom and staring off toward the trees where Tim and the second man scampered into the safety of the woods.

"We should join them. Get ready to run again," Brody said.

"What about Donnie? He'll need to be transported back to the—" *Morgue.* She couldn't bring herself to say the word.

Brody rubbed a hand over his face. "Someone will come back for him. Once everything is safe."

He reached over to squeeze her shoulder, and somehow the sympathetic gesture broke her. She couldn't catch the sob that rose up from her chest or the tears that poured from her eyes any more than she could bring Donnie back to life. She'd lost patients before. It was an undeniable and heartbreaking truth of emergency medicine. She saw some of the most gravely injured and desperately ill cases the hospital handled. But Donnie's death felt more personal somehow. More tragic. More…real.

She heard rustling sounds, and then Brody's arms were around her. "I know. I know. It's okay," he crooned softly, the pat, meaningless words still comforting.

Or maybe it was just Brody's presence. The shared moment. Knowing she wasn't alone.

She could have gone on huddling close to Brody and weeping on his shoulder over the appalling loss of life, the horror of their situation and the feeling of professional failure that wrenched inside her, but the shooter took away that option.

As gunfire began peppering the hillside again, the flying bullets came dangerously close to the spruce where she and Brody hid. The thick branches of the evergreen were good for hiding but not helpful as a shield.

When a shot landed a foot from where Brody set his backpack, Anya gasped. She swiped an arm over her face, drying her tears and gave Brody a look that said she knew what had to happen.

Together they shifted position, their attention on their destination as they linked hands.

"Ready?" he asked.

She inhaled a deep breath for energy, for composure. For luck. And nodded.

"Go!"

Jerry met Brody and Anya as they entered the cover of the hardwoods and scrub brush where several of the searchers hid behind trunks of larger trees. "Your downed man?" he asked.

Brody shook his head. "Didn't make it."

Jerry's jaw hardened. "Who?"

"His name was Donnie. He was with the SAR team."

With a heavy exhale, Jerry bowed his head and closed his eyes for a moment before rallying and narrowing an all-business look on Brody. "Needless to say, this search is over. Let's get everyone rounded up and off this mountain before anyone else gets hurt."

"Has anyone called the situation in to the police?" Anya asked, her back to a beech tree that didn't fully shield her.

Another volley of gunfire warned them the shooter wasn't finished.

"What is this guy's deal?" Brody grated. "He can't *not* know he's shooting at people. He long ago passed the threshold of mistaking movement for wildlife."

Jerry's radio crackled, and a voice said, "Team leader, report?"

"We're still taking fire. I have six—" he paused and glanced around the area where other searchers were crouched behind trees or lying on the ground behind small boulders "—no, seven souls with me."

Brody, too, scanned the wooded hillside, locating other members of the search team.

"I have most of the crew with me. Law enforcement has been apprised of our situation and is en route," said the voice on Jerry's radio.

"Good. If you haven't already, abort your search and get your people out of here," Jerry said.

Something beyond the copse of trees, down the hillside, caught Brody's eye. Careful to move from the cover of one tree to the next, he crept forward to find an angle with fewer branches obscuring his view. Was that a... *cabin?*

"Brody? What's wrong?" Anya asked.

Wiggling his fingers, he waved her to him. "C'mere. Take a look at this."

She joined him, sidling up close to him behind the wide oak where he'd taken cover. He aimed his finger toward the small wooden building nestled in a clearing below them.

"Was that...?" Cutting herself off, Anya dug in her pocket for the small topological map they'd been given at the start of their search. "That's not on our map. Do you think anyone has searched it for Sophie?"

"I'm wondering if that's where our shooter came from. We could have run across the camp of an extremist who prefers living off the grid and thinks the government is out to get him."

"Cameron, let's go!" Jerry called. The other five searchers who'd taken cover in the woods were already headed through the trees in an approximate direction of the operation base at the foot of the mountain.

"Hold up, boss. Look at this." Brody hitched his head, signaling Jerry over.

Crouching low, despite the fact the gunfire had ceased, Jerry scuttled over to Brody and Anya. "What do you have?"

Brody again pointed out the cabin, just visible through the dense underbrush and low-hanging branches. "If you were a hiker, lost on this mountain, and you found that, where would you take shelter until rescuers came?"

"You think Sophie's down there?" Jerry asked.

"Can we really leave without checking?" Anya countered.

Jerry furrowed his brow and cast a glance in the direction the gunfire had come. "Seems more likely we found what the shooter was trying to protect."

"Jerry?" another searcher called back from the group that had already started their retreat. "Something wrong?"

"Hang on, Frank. I—" Indecision darkened Jerry's countenance.

Brody weighed his options. Beat a hasty retreat with the rest of the searchers and live with the knowledge the hiker could have been in that cabin, could have been rescued if only they'd taken the time to check the structure? Or take the chance of running into the shooter, up close and personal, if they approach the cabin?

The crunch of dry leaves drew him out of his pondering as the other searcher, a balding man who appeared close to Brody's father's age—Jerry had called him Frank—drew close to join their discussion. "What's the problem?"

Jerry showed Frank the cabin.

Anya touched Brody's arm, drawing his attention, while the older men discussed the find and their next move. "I can't in good conscience leave without giving the place at least a cursory search."

Brody clenched his back teeth. He'd come to the same decision himself, but he didn't like the idea of Anya putting herself at risk. "I don't think you should—"

A flash of bright light at the cabin, like the sun reflecting off metal, caught his attention, stopping him mid-sentence.

"Did you see that?" he asked the others.

Then the flash came again, along with the faint cry of a female voice.

Brody's pulse stumbled, and Anya grabbed his arm, squeezing hard. The look on her face said she'd heard the cry, too.

"Someone's down there!" She lifted her chin and sent Jerry a determined look. "We have to go down and check. I'm not leaving until I do."

Brody squared his shoulders and readjusted his backpack. "I'm going with her."

"Cameron, I'm not sure that's—"

"I'm going, too," Frank said, interrupting Jerry. "As

a father of three girls and a retired cop, I have to follow through on this."

Jerry sighed, raised a palm. "I guess we're all going then. But carefully. Don't go charging in there blindly. Let's use common sense and caution, huh?"

"Naturally," Brody said, putting a hand under Anya's elbow as she stepped over the trunk of a fallen tree and started her descent.

After Jerry radio their intentions to the other searchers, the four picked their way through the scrubby underbrush, rocks and vines until they reached the nearest point of the tree cover to the cabin. In order to reach the wooden structure that was about the size of a two-car garage, they'd have to cross a grassy field. Translation: no protection if the shooter spotted them and decided to continue his target practice.

"Do we just…make a run for it?" Anya asked.

"I don't see another option," Frank said. "Although you should probably—"

Anya shot up a hand, her palm toward the retired cop as she said, "Stop right there. If you're about to make a sexist comment or play the overprotective dad type and tell me to stay behind, I swear I'll…"

Frank arched an eyebrow and gave her a crooked grin. "Once a protective dad type, always a protective dad type. No offense intended."

Brody scratched his chin, an awkwardness skimming through him. He'd been about to suggest Anya stay put himself. Did that make him sexist or overprotective? And was overprotective really such a bad thing?

Jerry eased to the very edge of the woods, scanned the area and muttered, "Here goes nothing." Without further hesitation, he sprinted across the field.

Brody followed, the tall grass and uneven ground making it more difficult to run the short distance than normal. He passed Jerry, and as he reached the corner of the cabin. He skidded to a stop and just avoided crashing into the side wall. No gunfire.

He turned to glance back across the field just as Anya stumbled to a stop. He spread his arms and caught her, helping break her sprint. The last across, Frank, was just on her heels. Winded from the dash, the four pressed their backs to the sun-heated side of the cabin for a few seconds. Nodding silently to the others, Brody eased to the corner and peered around to the entry. Jerry went the opposite direction and checked cautiously around the back corner, Frank following close behind him.

As Brody took the measure of the front of the cabin— an empty porch, a tree stump with a hatchet stuck in it and evidence of earlier wood splitting, an impressive garden spot with young plants already sprouting, a rusted barrel with a dirty rag hanging over the edge— the cry they'd heard before came again. The woman's shout was louder now that they were closer to the house. "Help me!"

The voice was ragged, as if the woman had been screaming at full voice a lot lately. Brody's gut somersaulted. Even if they hadn't found the lost hiker, they'd definitely stumbled across a serious situation.

From behind him, Anya grabbed his arm. "We're going to need police backup. Probably an ambulance. I dropped my radio when I was helping Donnie. You need to make the call."

Frank must have heard her or been thinking along the same lines, because he heard the older man's voice speaking into his radio. "…need law enforcement and medical support near last point of search. A rough wood structure approximately one klick east of where shooter was positioned. Over."

Brody glanced at Anya. "Would it do any good for me to advise you to wait here?"

She arched a black eyebrow. "No."

He sighed. "Stay close then. Keep low. Just in case."

She nodded her agreement, and he made his way slowly around the corner, walking duck-like to the only window on the front of the cabin. He peered inside, but the unlit interior was difficult to make out. He saw no obvious signs of life in the one large room.

"I'm going in," he said.

"Unarmed? What if it's a trap or someone is hiding, waiting to jump you?" Anya's fingers dug into his forearm.

"Well…" He scanned the ground, looking for a thick stick at a minimum that he could use as a weapon. When his gaze landed on the hatchet, he scuttled over to it, staying low and yanked it from the stump. Rushing back to meet Anya by the door, he said, "Better?"

Her eyes rounded. "Let's just hope you don't need it, huh?"

"Definitely." He keyed the speak button on his radio and said quietly. "Jerry, you there? I'm going in the front door. Is the back clear?"

"Back and east side. We'll join you inside in a second," Jerry replied.

Pressing his back to the wall and holding the hatchet ready in his right hand, Brody pushed on the front door with his left hand. The door swung open. When no one fired a gun or sprang from the shadows, he peered around the edge of the door. The room, now illuminated by sunlight from the open door revealed a sparsely furnished room with a table and a couple of chairs. An old potbelly wood-burning stove. A cot with a rumpled blanket. A milk crate with split wood. A few shelves lined with jars and plastic storage containers.

"Help! Please, someone!" the hoarse cry came again, though Brody saw no one.

He turned, speaking over his shoulder to Anya. "I don't get it. There's no one in there. Do you think it's a recording? A lure to get us to go inside?"

Frank and Jerry came around the other side of the cabin, walking slightly hunched over as if preparing to drop to the ground should gunfire ring out again.

"Whatcha got?" Jerry asked.

"Nothing. No one. It's clear someone spends a significant amount of time here, possibly permanently, but… I don't see the woman."

"Well, the shooter isn't going to stay gone forever. If we're going to search the place, to be sure we didn't miss something, we need to hurry," Anya said, pushing past Brody, before he could do anything to stop her.

With an exasperated look to Jerry, Brody followed Anya inside. He paused only briefly as he entered the dark one-room cabin to let his eyes adjust to the dim light. Once inside he became aware of a foul odor. Unwashed body? Human waste? Rotten food? Maybe a little of all three.

Clearly Anya smelled it too because she covered her nose with her hand and grimaced. "Hello?"

The briefest of silences followed before the female voice cried, "Hello? I'm here! Who's there? Help!"

The four of them turned slowly, searching for the source of the voice.

"We're here to help, but…where are you?" Anya called.

"Down here! In the cellar!"

Cellar? Again the four searched, looking for stairs or some sign of a closet or…

Frank began tapping the wood plank floor with his foot. "Maybe there's a trapdoor somewhere or the floor planks come up."

With a bit of searching, moving chairs and the cot, Brody shoved the milk crate with split logs aside and found a two-inch hole in the flooring. "Over here!"

He stuck his fingers in the hole and pulled up. A section of floor two feet by three feet lifted up, hinged near the wall. A stronger waft of the foul odor he'd smelled rushed up, and he winced. He heard a sob and could barely make out the pale face of a bedraggled woman roughly five feet below him. "Sophie Bane?"

"Yes! Yes! Oh, my God! Thank you! Please, please, get me out of here! He'll be back any minute. I know he will!"

"Does someone have a flashlight?" Anya asked, flopping onto her belly to peer down into the hole.

Jerry and Frank crowed close to gaze into the dark hole as well.

"We're going to get you out, honey. Hang on!" Frank called down.

Setting the hatchet and his radio on the small table, Brody shoved the straps of his backpack off and rummaged in a pocket until he found the small flashlight he carried for searching dark crevices, drainpipes and, apparently, cellars. When his boss stuck out his hand, he handed the flashlight to Jerry.

Sophie shielded her eyes as the beam of light shone around her, illuminating the ten-foot square hole and the shelf-lined walls. The shelves were loaded with jars, cans and boxes. But Brody saw no ladder or other means for Sophie to climb out, given the trapdoor was in the center of the ten-foot square and the nearest shelf was at least four feet away.

He met Jerry's gaze, and without speaking, his boss gave a nod of understanding. How did they get Sophie out?

"I'll go in," Brody said, shifting to dangle his legs into the pit. "Sophie, stand clear! I'm coming down to get you."

"Wait. Couldn't we just give her a chair or—" Anya started.

But Brody had already scooted, lowering himself into the cellar until he hung with his hands gripping the edge of the wooden floor. He dropped the final four feet or so, feeling a twinge in his once-injured leg. His knees buckled, and he toppled back on his tush. The source of the bad odor became apparent as soon as he rose to his feet and faced Sophie. In the shaft of light from the trapdoor, he appraised her condition. Her eyes held a wild gleam, her hair was matted and dirty, her clothes soiled, her face shadowed with stress and likely dehydration. "How long have you been down here, Sophie?"

She shook her head. "I… I don't know. I…days…"

Her gravelly voice told him a great deal of the last several days had been spent screaming for help.

"When did you last eat? Drink?"

Again, her head shook weakly. "I don't…"

When she swayed, he rushed forward to catch her. "Whoa. Steady there." He felt her shudder, and his heart squeezed. The horror and pain of what she'd endured was more than evident, and he wanted to bay like an animal himself in shared anguish. Especially when he reflected on how his niece had recently been kidnapped and held captive. Thank God Fenn had been saved. And thank God they'd found Sophie before it was too late.

"Hurry," she whispered hoarsely. "He'll be back. He always…comes back."

He nodded and tipped his face toward the trapdoor to call, "Heads up. I'm going to give her a boost, but she's weak. She'll need to be pulled up."

"Right." Jerry said as he and Frank got on their bellies with arms out to grab Sophie.

"Anya?" Brody added.

Her face appeared in the opening over his head. "She's in bad shape. Dehydrated. Starving. Probably rather disoriented."

"All right," Anya said.

Brody put a gentle hand on Sophie's shoulder. "We're gonna get you out now. I'm going to give you a boost up, and those men up there are going to help pull you out. You understand?"

Her eyes rounded, and her chin trembled. "But he… he will be back. He won't let me—"

"You're safe now, Sophie. I'm not going to let him hurt you. But we have to get you out of this pit. Okay?"

Finally, she gave a head wobble that he took for assent. Crouching, he slapped his bent knee. "Can you climb? Use my knee as a step and I'll push you up. Hold your arms up for Jerry and Frank to grab. Got it?"

Though the effort took a few tries, the three of them

finally got Sophie out of the cellar. That only left the question—how did he get out?

As soon as Sophie was out of the underground hole, Anya sat the frightened young woman on one of the hard chairs. Anya had a canteen of water ready and handed it to her. "I know you're thirsty, but just take sips or you'll end up throwing it all back up."

Sophie clutched the canteen with two hands and tipped it up to drink with trembling hands. Anya had to pry the water bottle away from her when it was obvious Sophie was gulping too fast. "You can have more in a second. Are you injured anywhere? Did he hurt you?"

Sophie only glanced around the cabin, squinting from the light, and shaking so hard Anya was surprised she couldn't hear the poor woman's teeth clicking. "Get…out."

"What's that?"

Sophie met Anya's eyes with a gaze full of terror. "Have to go! We…have to get…out!"

The lost hiker's panic caused a swell of restless nerves in Anya's gut. "Gentlemen, I have to agree with Sophie. The guy that was shooting at us wasn't that far away. He's bound to be back here any—"

Boom!

The thundering sound outside shook the ground. The window, the jars on the cabin shelves rattled. A low rumbling followed. Continued.

Sophie screamed, then started hyperventilating.

"What the hell is that?" Brody called from the pit.

Frank rushed outside and returned with a stricken expression. "Landslide to the west where we just were.

By the sound of it, I'd say man-made. The son of a bitch must have set off an explosive of some sort to start it."

"What!" Jerry barked.

Explosives. Gunfire. A hostage.

A feeling like bugs on her skin chased through Anya as she cast a stunned look around the cabin again. The itchy sensation sharpened as she heard Sophie repeating, "Get…out!"

Alarms blared in Anya's head. A sense of urgency that she had to battle to keep from panicking raged inside her. "Gentlemen," she said with far more calm than she felt, "we need to get the hell out of here and off this mountain. Fast."

Frank and Jerry exchanged a look, and Jerry jerked a nod. "Agreed."

Jerry moved to Sophie's side and said, "Ma'am, can you walk?"

"If she can't then we'll carry her. But we need to *go!*" Frank said, jamming his shoulder under Sophie's armpit and draping her arm around his shoulders. "Come on, honey. You can do it."

Anya scrambled over to the trapdoor and peered down. "Ya hear that? We gotta hurry!"

"Way ahead of you," Brody said, crouching. He sprang as high as he could, trying to grab the edge of the flooring to hoist himself out.

And missed.

Rubbing his hands on his pants, Brody crouched again. Jumped. And missed. He cursed and angled a look at her. "How about that chair you mentioned before? I need a boost."

Jerry and Frank were speed walking—practically

dragging—Sophie out the front door of the cabin. Jerry called over his shoulder, "Move it, Cameron!"

"Right behind you!" Brody shouted back as Anya dragged the chair over the trapdoor. She lowered it into the breach, and Brody took it from her. "Anya, get out of here! Go!"

She shook her head, something deep inside her telling her not to leave without him. "When you do."

He planted the chair, climbed up, jumped. But his push off knocked the chair over, and he toppled.

Anya's heart sank, and wings of panic began to flap in her chest. "What if I hand down more things for you to climb on? Like the crate the firewood is in and…the other chair. And—" As she was turning, surveying the room for possible means for Brody to build a mound tall enough to climb out, she heard another dull boom.

Then another. Louder. Closer.

Dread bunched in her belly as she ran outside to look. And had her fear confirmed.

Jerry, Frank and Sophie were only halfway across the meadow headed for the tree cover. Even as she watched, another explosion shook the rocky hillside just above the cabin. A large swath of dirt, granite and woodland sheered off the slope and tumbled down. Gaining speed. Taking out more land and trees as it raced downhill. Toward Sophie and the men. Toward the cabin.

The thundering of the landslide echoed in her terror-stricken heart. Instantly, she knew three things. The landslide would bury the cabin. She couldn't outrun it. She was probably about to die.

Somehow, from somewhere, she found the wherewithal to dart back inside the cabin. "Brody!"

The rumble of thousands of tons of dirt and rocks

grew louder. Adrenaline surged through her. She had only seconds to decide…

"Anya, get out!"

Instead, she darted to the opening of the cellar, dropped to her bottom. She grabbed the trapdoor, tugging it closed as she jumped inside the pit next to Brody.

"What the—" Brody began.

Above them the rumbling was deafening. The shelves around her, the ground under her shook like an earthquake. The tremors so violent she couldn't stay on her feet. When she crumpled, she instinctively balled into the fetal position and covered her head with her arms. Then Brody was there, curling his body around hers and adding his arm to shield her.

They stayed huddled that way for several minutes. Until the earth quit vibrating. Until the rumbling was silent. Until all she could hear was Brody's ragged breathing answering her own.

Finally he sat up, moving away from her. "Are you all right?"

"I… I think so." She blinked, trying to make out anything in the pitch-black cellar. "But I think…we're buried. We're trapped."

She heard Brody sigh. "I'd say you're right."

Chapter 4

"So...now what?" Anya asked, though she had a sick feeling in her stomach that she knew the answer to that question. And didn't like the answer one bit.

"I think our first step is to assess all aspects of our situation."

Brody's disembodied voice through the blackness gave her some measure of comfort, made her feel less alone. Yet the complete darkness, the I-can't-even-see-my-hand-in-front-of-my-face darkness chilled her to the core.

The word *entombed* filtered through her brain, unsettling her further. Oh, God! They were freaking *buried alive*!

When she realized she was starting to hyperventilate, Anya groped blindly in the dark for Brody. Finding him, she curled her fingers into his shirt, reassured by his presence. She forcefully slowed her breathing. Deep inhale, slow exhale.

"Anya?"

"Yeah, I'm here. Just…trying not to panic." She took another deep breath through her nose and blew it out through pursed lips.

"Yeah, panicking won't help. Information is what we need now."

"Okay. What information?" She could follow Brody's lead. Sure. The distraction might even be just what she needed.

"Well, for starters, let's see if we really are trapped. Maybe we can force the trapdoor open, manage to dig out…something."

Anya considered his suggestion. "How do we do that? You couldn't reach the edge of the floor earlier in order to pull yourself up. We're at the bottom of a pit that's, like, ten-feet deep."

"But you handed down the chair, remember? It's here somewhere. And there's two of us. Maybe you can reach the trapdoor if you get on my shoulders, while I stand on the chair and—"

A mirthless laugh bubbled from Anya.

"What?" Brody asked.

"You just described a version of the scenario I hear about twice a day, three or four times if it's a weekend."

"Huh?"

"'I was climbing on a ladder to get the Frisbee off the roof.' Or, 'I thought I could clean the cobwebs from the top of the cabinets if I stood on the counter.' Or, 'I jumped down instead of using the ladder. It didn't look that far.'" She rolled her eyes even though she knew he couldn't see it. "So many trips to the ER with broken bones and worse start with a tale of reckless climbing or jumping or ladder user error."

She heard a sigh. "Do you have a better idea?"

Anya drew her bottom lip between her teeth. "No. But aren't we asking for trouble, climbing on a questionably sturdy chair, in the dark. And that's before you try to put me on your shoulders."

Brody was silent, and she shook the fistful of shirt she clung to like a lifeline. "I'm not saying no. I mean... do we have any other option?"

"Sit around and wait for rescue that may or may not come. Surely someone will report the explosions, the landslide, the fact we didn't return to base and come looking for us, but...how long will that take?"

A new thought occurred to her that seesawed in her gut. "Brody."

He must have heard the change in her tone, the gravity. The horror.

"What?"

She pressed a hand to her chest as a raw ache gnawed her heart. "Jerry and Frank. Sophie."

She sensed his stillness, as if he were holding his breath. He muttered a curse word softly.

"When I looked outside after the first detonations... they were in the middle of that open field when the second explosions started the rockslide above the cabin. I rushed back inside, so I can't be sure, but... I don't see how they could've..."

She heard the scuff of his feet, felt his body turn toward her. Then his hand was on her arm. "Let's pray their death was instant. That they didn't suffer." His huff of frustration sounded broken, grieved. "What a disaster."

"Yeah." She put her hand over his. "I'm sorry."

He gave her arm a squeeze then seemed to rally, his voice more determined sounding when he said, "Right. Well, we can accept we are trapped and wait passively, or try to find a way out. I won't ask you to put yourself at risk, but maybe we can feel around and find something else I can climb on, or stack the chair on—and, yes, I know that what I'm suggesting is a recipe for a broken bone or five. I'll take the risk. You don't need to."

Anya squared her shoulders, a gesture that made her feel more confident even if he couldn't see it. "I'm willing to assume my fair share of risk if it means getting us out of here."

"Anya, you don't have to—"

"Brody," she returned. "Don't play martyr. I'm going to pull my weight. I'm just trying to figure everything out."

"Martyr?"

"Okay, poor word choice. Let's just…" Remembering her phone was in her pocket, she dug it out and woke the screen.

"You have a phone?" he said, his tone dripping with relief and an unspoken *well-duh*.

"Don't get excited. I only have—" she checked the signal "one bar. No…it just flashed no signal. Wait. One bar again." She glanced up in the dim glow of her phone screen to his hopeful expression. "I wouldn't count on a call or message getting in or out."

"Yeah. If we weren't remote enough on this mountain, the piles of rock and dirt on top of us aren't helping the signal get out." He patted his pockets and buzzed his lips in frustration. "But at least you have your phone. My backpack, my radio—basically everything I was carrying—I set aside up top before I climbed down here. I got nothing. No water, no food, no communication."

"I have another protein bar and a few hard candies. But look." She opened the settings on her phone and turned on the flashlight accessory. Shining it around the cellar, she put the spotlight on the shelves around them. "Our sniper had laid in supplies for himself." She shone the light on the row of jars nearest to her. "This looks like peaches, and there's tomatoes. Here are cans of corn, tuna, beans, pineapple. We won't starve."

"May I?" Brody took the phone from her and used the light to explore the shelves nearest him. Matches. Small cans of propane fuel. Boxes of rifle cartridges. Batteries of various sizes. A couple bars of soap. In the corner, behind the shelves, a shovel leaned against the dirt wall.

"Hermit supplies," Anya mumbled. "He was planning to live here off the grid for a while."

Brody turned off the flashlight app and put the screen to sleep.

"Wait. Why'd you turn it off?" she asked as he put the phone back in her hand.

"The flashlight uses the battery pretty fast. We should only use it when we have to. Better that we have it for the possibility of getting enough signal to get a message out."

Anya groped in the dark until she found the rickety wooden chair she'd handed down to Brody earlier. Taking a seat, she woke her phone again and studied the screen. "Good news is I have ninety-five percent of battery left. I'd just charged it in the car driving over. Reception is just one bar, but let me see if I can call out."

She tried five times to place a call to 911. Three times each to call the number Brody gave her for his sister

Emma, who always had her phone close by, and for his parents' landline. Nothing. Next, she tried texting his sister. Texting her best friend, Chloe. Texting the head of the SAR group. Each time she got a message back that delivery had failed.

With a dejected grunt, she stowed the phone in her cargo pants pocket again and said, "All right. Let's try your idea to reach the trapdoor."

"Right. But if we want to avoid one of those ER-worthy mishaps that you mentioned, you better fire the flashlight app back up."

"Way ahead of you, buddy," Anya said as she did just that and propped the phone against a jar of peaches so that a dim glow filled the cellar and the main beam was angled toward the ceiling. "So do I get on your shoulders first or wait until you're standing on the chair?"

"Let's try shoulders first." He squatted and she hooked her legs over his shoulders and leaned forward over his head for balance. This close to him she could smell the scent of clean sweat, remnants of a crisp, herbal shampoo and a pleasant woodsy odor she assumed was his deodorant. She wanted to bury her face in his hair, in the curve of his neck and fill her nose with the good smells. Especially if they'd help cover the rancid odors of human waste and mildew that hung in the air.

He anchored her with one wide palm spread on her thigh while his other hand steadied the chair as he carefully climbed on it. Anya overcorrected for his step up, and she lost her balance on top of him. He tried to catch her, but she slid awkwardly over his head. Fortunately, she landed feet first, breaking her sloppy fall before dropping onto her bottom.

"Anya!"

She waved and flashed an embarrassed grin. "My fault. I leaned too far forward."

"Are you hurt?"

"Just a bruised ego."

He lowered his sandy eyebrows in concern. "Maybe you're right about this being too risky."

She dusted the dirt from her hands and shook her head. "I can do this. Let's try again. If we have no luck or it seems too difficult after a try or two, we won't push it, but… I don't want to give up because I'm a klutz."

Brody continued to stare at her as if assessing her in some way. Finally he rubbed his hands on the seat of his jeans and crouched again. "Okay, cowboy up!"

She chuckled. "Yeah, only if my steed is well broken. I'm not an experienced rider."

Still squatting, he twisted to cast a suspicious, somewhat sultry, look over his shoulder. "I've been ridden a fair amount, but I still have some bronc left in me."

A choking sound sputtered from her throat, before she muttered, "Are we still talking about the same thing?"

His grin turned puckish. "What do you think?"

"I think…we should keep our minds on the task at hand."

He turned back around and patted his shoulder. "Have it your way."

Anya swung her legs over, one at a time, as she once again settled atop Brody's broad shoulders. But no amount of trying was enough to ignore the sexual innuendo of his teasing. Her hands shook as she grasped his head, his shirt, her legs hooked around his chest to help stabilize her. Images flashed in her brain of straddling Brody in a bed, his hips bucking beneath her.

When she felt a little light-headed, her head spinning a bit, she grabbed a fist full of his hair near his ear.

He grunted. "Ow. You okay?"

"Uh, yeah. Yeah…"

He stepped onto the chair then. Slowly. Carefully.

The chair creaked. Brody straightened, standing taller. Anya held her breath.

"Okay. I've got your legs. See how far up you can reach," he said.

Anya angled her head to look up at the trapdoor. It was about a foot above her, and she cautiously stretched an arm to push on it.

The wooden panel didn't budge. Frustrated, she tried again with both hands. Still nothing. There was simply too much weight, too much debris or rock or whatever, sitting on the door to open it. A crushing despair settled on her, as sure as if one of the rocks from the landslide had fallen on her. They were, indeed, buried. Trapped.

When a thread of panic tried to strangle her, she gritted her teeth and dug deep for the strength that kept her going through particularly trying days in the ER. She searched for the extra ounce of energy and hope that buoyed her when she'd been on her feet for twenty hours and had seen nothing but death, pain and hopelessness her entire shift. Drawing a deep breath, she seized the spark that flickered inside her. Planted her hands on the door again. Shoved.

Giving the effort all of her strength, she strained against the unyielding barrier until loose dirt rained down through the blocked two-inch hole that Brody had used to open the panel.

"Oof," Brody said and made a spitting sound. "That went in my face."

"Sorry."

"Does that dirt shower mean you're having some luck?" The hopeful note in his voice wrenched inside her.

Anya's back slumped, and she lowered her arms to hold on to Brody again. "No. Afraid not. It won't budge. Not even a little."

Under her legs, she felt his body wilt with his own disappointment. "Well…hell. It was worth a shot. Hang on. Getting down."

Once he'd climbed off the chair, he helped her off his neck, and they stood in the dank cellar staring at each other for long seconds. A mutual understanding of their predicament passed wordlessly between them. When he stepped closer to her, she reached for him. He tucked her firmly against his chest, his chin resting on the top of her head.

Anya pressed her ear to over his heart, heard the steady thump of a strong sinus rhythm and curled her fingers into the sweat dampened shirt at his back. He squeezed firmly, almost to the point of restricting her breathing. Or was that just her natural reaction to being held by him, snuggled securely against his brawn?

Maybe it was the shock of reality stealing the air from her lungs. They were stuck. Prisoners of the sniper as surely as the missing hiker had been. But would they be found, dug out of the landslide before…well, they had a good bit of food. And the juices in the jars would provide hydration for a while. But…

As she backed out of Brody's arms and picked up her phone to turn off the light, she asked quietly, her voice trembling, "How long do you think the oxygen in here will last?"

Chapter 5

Brody's pulse leaped. Damn! He hadn't considered the air supply, had taken for granted the ability to breathe—as one does until that ability is threatened.

"I—I don't know." He tried to remember if, in news reports about trapped miners, he'd ever heard estimates of how long someone could survive without a fresh air supply.

"The air we breathe isn't pure oxygen," Anya said. "And we don't exhale pure carbon dioxide, but I don't know the math behind the exchange or know when the CO_2 saturation becomes lethal."

At best, Brody estimated, they had a couple of days, but he didn't want Anya to panic. He'd already seen the fear in her eyes, felt the tremble in her limbs and heard the quiver in her voice. His job was to reassure her. Take care of them both. Make sure they survived this disaster. He simply refused to believe that this fluke event was how he'd die.

He placed a hand on each of her shoulders and met her gaze evenly. "All right. First order of business has just become ventilation." He angled his head to stare up at the trapdoor, the two-inch gap in the wood through which the rain of loose dirt had tumbled down on them.

"Our best bet is probably that finger hole in the door." He took her phone from where it was propped on the shelf and climbed on the chair again, raising the light to get a better look.

"It's blocked. The door wouldn't budge. There's a whole hillside of dirt, rock and collapsed cabin sitting on that trapdoor, Brody."

"Maybe. And maybe there's enough loose dirt for us to dig a small hole through whatever is sitting on top of the trapdoor." He stretched an arm up, but his fingers came just shy of reaching the hole to test his theory. "If too much weight were tumbled onto the door, why didn't it cave in?"

Anya groaned. "Oh, don't say things like that! You'll jinx us."

He glanced down at her and met her anxious look. "No jinxes. Just trying to reason things out." Climbing down from the chair, he shone the phone's flashlight around the small cellar again. "I think I saw—jackpot!"

He hurried over to the shelving where the dry goods and fuel canisters sat. Reaching behind the metal shelves, he grabbed the shovel.

Anya gasped. "Are you thinking we can dig our way out of here?"

He didn't miss the note of hope that overrode the skepticism in her voice.

"In a sense. But not how you're probably thinking." He climbed back on the chair and used the handle of the shovel to poke at the dirt in the finger hole. Another small cascade of dirt rained down. "If we can even make a channel the size of this shovel handle through whatever debris is on top of the door, we'd at lease have some ventilation."

"Yes! Oh, Brody, you're a genius!" The relief and admiration that filled her voice stroked Brody's ego. But he quickly set the mood boost aside to face the reality that he was a long way from moving his idea to fruition.

While Anya held the phone with the light properly aimed, he poked at the hole again. More dirt came through, tumbling to the floor of the cellar. But each successive jab resulted in less and less loose debris. He paused from the task, dismounting the chair and regarding the shovel handle with a frown.

"What's wrong? It was working. Why'd you quit?"

Brody scratched his head where dirt had fallen on him and made his scalp itch. "The blunt end of this shovel is just packing the dirt tighter and harder. What I need is a point or blade that can chop through the debris."

Anya turned the light to scan the cellar again. Brody joined her search, but it quickly became evident their choices were basically nil.

"Okay," Brody said rubbing his chin, "time to be resourceful."

Anya pinched her bottom lip and her expression grew pensive. "Break a jar and use a shard of glass?"

Brody shook his head. "I don't think the glass would be strong enough. And how would we attach it to the shovel handle?"

She stepped over to the shelf behind him and pushed aside a large bottle of bleach. Lifting the roll of silver tape behind the bleach, she presented to him with a lopsided grin. "How do most men fix broken stuff? Duct tape."

Brody returned a smile. "Of course. Still not strong enough. But I have an idea." He dug in his pocket and withdrew a pocketknife. "The other item most men are never without."

"So you're going to tape the knife to the shovel?"

He shrugged. "Actually, I was thinking I could whittle the blunt end into a thin flat tip with a point like a spear. But let's call taping the knife on plan B. 'Kay?"

She flipped up one palm. "Works for me."

With a flick, Brody opened the knife to his best blade and sat down with the shovel handle to start whittling and reshaping the knobby end. Slowly the tip began to resemble the tool he'd imagined. When he finished crafting a sturdy but pointed blade, Brody stood and mounted the chair again. He grunted and rubbed his thigh as he climbed up.

"Your leg is bothering you," she said, not a question.

"It's aching a little. I've used it more today than I have since my accident. And the jump in here jarred it." He noticed her wrinkled brow and shook his head. "But it's fine."

She angled her head and narrowed her gaze in a way that suggested her skepticism, but she said nothing.

Brody tested his homemade gouger, jabbing at the dirt-packed hole and loosening the debris that blocked the trapdoor. Again loosened soil trickled down, landing at his feet, in his hair and on the dirt floor of the cellar. When he stopped at one point to wipe his sweat-damped palms on his jeans, Anya poked his back. "Let me take a turn. You rest a little while."

"I'm good."

"Brody, I'm serious. Let me help."

He studied her face in the dim glow of the phone's flashlight. He could refuse her again, but he sensed her request was more than just an offer of help. Doing something, taking an active role in solving an issue facing them, meant feeling a tiny bit of control over their circumstances. And he knew well how the sense of helplessness sucked.

He stepped down from the chair and offered his hand to help her climb up. She took the shovel from him and went after the task, full bore. He turned off the phone light to save battery, but the soft clatter of dirt falling told him she was making some progress. Soon, though, the dribble dried up, and the thudding of Anya's jabs slowed. Turning the light back on and propping it on a shelf, Brody climbed on the chair with her and reached for the shovel. "Your turn to rest."

"I can—" She was mid-sentence when they heard the distinct *crack*. Her gaze met his. "Uh-oh."

He took the shovel handle from her and brought it down to examine. The tip had been dulled by the repeated thrusts into the packed dirt and rock, and the flat blade he'd carved had split.

"Aww, man!" she said, her tone rife with frustration.

"It was an old shovel. The wood was dried out. It was bound to happen." He poked the handle back in the hole to measure how far they'd burrowed. "We're about to run out of handle length. If we don't break through soon, we'll be back to square one."

"So what do we do about that?" Anya pointed at the cracked wood as he brought it down again.

"Plan B?"

With a nod, she hopped down from the chair and retrieved the duct tape. While she pulled a strip off and tore it with her teeth, Brody examined the cracked wood. Was he better off sharpening the handle again, reshaping what was left of the wood, or affixing the pocketknife with tape?

Opening the knife again, he scraped away some of the splintered wood in the crack until he'd crated a small gap at the end of the handle. Turning his pocketknife, he wedged the slim knife into the gap and held the tool out to Anya. He steadied the shovel while she tightly wrapped the silver tape around, over, back. She created a thick and sturdy binding, then raised her gaze to him. "Think that will hold?"

He chuckled. "Is the pope Catholic?"

She set the tape on the shelf and rubbed one hand with her other. "I have practice. You should see me wrap a sprained ankle."

Even in the dim light he could see the blisters on her palms. A niggle of something tugged at him. Pride for her valiant efforts? Remorse for her injury? Admiration for her determination and lack of complaint for her sore hands? He thought of the packet of antibiotic cream in the small first aid kit in his backpack...which was buried somewhere in the debris overhead. Maybe they could find something else down here in the sniper's supplies that would keep her blisters from festering.

"Well, give it a go." She waved a hand, indicating he should test the pocketknife-tipped shovel-handle-cum-hole-poker.

Brody resumed prodding at the dirt blocking the trapdoor, and the rain of loosened soil fell again. Anya doused the light, and Brody continued working in the dark, blindly jabbing and praying each poke would be the one that finally broke through.

He'd lost track of time, his mind wandering and his shoulder muscles aching, when Brody sensed a change. His thrusts met less resistance, and a thin beam of pale light seeped down from above. A jolt of adrenaline revived him as hope and excitement surged in his blood. "Anya, look! I think we did it!"

He heard a scuffling as she climbed to her feet from where she'd sat waiting in the dark.

Brody twisted and jabbed as hard as he could, and the small hole grew larger. Light and air greeted him through the two-inch hole he'd created. And relief. It might not be much, but even that small tunnel through the pile of debris and soil gave them the ventilation hole they needed to refresh their supply of oxygen. If—

If they could ensure that the narrow channel to the surface didn't collapse on itself and fill in again.

"You did it!" Anya gave a happy squeak and bounced on her toes in the narrow stream of light. As he withdrew the shovel handle carefully, praying he didn't disturb the walls and create the very problem he was concerned about, he heard her sigh and say, "Fresh air. Thank God. And now it won't be so completely dark anymore. I have to say, the total blackness down here was giving me the heebie-jeebies."

"That little hole isn't worth much for light, but at least we have ventilation."

For now. He chose not to tell her how precarious the narrow tunnel to the other side of the landslide pileup was. Shifting rocks, rain or just gravity could cause the hole to fill in again.

Brody rolled his shoulders and neck, which were stiff and sore now after the awkward position needed for the task. "Okay, so where do we stand now?"

"Still in a pit," Anya said, her tone both wry and confused.

"I mean…where's your phone? Any replies to your texts? How much battery is left?"

"Oh, uh…" She woke the home screen. "No replies. Eighty-nine percent battery left. No signal."

Brody turned, squinting in the minuscule light to look at the jars on the shelf. "I'm thirsty and could use a snack. What do you say we treat ourselves to a jar of preserved peaches?"

"I have a protein bar, too." Anya used the phone to illuminate the jar Brody had selected.

"Save it for now. Huh?" Brody said. He twisted the lid of the canning jar in his hands, and it gave a soft pop as the pressure seal was broken. He raised the jar to sniff it. The sweet mellow scent of peaches rose from the jar to greet him, a welcome smell to counter the bad odors around him. "I think it's all right. No spoilage. Wanna drink first?"

"Naw. Go ahead."

Brody tipped up the jar, and the syrupy juice the peaches had been canned in bathed his tongue in a honey-sweet wash that did little to quench his thirst but gave him a boost of energy. With his lips, he caught a slice of peach that slipped out of the jar, and he munched the soft fruit while watching Anya frown at the dirt under her nails, visible in the glow from her phone screen.

"You okay?" he asked, then tipped the jar up to try to catch another chunk of peach.

She hummed. "Just thinking how hard I'll have to scrub to sterilize my hands enough to return to work."

Brody was about to stick his hand in the jar to fish out a slice of fruit, when Anya said, "Do you have any idea how much bacteria and fungi are in dirt?"

Brody looked at his own filthy hands and discarded the idea of touching the peaches. Tipping the jar up would be messy, but it might be more sanitary. After catching another slice of peach in his teeth, he offered the jar to Anya. She took it, drank some juice and finagled a slice out, then handed the jar back.

After wiping her hands on her cargo pants, Anya shone the camera around her until she found a clear corner where the shelves didn't block the dirt wall and the floor was unobstructed by clutter. She moved to the corner and sat down, leaning her back against the cellar wall. She glanced at the phone again. "Oh! One bar!" With flying fingers, she tapped her screen. "There. Sent another text to Chloe and one to your sister Emma before the bar disappeared. Cross your fingers."

He ate another peach slice before screwing the lid back on the jar and moving to the corner to sit on the dirt floor beside Anya. She put the phone screen to sleep, and the suffocating darkness swallowed them again.

She sighed and leaned against him so that their shoulders and hips touched.

He had to admit, the casual contact made him feel less alone in the black pit, less overwhelmed by their situation. He heard her exhale, a gush of breath that reverberated with fatigue, frustration, boredom and held an edge of barely contained fear. A lot like what he was feeling. "Can I ask you something?"

She shifted a little, and the contact between their hips disappeared. "You just did." He snorted in reply to her quip, and she added, "Yes. Ask me something."

"You've texted your friend and my family but...not your boyfriend. Why not?" He tried to make his voice sound casual, as if it was simply a curiosity to him that she hadn't mentioned the boyfriend and not a personal fact-finding mission. "Isn't he going to be worried when you don't come home tonight?"

She said nothing for several seconds. "How did you know..."

When her voice trailed off, Brody shrugged. "You turned down my highly romantic marriage proposal in the ER last summer because you were involved with someone."

"Oh, right. Well." She cleared her throat. "If you wanted to ask me to marry you again, you might get a different answer. The boyfriend is gone."

"By 'gone' do you mean he...moved?"

"More like moved on."

Even though she was clearly trying for a light delivery, he heard something in her tone that plucked at him, gave him pause. She'd been hurt. That much was clear.

"Oh," he said finally, a couple beats too late. "I'm sorry."

"Yeah, well...better that I find out he didn't have the same view of our relationship as I did before I invested any more of my time or heart in him. Right?"

"Um, right." Yep, definite hurt behind her tone. Brody didn't consider himself particularly tuned in to the nuances of body language and voices the way his sisters were, but he couldn't deny what he sensed from Anya. Maybe it was just that the darkness had fine-tuned his hearing. Or maybe his interest in knowing and understanding Anya made him pay more attention to subtleties. Regardless of the reason behind it, his instinct to protect and provide compelled him to drape an arm around her shoulders and draw her closer.

After an initial twitch of surprise, Anya relaxed against him.

He searched for the right words to offer comfort or condolence. What would Isla say? His younger sister was the most empathetic, gentle soul he knew. He tried to conjure his sister's voice, her previous advice in his head. Isla would have something heartfelt, pertinent and eloquent to say. Instead, he heard himself mumble the all too trite, "His loss."

Trite but true. He couldn't imagine what Anya's ex could have objected to about her. But the second half of the trite saying also came to mind. *My gain.*

A quiver of something alluring rippled through him. Anya was unattached. Brody definitely still found her attractive and witty and intelligent. When they were rescued—when, not if, because he was certain rescue crews would come looking for them by nightfall—would Anya be open to exploring a relationship with him?

Anya hadn't said anything for a while, he realized, and given the darkness hid her expression, he could only guess at her mood.

"You okay?" he asked.

"With Mark leaving or in general?"

"Either. Both. But mostly, right now."

"Like Mark, I've moved on. And right now? Hmm.

I'm alive. I have company. We have food to survive on, so… I'm trying to stay positive."

He squeezed her closer in an encouraging side hug. "Good."

She rested her head on his shoulder, and they fell silent in the oppressive darkness. The only sound in the cellar was their breathing. After a few minutes, Anya said, "So…"

"So…what?"

"So now we wait," she said, but he also heard the hint of an unspoken question: Is there anything else we can do to facilitate our rescue?

Or was it simply that his own brain had shifted to that question? Anticipate trouble. Solve problems before they come up.

Isla had spent most of last Sunday's family dinner talking about the book she'd read on "upstream problem solving." She'd been bubbling over with ideas for how Cameron Glen could employ this proactive business management. Brody hadn't had the heart to tell his younger sister that he'd spent his entire life thinking, planning and executing everything upstream. Anticipating and solving problems was wired in his DNA.

But for all his analyzing their situation, Brody hadn't come up with anything else they could do at the moment. He blew out a sigh that buzzed his lips. "Yep. Now we wait."

He closed his eyes, stretched his legs out in front of him and crossed his ankles. After waking early that morning, hiking up the mountain with the search party, running from the sniper, jumping in the cellar and jabbing an air hole for fresh air, Brody decided he'd earned a rest. He closed his eyes and leaned his head back and was drifting off when Anya spoke again.

"Brody?"

"Hmm?"

"Just tell me that what we're waiting for is *not* the sniper to show up here and finish what he started."

After watching the searchers scramble for cover like ants when their hill is disturbed, Sol Guidry had spotted the strays that went into the tree cover and known he might have to take more extreme measures to protect himself. When they'd entered his cabin and emerged with the woman hiker, he'd known he had to take them out. Had to cover his tracks. He'd prepared for the worst months ago, but having to obliterate everything he'd worked for these past years infuriated him. The nosy searchers deserved what they got for putting everything he'd created in jeopardy.

That the denotations he'd rigged did their job perfectly gave him little pleasure. Not when their deployment set him back, left him starting over from nothing.

He rubbed his eyes and replayed the sight of his captive and the two men racing for their lives as the crumbling mountainside chased them. A small smile tugged a corner of his mouth. That much had been enjoyable. A sliver of sweet revenge amid the destruction of so much else.

Some of the searchers had escaped when he started firing, though. They'd report what happened, and more law enforcement would arrive before long.

But what about his treasures, his collection, his secrets?

He gave the rubble and ruin of what had once been

his safe house a last look. The structure had been leveled by the landslide. Hewn logs and splintered boards reached through the tumble of dirt and rock like bony hands reaching up from a grave. The cabin had, for the most part, been destroyed. Irritation, like a boiling acid, gnawed him over his loss. He'd have to start over. His location had been compromised, and even if he could dig out his possessions, he couldn't stay on this mountain any longer. He had to disappear—but not before making sure his greatest vulnerability, the truth he had to protect at any cost, had been sufficiently buried. And that the searchers who'd intruded on his hideaway could never tell what they'd found.

Chapter 6

"I know being thankful that we're still alive should be enough, but this waiting to see if rescuers will reach us before a crazed sniper does is nerve-racking," Anya said.

Brody hummed his agreement. They'd been sitting in the dark, waiting for what felt like several hours but had probably been less than one. "I was just thinking how tedious it was not to have anything productive to do to get us out of here. I'm not good with idle time. I much prefer action and problem-solving to meditation." He scratched his cheek, where drying sweat was making him feel itchy. Or was it just the prickly sense of uselessness that had him fidgeting? "We need a distraction. A discussion topic or something else to do to pass the time. The more practical, the better, in my opinion."

"What if we played a game?" she suggested. "I can't

say how practical it is, but it's better than getting stir crazy."

"Sure. Why not? But not twenty questions. That one's too tedious for me."

"Then how about we play Random Questions?"

Brody lifted an eyebrow in silent skepticism. "Random Questions. Is the name self-explanatory or is there a wrinkle or twist to this game I should know about?"

"Well, since I just made it up, I can't say there are any twists I've considered."

He snorted a laugh. "Just made it up?"

"Would you rather play Truth or Dare?"

"Why does it have to be a game with any rules? I'm an open book. Ask me what you want. I'll answer." He heard a little humph of discontent and grinned. "Okay, but for every question you ask me, you also have to answer the same question about yourself. And vice versa."

"One rule. You have to answer, and you have to be honest."

"That's two rules," he countered.

"Then two rules. Oh, and let's say you get one pass."

"So three rules," he said, unable to hide his amusement in his tone.

"Yes. Three rules. Do you agree?"

He flipped up his hand in acquiescence, then remembering she couldn't see it, he said, "Sure. Fire away."

"Tell me about your family."

He chuckled. "That's not a question. That's a sweeping info grab. Want to be more specific?"

Her sigh filtered to him in the blackness. "Fine. In that case, how would you say your family has shaped who you are?"

He blinked and gave a snort of surprise. "Wow. From

overbroad to deeply personal and analytical in under a minute."

"You said to be more specific."

"I did. Fair enough. Okay, let's see. Having had three sisters growing up has made me value having my own bathroom."

She was silent for several seconds before she said, "That's it? That's all you have to say about the influence your family had on you?"

He chuckled. "I answered honestly. You didn't make a rule about the length of answers."

Anya made a grunting sound. "Touché. But I was hoping to learn more about you than you having sisters, volunteer with the fire department and have breathtaking blue eyes."

His pulse tripped. *Breathtaking blue* was a rather intimate way to describe their color. And did he detect a hitch in her tone when she used the term? He filed away that hint of her attraction toward him. He was not one to take advantage of a situation or a woman's vulnerability to score points for himself. And being stranded down here in this black pit definitely left Anya vulnerable.

Rubbing his hand on his thigh, he gathered his thoughts and considered her question on a deeper level. "Growing up in my family taught me…" He twisted his lips as he mused. "The value of home. That home was more than a house. It's the people. Home is about traditions and heritage and history." She didn't respond, and he nudged her with his elbow. "Your turn. How did your family influence you?"

"Oh, well… I pursued nursing largely because my dad is a doctor."

"What specialty?"

"Neurology."

"So he's…a *brain surgeon*?" Brody said with a little chuckle of amazement.

"No." Her tone was wry. "He doesn't do surgery. He treats things like Alzheimer's, strokes, ALS, Parkinson's."

"Still pretty impressive. So he encouraged you to go into a health profession?"

"Well, let's just say he strongly, uh, *encouraged* my sister and me to make straight As, and be proficient in a number of skills, so that I was fully prepared for whatever career path I took. And by *encouraged*, I mean expected. Insisted on. Drilled us with the importance of excelling in all things."

"Huh. And what skills are you proficient in?"

"I wouldn't say I was proficient, especially since I haven't practiced in years, but I play piano. And soccer. And I was on the newspaper staff in high school and college, where I minored in English composition, so maybe I could fall back on journalism if I burn out in nursing?"

"Wow," Brody said, his mind goggling. "Whereas I never went to college. Just straight into landscaping. I built my current business with help and advice from my dad and brother-in-law. By the time I created Cameron Landscaping, I had a preestablished client list from my summers as a teenager mowing lawns and doing yard work both for Cameron Glen and people who saw my signs around town."

"Mmm," she hummed, sounding unimpressed, and Brody wondered if the blue-collar nature of his primary profession was somehow off-putting to her, considering her broader education and highly skilled job. He closed his eyes, even though the darkness meant the action changed little for his senses, but it still helped him focus his thoughts.

He'd never second-guessed his choices. He loved being outdoors, loved making things grow, loved the freedom of being his own boss. And between the Christmas tree farm he ran for the family, his landscaping company and the random odd jobs he picked up in off-seasons, he was doing well financially, thankyouverymuch. So why did her approval, her validation matter so much to him?

"So do you think your family's heritage and traditions matter more than… I don't know, love?" she asked, rousing him from his musing. "More than opportunity? Or responsibility to one's…*self*?"

"What?" He blinked his eyes open, and turned his head toward her, only able to make out the vaguest outline of her from the thin light coming from the ventilation hole.

"Earlier you said your family taught you the value of heritage and history and that home was about traditions. But isn't home more about being loved and feeling accepted and valued for who you are?"

"Well, sure. Of course love and support are important." He wished he could see her face, the emotion in her eyes to get a better read on where she was coming from with her question. He heard something in her tone that felt off, but he couldn't pinpoint what might be bothering her. "That's kinda understood, isn't it? I figured you were looking for more than a cliché you'd find on the kind of kitschy home decor my sisters have all over their houses. 'Home is where your heart is,' and that ilk."

"Oh. Okay." But her tone didn't say things were okay. Her tone said something was troubling her. Something deeper than how to define or qualify the attributes of a happy home.

"Anya? What are you asking? What do you mean by a responsibility to one's self? Like self-esteem? Personality? Personal values?"

"I...well, all of that. Yeah, and...never mind. I was just..." He felt the swish of her hair against his arm as she shook her head. When had she taken her hair out of her braid?

"Hey, the rule was honesty. Remember?"

"Are we even playing my made-up game anymore?"

"Does it matter? Can't we be honest with each other without games?"

"Well, yeah..."

"So why did my point about heritage and history bother you?"

"It's just..." She huffed a sigh. "Being from an Indian family while living in an American city, I've always felt like I was walking a line between two worlds. I wanted to make my traditional grandmother happy and meet my parents' expectations, while also wanting to blend in with my friends and feel accepted by others for who I was and not—" Her exhale sounded louder than normal in the dark of the pit. "Geez, this went off the rails. How did we get so deep in the weeds?"

A chuckle swelled in his chest. "You're the one who suggested a game."

Her response was a low hum-growl of irritation. "I change my vote. Let's go back to professions and eye color. My favorite color is red, but I went through a pink phase as a kid."

He reached toward where he knew she was sitting and found her cheek with what he intended to be a platonic pat on her shoulder.

She yelped and swatted at his hand.

"Easy! It's just me."

"God! Give me warning before you do that. I thought it was a spider or a mouse or something."

"No critters. Just me. Heads up...incoming again." He grazed his hand along her cheek, under the cascade of her thick hair until his palm rested on her nape. He squeezed the tense tendons there, and she sighed. The whisper of her breath in the darkness sent a quaver through him that heightened his senses. He became hyper-aware of the soft veil of her hair against his skin, the silkiness of the skin beneath his fingers. What he'd intended as a simple kindness to help relax Anya suddenly became saturated with sensual overtones for him.

"Oh, don't stop. That feels good," she said, a moan of pleasure behind the words that sent another flash of heat through his veins.

He took a beat to clear his throat and refocus his train of thought before he said, "No doubt. Your muscles are as tense as piano wires."

"Imagine that," she said dryly.

"Maybe you should stop imagining we're sharing this cellar with spiders and mice."

"Maybe I'll try. Maybe you should tell me about your family, so I can distract myself."

Brody laughed. "Point for Anya. Now let's see..." He continued massaging her neck as he collected his thoughts. "I have a large family, as you might remember, since they all kinda flooded the hospital at some point or another after I shish-kebabbed my leg."

"Yes. I remember sisters and their husbands and at least one niece. The one you rescued. Uh, your parents... Who am I missing?"

"A younger brother. We adopted Daryl when he was a toddler. His mom and mine were close friends and had been for years. When his mom, a divorcée, was diagnosed with late-stage cancer, my mom volunteered to help with Daryl. We took him in when she grew too sick to take care of him, and at some point, my mom and Rosalee had a heart-to-heart conversation where my mom promised to raise Daryl. Papers were signed before Rosalee died making our family his legal guardians, so formal adoption was the next natural step a couple years later. The judge tried to balk because Daryl is black, but mom wouldn't hear of it. She told that judge in no uncertain terms that Daryl was every bit a part of our family, and he'd better not let race be a factor in his decision. Daryl belonged with us, and she would keep fighting the courts until he was legally ours."

"Hmm, so your mom is a warrior? A crusader?"

Brody frowned, never having thought of his gentle and loving mother in such militaristic terms. "I...no. I mean, she has the strength and determination and intelligence to fight public battles or lead championing causes, but she's not that brash or outspoken. I guess the difference was she was standing up for her child. Her family. When it comes to family, she'd move mountains to defend and protect. She is the truest form of nurturer. She loves to feed us, and babysit grandkids, and raise her garden and teach us all to appreciate the little things in life. She's happiest when she is baking cookies with her children or grands and passing on family recipes. Especially Scottish ones."

"Scottish?"

"Oh, aye," he said, employing his best Scottish brogue. "My Nanna, my paternal grandmother, lives with Mom and Dad. Nanna was born in Scotland and lived there until she married Da just after World War II. Da's family was also Scottish, but they had been living here in North Carolina for a generation or so. They bought the hundred and fifty acres of land where Cameron Glen is now and had the idea of building and renting vacation cabins on the property as a source of income."

"Cameron Glen, huh? Seems like I've heard your place mentioned before around town. You sell Christmas trees?"

"Yep. And rent cabins. And have a produce stand on weekends in the summer. I'm not really involved with the produce stand. That's mostly Isla, Nanna and Mom." Beside him, he felt Anya stiffen, and he wondered what it was about produce that would have evoked such a reaction. "Is something—"

"Shh. I heard something," she whispered.

Holding his breath, he strained to listen. From the small ventilation hole they'd made to the surface, he heard the quiet clatter of tumbling rocks, the low thud of booted footsteps and the creak of shifting timber. A grunt.

He placed a hand on her leg and squeezed as if to say, "I hear it, too."

Someone was up there. But who? Rescuers? A bear? The sniper?

Only one way to find out. Brody stood and moved directly below the air hole. Cupping his hands around his mouth, he shouted, "Hello? Anyone there? We need help! We're trapped down here under the rubble."

A grumbled curse filtered down from above. A shadow moved at the top of the narrow air hole that was too small to see anything of consequence. Then something blocked the light coming from the air hole, and Brody took a step toward where he had left the shovel, meaning to reopen the gap or somehow signal whoever was above.

Instead, an ear-shattering blast tore through the cellar.

Anya screamed. Brody cussed and stumbled back to Anya.

Another shot rang into the dark hole where they were trapped with nowhere to take cover.

Brody fumbled in the blackness to find Anya. She'd already instinctively curled into a ball, and he lay across her, determined to do anything he could to protect her. Another shot and the sound of glass shattering, as if one of the jars on the shelves had shattered.

Things grew quiet for a moment, and somehow Brody knew it was essential that he and Anya remain absolutely quiet. They had to give the impression they'd been killed, or the sniper's fire would continue…until they were, in fact, dead.

Beneath him, Anya drew a breath that carried a half whimper of fear, and he hurriedly pressed a hand over her mouth. In his quietest voice, he whispered in her ear. "No sound. None."

Her head moved. A nod of understanding. Though neither of them so much as inhaled, her body was trembling, and Brody tried to calm the powerful thrash of his heart, convinced the loud thumping in his ears was audible above, too.

The silence was shattered by two more shots fired into the black pit where they huddled. More jars shattered. Something stung Brody's cheek, but he didn't move. Didn't breathe.

A male voice above them grumbled something, adding a vile epithet, clearly intended for him and Anya. He felt Anya's body jerk in silent sobs or spasms of fear, but she made no noise.

Finally, the shadows above shifted again. Once more, a thin beam of light streamed in the ventilation hole. Shuffling sounds. Silence.

Then something new rained down through the air channel. Brody frowned, trying to discern in the darkness what new threat or evil they were facing. Anya too raised her head, angling it toward their source of fresh oxygen.

Her hand gripped his arm, her fingernails digging in. An instant later, he realized what she must have sensed. The tumble from above was dirt and pebbles. The sniper was burying their ventilation hole, ensuring that if his bullets had failed to kill them, lack of air would do the job all too soon.

Having listened for several moments for any signs of life from below—and being pretty certain his shots had finished off anyone underground—Sol kicked soil and debris from his ruined cabin over the small hole he'd fired through and stomped down the loose dirt.

Satisfied he'd done all he could to be rid of the bastards who'd breached his safe house, necessitating its destruction, Sol collected his hunting rifle and Ruger pistol and headed out. He had little time before a wide variety of law enforcement came swarming over his mountain looking for survivors, looking for evidence, looking for *him*. His job now was to vanish. Finding another isolated spot where he could live off the grid and not raise suspicion would take time. Until then, he had to hide in plain sight, which was a bit trickier.

Sol started his hike down the mountain, climbing over the rubble of the landslide he'd created, heading for the more rugged eastern slopes where he'd be less likely to encounter rescue teams coming up the mountain. As he ducked into the tree line, he gave his handiwork one last look. Yep, the cabin was sufficiently buried—along with anything and anyone who could bear witness against him.

Chapter 7

"He plugged the air hole!" Anya whispered minutes later when they dared to move. A timbre of frustration—and a grain of despair—thickened her voice.

"Yep," Brody said, sounding equally disgruntled.

Not wanting to give in to the fingers of fear that strummed her nerves, she took a deep breath and exhaled slowly, shook the tension from her hands. "So we open it up again. Where's the shovel?" She dug the phone from her pocket and switched the flashlight app on. "I'll go first."

Brody caught her arm as she shoved to her feet. "Careful. There'll be broken glass around from the jars he shot up."

A fresh shudder of spent adrenaline rolled through her when she realized how lucky they were not to be gut shot…or dead. She aimed the light to the shelves and found the puddle of preserved peaches, pickles and broken glass. Swinging the beam around the confined space, she found splattered tomato puree dripping like bloody gore from one set of shelves and more shards of the broken jars glittering like diamonds all across the dirt floor. "Geez, what a mess."

Anya glanced to Brody, who was rolling to his feet, dabbing with his fingers at something red on his temple. She lifted a corner of her mouth, prepared to tease him about wearing tomato, when she realized the red was a deeper tone. Crimson.

Blood.

"You're hurt!" She surged toward him to examine his wound. "Were you shot?" With an encompassing scan, she searched his length for further evidence of injury.

"Can't say what got me. Probably just glass." He held out his arms, turned up his palms, and Anya saw the multiple tiny cuts left by flying fragments of the shattered jar. But no sign of a bullet wound—thank God. "Are you okay?"

She checked her own arms and felt her cheeks for signs of blood. Nothing.

Because he covered you with his body, shielded you, protected you. Gratitude swelled in her chest, and something sweet and warm coiled in her core. *Her protector.*

Brody picked tiny pieces of glass from his skin with the tips of his fingers, flicking them aside. "Get the shovel. We need to both open the ventilation hole again and scrape this broken glass to one side of the cellar. Maybe bury it with dirt, so we don't cut ourselves again in the darkness."

"First things first," she countered. Rising on her tiptoes, she placed a quick kiss on his cheek. "That is for your gallant gesture of covering me when the shooting started. You are a true gentleman, sir."

He tossed a quick smile her way. "Call it habit or instinct. I've been looking out for three sisters my whole life. Now two nieces, as well."

"Mmm-hmm. I remember that it was rescuing your niece that landed you in the ER."

"That was less chivalry and more klutziness on my part."

"Not to hear your niece tell it. You're her hero."

"She's five and easily impressed."

"I'm not five. And I'm impressed. And grateful."

"Hey, it earned me a kiss. I'd do it again in a heartbeat."

She felt herself flushing as she pivoted to search the shelves for something that contained alcohol or some other germ killer. Did the hermit sniper keep a first aid kit down here? Spotting a bottle of Evan Williams on the bottom shelf to her right, she opened the bourbon and said, "Hold out your arm. The last thing you need is for any of those cuts to get infected before we get out of here and you get proper wound treatment."

"Shouldn't we get that vent hole open first?" he said, tipping his head to look up where their precious fresh air had once come.

"This will just take a second. Even now, bacteria from all this dirt and grime are burrowing into your body, ready to wreak havoc." She wiggled her fingers motioning for him to hold out his arms.

"Hang on." He took the bottle from her and tipped it up for a swallow, smacking his lips and exhaling loudly when he finished.

"Oh, come on, soldier. You've had a rod through your leg. Don't tell me the sting of a few cuts has you shaking in your boots?"

"Naw. The stings I can handle. Just hate to see perfectly good bourbon go to waste."

He had a point. No need to overdo it.

She set the bottle on the ground and untucked her T-shirt, finding what she deemed the cleanest part. After handing him the phone to hold and tearing off a square of her shirt to make a rag, Anya doused the fabric with bourbon and swabbed the cuts with gentle strokes. She followed up with tiny splashes of the liquor, to be safe, then recapped the bottle. "There. Not ER standard measures but hopefully enough."

He set a hand on her waist and nudged her close... and kissed her forehead. "Thank you. Once again, your care was top-notch."

Even without swigging the bourbon, a muzzy, intoxicating thrill raced through her. If such a simple peck on the face had her this giddy, what would a real kiss on the lips do to her? Had Mark's kisses ever given her such a deeply pleasurable visceral reaction? Not that she could remember...which meant *no.*

"Okay, let's do this." Brody passed her back the phone, retrieved the shovel, and checked the knife still strapped on the handle. Next, he grabbed the back of the chair and planted it in the center of the cellar again. In the dim, refracted glow of the mobile phone flashlight, she saw him frown. He wrapped his hand around her wrist, angling the flashlight beam onto the seat of the chair. The seat now sported several large splintered holes, and one leg had a chunk missing. He grunted and put one foot up, testing the chair's strength before moving his other foot up. The chair creaked but held his weight.

While he hacked at the clog of dirt blocking the air hole, repeating the tedious process they'd only just finished an hour or so before, she used her boot to scrape as much of the broken glass and splinters of wood from the chair into a pile in the corner. After a few minutes they switched jobs, taking turns as before until finally they had a new ventilation hole made. Even with turning off the flashlight app now and then to conserve battery, the light needed to complete the cleanup and hole jabbing process sapped another twelve percent of her battery. She used an additional one percent to attempt to send another text message to her search group leader, another to Chloe and another to Brody's sister.

As Anya stashed the phone and took her spot on the ground, sitting next to Brody as they resumed the wait for rescue, a frisson of anxiety slithered through her. What would they do when the phone died? Without light, without a means to signal the outside world—the only things giving her hope in the bleak, dark pit…

She leaned into Brody and amended the last thought. Not the only things. She had Brody, and he was a tremendous source of comfort and reassurance. Anya closed her eyes and settled in for a nap, exhausted by the day's efforts and emotional turmoil…and found that despite her circumstances, she was smiling. Because of Brody.

Anya was surprised at how quickly time became elastic, sitting in the dark, no cues from the sun to tell the time of day. Boredom and anxiousness to be rescued slowed time to a crawl. Brody, his arm draped loosely around her shoulders, had grown still, quiet, his breathing deeper a few minutes earlier, and when she whispered his name quietly, she got no response. She didn't need to wake her phone screen again to know it was not much later than eight o'clock. She'd checked the time every fifteen minutes or so for the last three hours, and finally resigned herself to the creeping clock.

She propped against Brody, shifting her hips to get more comfortable and resting a hand over the steady thump of his heartbeat. That *bu-bump* under her palm reassured her, helped her relax enough to search for sleep. The subtle scent of him near her nose sparked an awareness beyond the most obvious. She leaned into that tingle as it spread through her. Analyzed it. The darkness. The warmth of him close to her. The sound of his breath. The texture of his skin. Softness of his shirt. Deprived of vision, she feasted her remaining senses on him, and a sweet mellowness expanded in her core. If she had to be trapped in a remote mountain pit, she could do a lot worse than having Brody for company.

She apparently drifted off for a while, because some time later, Brody roused, and his movement woke her. The engulfing darkness confused her for a few seconds, until her groggy brain recalled her situation, her location. "Brody?"

"Sorry. Didn't mean to wake you, but my butt was getting numb. I had to reposition."

"It's okay."

A dim but surprisingly bright light flared beside her with a bluish glow, and she blinked against the glare as she angled her head to find Brody's watch lit.

"What time is it?" she asked.

"One a.m."

She sat up, rubbed the crick in her neck, arched her back, and then groped to her feet to stretch more fully. She heard the scuffling of feet, and he gave a quiet groan before she sensed him standing near her. She dug the phone from her pocket and switched it on, aiming it at the dirt floor when the light glared in her dark-adjusted eyes. "I need a snack. You?"

"Sure. Surprise me."

She picked a jar of green beans off the shelf and struggled to open it. "Man, the things you take for granted until you don't have it. Like Frosted Flakes or Oreos for a midnight snack."

"Or a bathroom."

She raised a startled glance to him, and suddenly, because he'd mentioned it, she had to go...badly. "Oh, geez."

He lifted the empty peaches jar. "How's your aim?"

She sputtered a chuckle, then gave in to a full belly laugh. "Oh, geez!"

He nodded. "Right?"

They turned their backs for each other, so they could both take care of their business with relative privacy. Once finished with that task, he took the green beans from her, twisted off the lid and passed them to her. "Pretend they're chocolate."

She snorted. "Ooookay." She tipped the jar to eat a few beans, and while they were a far cry from chocolate cookies, she was grateful to have food at all. After passing the green beans back and forth with Brody a couple times, Anya turned off her phone and settled again on the floor next to him. "So...you said you were a volunteer fireman and full-time landscaper slash business owner. How big is your company?"

"I have a couple of employees but do most of the work myself."

"Pardon my ignorance but...what does that involve besides mowing and planting flower beds?"

"Well, a large part of it *is* mowing and planting flower beds, but I have a contract with my brother-in-law who has a construction company. I handle the planning and execution of landscaping for his new builds. I decide things like where to put trees for energy efficiency or create privacy, increasing curb appeal, ease of maintenance. My family hires me to keep the grounds at Cameron Glen neat and flourishing." He paused as he took the green beans back from her. "Sometimes I wonder what I might have done if I'd decided to go to college, but the thing is I've always loved being outside, playing in the dirt."

"More power to ya then. I hate yard work, and I have a black thumb. I can't even keep my air plants alive."

"What! How do you kill an air plant?"

"Well, in my defense, it was really my cat that killed it. She nibbled on it, played with it. When it started looking really sad, I just gave up and threw it away."

"The cat?" he said, a teasing note in his tone.

She laughed. "No. The air plant, goofball. Whiskers is at home now wondering where the heck I am and pacing the kitchen floor, expecting her dinner." Her shoulders dropped as she thought of her gray-and-white cat waiting at home for her. She experienced a pang of longing for her furry friend's company and considered how long Whiskers could get by without her. She'd had a full bowl of dry food when Anya left that morning. If Anya didn't get out of this pit, would Chloe think to take care of Whiskers? Her best friend had a spare key to Anya's place. Surely…

"I've been thinking about getting a dog," Brody mused, pulling her from her worries over Whiskers.

"Why don't you?"

"Good question. Don't really know why I'm waiting. I guess I've just been reluctant to make the commitment. I kinda like being unencumbered, free to drop everything and head out of town on a moment's notice, have nothing more pressing than choosing a series to binge on my days off."

Reluctant to make the commitment. Anya's heart stilled as those words reverberated deep inside her. If she'd been harboring any illusions of pursuing a relationship with Brody if, no, *when—stay positive, Anya—* they got out of this hole, those few brutally honest words gave her pause. She had no interest in investing herself in another man who couldn't commit. Shoving aside the ache these thoughts brought on, she refocused on what Brody was saying.

"…family says I'm the quintessential bachelor, living the life of a guy without responsibilities, but I don't know if I'd go that far. I'm responsible. I have a business to run. Clients to make happy. A mortgage to pay. Maybe I don't always eat vegetables at dinner or wash my laundry before I'm out of underwear, but…pff. So I go commando one day while I catch up on washing. So what?"

Anya's pulse ticked harder at the suggestion of Brody going commando. Her mouth dried a little as, working to keep her tone light, she asked, "And where in your wash cycle were you yesterday when you dressed for the search?"

He gave a low, devilish chuckle. "Are you asking me if I'm wearing underwear, Ms. Patel?"

She laughed, even as she felt her cheeks flash hot. "I think I did. I guess the dark makes me bolder." When he said nothing for several seconds, she laughed again. "You're not going to answer? I have to imagine?"

"Well, you could…check for yourself."

The air whooshed from her lungs, and she wheezed, "I…what?"

His hand settled on her knee, and she jolted at the contact.

"I dare you. Double-dog dare you," he said, his tone thickly mischievous.

"Brody! What are you, eight years old?"

"Yep. Are you chicken?"

Okay, she thought, allowing the darkness to embolden her. "Not me."

She ran her hand down his chest until she reached his waist. Gathering the edge of his shirt in her fist she tugged it up. The wiry hairs on his belly tickled her fingers as she felt blindly for access under top of his jeans. She thought she heard his breath hitch as she slipped her hand under the button of his fly, a slow cautious quest. She quickly discovered the elastic band of undershorts and pulled her hand out. Did that mild stab in her chest mean she was relieved or disappointed?

Before she could analyze further, the hand on her knee slid up the front of her thigh, over her belly to the waist of her cargo pants. She felt the scrape of a knuckle against her midriff as he dipped a finger inside. "What about you? Silk? Cotton?"

Gulping air silently, she quipped. "Go ahead. Find out."

His fingers delved deeper, and his knuckles flexed against her skin as he explored the texture of her panties. "Hmm. Cotton. Very practical."

"And cooler for a day of hiking. I have prettier ones, silkier ones, at home." Again, heat bloomed in her cheeks. Why was she telling him this?

Why not? an impish voice in her head prodded. *What's the harm in flirting?*

"Mmm. Nice," his voice was a purr as he flattened his warm palm against her belly. A moment later, he drew his fingertips up her side, over her ribs, to her throat. Even through her shirt, the trailing of his fingers set her on fire. At her neckline, he smoothed the callused pads of his fingers along her collarbone. The tender caress was seductive, mesmerizing. A sweet lethargy stole through her, and she allowed her head to loll back against the wall. She savored the gentle stroke of his fingers and the tingles that spiraled through her blood.

"I'm trying to remember exactly how you were dressed today," he murmured. "I was focused on your eyes, your smile, the way your nose wrinkles when you squint in the sun. The way wisps of your hair escaped your braid and brushed your cheek."

She tugged up a corner of her mouth, charmed by his admission.

As his fingers trailed along her throat, he murmured, "Hmm. No necklace. I thought I remembered jewelry."

"I have—"

"Shh, don't tell me. Let me discover…" His fingers traced her cheek as they moved to her earlobes. "Ah, studs. Some kind of gemstone. Sapphires?"

"Nuh-uh," she hummed, reluctant to even rouse enough from her repose to even grunt her response. "Rubies."

"Right. 'Cause you like red."

A different sort of pleasure filled her. He'd paid attention, remembered. Mark couldn't even be bothered to remember how she drank her tea…or her birthday. "Mmm-hmm."

Brody ran his thumb around the shell of her ear, then massaged the whole ear between his fingers. *Wow, who knew your ears were such a sensitive erogenous zone?*

She wanted to whimper a protest when his touch left

her ear and ventured elsewhere, but the soft exploration of her temples, eyebrows, the bridge of her nose and lips was so intimate and arousing, she could do no more than sigh her pleasure.

When he caught her chin in his palm and tipped her face up, she followed his lead willingly, pliant to his guidance. Then his nose bumped hers and hot, chapped lips closed over her mouth.

A bolt of adrenaline shot through her, but rather than spoil her relaxed and heady mood, the electric surge heightened the crackle of every nerve ending, wound the coil of desire tighter in her core. She parted her lips for him and met the tip of his tongue with her own.

When he slid his arms around her and eased her more fully prone on the dirt floor, she went easily. Finally, he shifted one leg over hers before settling in the cradle of her hips, pressing his weight, his groin against hers. Anya arched up, craving the contact, telling him with her body that his kiss, his hands, his body were everything she wanted.

His fingers stabbed her hair, and he held her head still as his mouth angled and explored hers, the kiss deepening. Her hands scrabbled at his back, yanking the shirt out of her way so she could smooth her palms against the play of muscle and sinew in his shoulders, along his spine.

Now, all shyness discarded, she plunged a hand under his jeans, inside his briefs to cup one taut buttock. In one controlled move, he rolled, bringing her with him as he moved to his back and positioned her on top. Breathless, she raised her head, straddling him and staring down in the darkness. She saw nothing in the blackness but felt his panting as a warm stir of air on her cheeks.

"Do you have…protection…with you?" she asked.

He exhaled more heavily, the sound frustrated. "No. I had no reason to think… I mean, I'm healthy. That's not a worry."

"Same here," she reassured him.

"It's just…geez."

Anya struggled to clear her lust muddled mind enough to make mental calculations, remember where in her cycle she was. Maybe…

But he was sitting up, scooting her off him, groaning. "I'm sorry. I shouldn't have…"

"I didn't complain, did I?" She raked her hair from her face with her hand, and after a few minutes of staring into the darkness, mindfully distracting herself from what she *wanted* to be doing, Anya woke her phone to check the time. Two o'clock.

Brody draped an arm around her shoulders and snuggled her closer. "You know, it's a proven fact that time passes slower every time you check the clock."

She grumbled her frustration. "I believe it."

"So…let's sleep. Huh?" He placed a palm on her temple to nudge her head to his shoulder. "They'll resume searching at first light, and with any luck, we'll be home by this time tomorrow."

Home—her bed, her cat, her clean pajamas. She smiled. "I like the way you think, Cameron."

"Ever optimistic. My dad says, 'If you have to be something, why not be positive?'"

Anya tried to conjure an image of an older version of Brody. Of any older man she'd met when Brody had come through the ER. "I don't think I met your dad last summer. Was he there?"

"At some point, my whole family came through the hospital to see me before I was discharged, but the day of the accident? I was too dopey on painkillers to remember much."

She angled her chin up, even though she couldn't see him. "What do you remember about me?"

"Besides you turning down my marriage proposal?"

She gave a humored snort. "Besides that."

"Your smile. When the pain was at its worst, I focused on your smile. You were a true angel to me that day. You kindness was comforting, and your cool competence was reassuring. I remember thinking I was really lucky you were on duty." He bent his head and kissed her hair. "Kudos, Ms. Patel."

"You're welcome, Blue Eyes."

"The search for a missing hiker near Kiper Mountain took a macabre and deadly turn yesterday, when a sniper opened fire on the searchers, killing one local man and injuring six others."

Sol raised his gaze to the television playing in the motel lobby where he was eating a bowl of cereal from the free breakfast bar. He hadn't stayed at the motel that night, but no one questioned him as he strode confidently into the lobby and helped himself to coffee, cereal and a banana. He had, in fact, slept in the woods behind the highway-side motel. Now, as he shoveled his purloined breakfast, he listened intently to the news report of the events on the mountain. What did the police know? Had anyone seen enough of him to give a description?

"…as they escaped the gunfire, searchers reported the detonation of explosives, which created a rockslide," the newscaster read somberly.

"Good lord!" the woman at the table next to him said, shaking her head, "What is this world coming to?"

Sol feigned dismay. "Terrible, huh?"

"Two members of the local SAR team and two Valley Haven volunteer firemen are still missing following the landslide. A new search for the missing rescuers will resume later this morning. Sophie Bane, the hiker who disappeared on Kiper Mountain three weeks ago, is still missing, but her family, who describe Sophie as an avid outdoors woman, holds out hope she is still alive."

Sophie Bane. Sol let the name roll through his mind. So that was her name. Pretty thing. He'd had fun taunting her, letting her know how her death would happen, seeing the flare of terror in her eyes. But if not for Sophie Bane, if not for the nosey searchers, he'd be at home in his cabin right now, instead of looking over his shoulder and rebuilding his life on the run.

He firmed his mouth in a snarl of disgust. If Sophie and the missing rescuers weren't already dead, he'd make sure they were by the end of the summer. Vengeance wasn't just required. It would be sweet and satisfying.

But his first order of business today was finding a place he could shower. On the mountain, it didn't much matter if he smelled bad. Personal hygiene wasn't a priority. But in America, out in society, if you stank, you stood out. People noticed you. And he had to blend in to keep a low profile until he settled somewhere.

Fortunately, the inattentive or indifferent staff of the motel provided his opportunity to bathe, as well as eat breakfast. As he left the lobby, sauntering down the cracked sidewalk in front of the rooms, the door to Room 106 stood open as the housekeeper walked back and forth from her supply cart, parked outside the door.

Sol strolled into Room 106 as if he belonged there and called a cheerful greeting to the maid.

She scurried out of the bathroom, rubber gloves on her hands, and blinked at him as if confused. "I'm so sorry, sir. I thought you had checked out."

Sol took a seat on the freshly made bed and swiped a hand across his forehead. "Not quite yet. I just went out for my morning exercise. A brisk walk is a great way to get the blood pumping."

She smiled, saying, "It is. I'll be out of your way in just a moment."

He gave her a charming wink. "No problem."

Five minutes later, he was in the shower, his clothes piled at his feet. He'd wash the shirt and pants with the bar soap after he finished scrubbing his body, then wear them wet, letting them air dry in the sunshine as he walked to his next stop.

Breakfast…check. Shower…check. Next up…a car.

He had to find a place to hole up for a few days until things settled down. Then he had a score to settle with the searchers who trespassed on his mountain and destroyed his life.

Chapter 8

The next morning, Anya woke to her muscles aching and her stomach growling. The darkness confused her for a moment until the nightmare of the previous day crashed through her brain, bringing a sinking sense of dismay. She reached for Brody, wanting the reassurance of his presence to buoy her spirits as he'd done yesterday. *Misery loves company and all that, huh?*

But he wasn't there. "Brody?"

"Oh, morning glory," he said and relief swamped her.

Relief? *What, you thought he'd been rescued and left you behind?*

No, she told the taunting voice in her head. This darkness is...disorienting. Unnerving. Wearing.

"Can I interest you in some breakfast beets?"

"Beets?"

"I picked a jar at random without the light, and that's what I grabbed."

"Ugh. I think I'll eat my protein bar." She rolled on her side to fish the protein bar from her cargo pants pocket. The bar had gotten flattened overnight, but it tasted better than canned beets. She woke her phone screen to see what time it was—8:47 a.m.—and check for missed messages—none. Of course not. Not with no cell signal up here on the mountain.

In the dim light, Brody moved back across the cellar to sit beside her. "It's a new morning. By now, they've organized rescue teams and law enforcement and will be out looking for us. We're going home today. Count on it."

"Oh, Mr. Be Positive, I hope you're right." She took a large bite of her protein bar and thought about what her family must be thinking. Had they heard she was missing? Had they driven to Valley Haven to wait for news or were they in Charlotte, sitting by the phone? "I hate to think how this is worrying my parents. My grandmother."

"Wow! You're a mind reader," Brody said. "I was thinking the same thing, right down to the grandmother."

"Well, not too surprising. New day. Talk of rescue. Of course our minds turn to our family, their worry."

"Families are all the same in a crisis. Huh? People really are more alike than different, big picture." His tone was musing, but she couldn't help wondering why his thoughts had gone to differences. Was he thinking about her being Indian, or was she paranoid, because it had ended up mattering more to Mark than he'd admitted at first?

"Yeah," she said, glossing over her questions.

"I think it's cool that you and I both had our grandmothers living with us, growing up."

"I loved having her around, especially since she was the one who indulged us when our parents were strict."

"Oh, definitely. Nanna spoiled us. Flat out."

"Snuck you extra money to buy yourself treats?" she asked, remembering her own Gran slipping her cash on the down low.

"Sometimes. Lots of baked goods. Generous birthday cash. Privileges that broke parental rules. It drove my parents nuts, but she was unrepentant."

Anya chuckled. "My Gran is eighty-five years young and still full of energy and opinions."

"Sounds like Nanna. I'd love for you to meet her," he said.

"I'd like that, too."

They were each silent for a moment before he said, "What generation of your family first moved to the US?"

"My grandparents. And like your family, my grandparents were very influential in keeping family traditions and our heritage alive and well, even as my parents raised us to assimilate in modern American culture." She paused. "Well, mostly."

"Mostly?"

"Yeah. My grandmother moved in with us when I was ten, and whereas Mom let us have hamburgers and mac and cheese as kids, Gran had Mom making traditional Indian meals more often than not."

"You don't sound too happy about it."

"I don't?" She sighed. "I didn't mean to sound dismissive. I know I was lucky to have my grandmother with us, and the food was fine. Delicious, really. I guess I was just thinking about the leftovers and how Mom insisted on sending leftovers with me to school for lunch."

"What's wrong with leftovers?"

She grunted. "Well, when you're already the only Indian kid in your school except your sister, and you just want to fit in, having a lunch seasoned with curry or turmeric or coriander kind of makes you stand out in the lunchroom. I had kids tease me about how my food smelled."

"They teased you?"

"Oh, come on, Brody. Kids always tease anything that is different. And my lunches of korma and lamb vindaloo were definitely different from the kids eating peanut butter and jelly or the school's pizza and corn."

"Ah, yes. Cardboard pizza and canned corn. I remember those. Personally, given the choice, I think korma for lunch sounds great."

"But would you have as a ten-year-old or a preteen?"

"Maybe not. But I would have empathized with you."

"Empathized? How so?"

"I told you my grandmother is Scottish, right?"

"Right?"

"Well, when I brought friends over, she thought it was great fun to have them try haggis or Cullen skink. Next thing I know, my friends have turned it into a joke, a dare on par with climbing the water tower or leaving a frog in the math teacher's desk."

A laugh tumbled from her. "What the heck are haggis and Cullen skink?"

"Haggis is a meat dish made from sheep's organs, oatmeal and spices."

"Which sheep's organs?"

"You don't want to know."

"Oh." Anya laughed, then after thinking about his answer, her tone darkened. "Ooh!"

"Yeah. Cullen skink is fish stew basically. I like them

both, but then I grew up eating them. My sweet Nanna never knew all those boys coming to the house were snickering behind her back."

"Aww." Her heart tugged for Brody's grandmother.

"She also fed them tablet, but they did like that."

"And tablet is…"

"Candy. Basically just sugar, butter and milk. Very sweet. Very rich. Sometimes flavored with whisky."

"Oh-ho," she said with a startled laugh, "I can see why that would be popular with your friends!"

"Right?" He gave a meditative sounding hum. "I hadn't thought about those days in a long time."

Her bottom was getting numb, so she shifted and leaned her shoulder lightly against him. In response, he tightened his grip on her hand and stroked his thumb along her wrist.

"So is real Indian food anything like what is served in Indian restaurants?"

"I suppose it depends on the restaurant. Ours is authentic, although Dad has added some more Americanized items to the menu to appeal to a broader customer base."

"Wait…do you mean to say your family has a restaurant?" His tone sounded intrigued, excited even. "In Valley Haven?"

"We do as of a few years ago. Dad's idea. It's in Charlotte, though, not Valley Haven. That's where I grew up."

"I thought you said he was a doctor? A neurologist?"

"He is, but he's also not one to miss out on a business investment opportunity. When Indian cuisine became more popular, my dad decided, why not? Mom already cooked enough for an army most nights, and he got my sister and brother-in-law to help run the day-today. They've done pretty well, despite struggles within the food industry of late."

"Cool. How's the butter chicken? That's my favorite."

"Excellent, of course," she said with a laugh. "But don't take my word for it. Head down to Queen City sometime and try it for yourself."

"Maybe I will," he said, and she felt his hand on her arm, sliding down to take her hand. "If you'll go with me. Show me around your old neighborhood? Introduce me to your family?"

"I—" She fumbled mentally for a moment. "Well… sure." Introduce him to her family? That sounded so… formal. Serious. As if they had *that* kind of relationship. Not that she didn't want to explore a relationship with Brody, but…

She'd introduced Mark to her family and been humiliated when he left her. Dismissed her. Essentially rejecting not just her, but her family as well. She still choked on that bitter pill when she remembered him. She wasn't sure she was ready to introduce anyone else to her family. And her heart wasn't ready to put that kind of faith in anyone yet…even if Brody's hand squeezing hers did send waves of warmth spinning through her blood, puddling in her core.

"It's great that your family has something they can work at together, build together, share in the day-to-day operation. Building Cameron Glen to what it is and maintaining it for the next generation has been… well, I wouldn't trade the experiences or the memories for anything." He made a happy sound sigh. "I got into landscaping initially because I was drafted to help my grandfather with groundskeeping at Cameron Glen. My dad stepped the property up from the level Da had established, and the vegetables and fruit trees became a lucrative summer side business to renting cabins."

Anya closed her eyes, content to listen to Brody's mellifluous voice, the joy that vibrated in his tone. If she tried, she could almost pretend she were somewhere besides this dank, smelly hole in the ground.

"And the Christmas trees? Whew! The first year we invited the public to come and cut a tree from the property, my dad and I realized what a market there was for fresh fir trees. We were sitting on the means to grow a commodity that would pay for itself several times over in few seasons. And the delay is only because you have to hold back some trees to give them a chance to reach larger size to meet the demand for taller trees."

Anya angled onto her hip and leaned into Brody as their conversation continued. As impatient as she was for rescue, she had to admit that just being with Brody, sharing memories, making lame jokes and whiling away the minutes in idyll chatter was…pleasant. Like the best parts of a first date, happening under the worst conditions.

Would there be a first date when they got out of this place? *When*…because his optimism was contagious, and she refused to accept that the rescue teams wouldn't find them soon.

Hours later, she repeated that affirmation, trying to say positive when they'd heard no activity above them yet. *Help is coming. Just hang on…*

Shoving to her feet, Anya stretched the kinks from her back and shoulders. "I'm getting hungry again. Want anything in particular?"

"Huh. Think Pizza Hut delivers up here?"

Anya laughed. "If only. Can I interest you in some canned corn or home preserved tomatoes instead?"

Brody mumbled something she didn't catch then said, "What are our other choices?"

As she keyed on her phone, she gave each leg a shake, too. Her right foot tingled a little, having gone to sleep after being tucked under her for the last half hour or so. When she'd turned on the flashlight app, she shone it over the jars and lined up cans reading labels and identifying fruits and vegetables in the Mason jars. "Looks like jarred okra, tomatoes, more peaches and green beans. Canned tuna, sardines—yuck—ravioli, corned beef hash—yuck, again—mayonnaise…" She crouched to check lower shelves. "Hmm, no. This looks like non-edibles. Motor oil, batteries, Sterno… wait. There are some jars in the back behind the Sterno." She stuck the phone in the waist of her cargo pants, so she'd have two hands to move the case of canned heating fuel. Once the box of Sterno fuel was out of her way, she took the phone in hand again and angled her head to see the jars at the back of the shelf. She frowned at the odd-looking contents as she dragged one of the jars closer to examine. If she didn't know better, she'd say that was—

Gasping, Anya released the jar and stumbled back.

"Oh, God! Oh, no no no no!" She wiped her hand on her shirt as if she could erase the memory of having touched the offending jar.

"Anya? What the—"

"A hand. A human hand."

Chapter 9

Brody narrowed his eyes on Anya, sure he'd misunder-stood, or she'd mistaken what she saw or…something. But the terror in her eyes was no trick of shadows cast by the light from her phone, which she'd dropped as she reeled back from the shelf as if she'd seen a demon.

He rolled to his knees and picked the phone up from the dirt floor. Angling it toward the lower shelf she'd been exploring, he crooked his neck to see for himself what was down there.

The beam from the phone glinted on the glass of a large canning jar, and he pulled it closer for a better look. Holding the jar up, he stared in disbelief at what was, unmistakably, a severed human hand floating in some sort of clear liquid.

His gut roiled, and an eerie shiver crawled through him. He muttered a choice word, his voice hoarse, and, with stiff movement, he put the jar on a higher shelf.

"Brody…"

"Hang on." He ducked his head and aimed the light to check the lower shelf again.

There were other jars. More strange contents. Swallowing the bitter taste of bile at the back of his throat, Brody carefully pulled out three more jars from behind the fuel supplies.

Anya scuttled up behind him, clinging to his arm as they examined the next jar. A heart, also floating in clear liquid. Anya put a hand to her mouth, and he felt the shudder that raced through her. "Is there more?"

He nodded and slid the next jar from its hiding place. It took a moment for Brody to realize what he was looking at. Ears. Small hoop earrings still through the lobes. He placed this jar next to the others on the higher shelf before drawing a deep breath for composure and reaching for the next jar.

"Geez, no more. I can't—" She waved a hand and turned away, stumbling a few steps back toward the corner where they'd been sitting.

"You okay?"

"Not really."

He moved to put a hand on her back. "You're a nurse. I'd have thought you'd have a stronger stomach."

She swallowed audibly and inhaled deeply. "Yeah, I've seen my share of blood and guts. Even dissected things all through nursing school, but that was different. It's not the body parts that bother me as much as… the implication of how they got in those jars. And for what purpose?"

Brody jolted. He hadn't allowed his brain to go so far as to consider all the gory aspects of what their find implied.

Now, with his heart in his throat, he returned to the lower shelf and brought out the last jar stashed behind the motor oil. Shining the light on this last jar, he knew he was looking at some sort of organ.

"Looks like a gall bladder," Anya said, and he cast her a worried look. "But why? What sick reason— And how—" She shook her head and groaned, "Geez."

"Anya, what are you thinking?" he asked, even though it didn't take too much brainpower to draw a straight line from their discovery to…evil.

"I'm thinking my earlier concerns about spiders down here would be preferable to this…whatever this is." She pressed a hand to her stomach, squinting as he turned the bright phone light on her. "Well, since he was holding Sophie captive down here, it's not a big leap to suppose he's held other people prisoner."

Brody exhaled slowly, letting Anya's theory roll around uncomfortably in his head. "Yeah."

"And…considering he has the…" she grimaced, "body parts saved in Mason jars like preserved peaches, it begs the question whether his intent was to keep them as trophies or—"

Rather than speak the gruesome and unthinkable, Anya pulled an expression of repulsion and angled her face away from the shelves.

"Maybe that's a reality we don't need to dwell on too long." Brody took a step toward Anya and gave her shoulder a consoling squeeze. "Until we're out of here, let's not make ourselves crazy with horror story scenarios. Right?"

She gave a shudder as if she could feel the brush of ghostly fingers down her spine, but lifting her chin, she whispered. "I'll try." She wrapped her arms around herself as if trying to keep from flying apart or warding off an unnerving chill. "Brody, that's just one shelf. What about…all these others?"

Brody followed her gaze as she cast her eyes from one shelving unit to another. One on each of the four walls, five shelves tall. His gut flip-flopped. What else, indeed. He wavered between the notion of playing ignorant for their sanity's sake and getting a complete picture to report to the authorities if—*when* they were rescued. The sniper, who'd clearly been living off the grid and keeping hikers as prisoners in this pit cellar, could easily have been responsible for more atrocities.

Brody rubbed his cheek, his two-day beard scratching his palm as he recalled the newspaper headline Emma had been discussing with the ladies in the high school office last week. His sister had been lamenting the lost hiker—Sophie—and when he'd tried to give her hope Sophie would be found, Emma had said, "They never found the two that went missing last year in the same area."

Brody's mouth went dry. Could they have found evidence of what happened to the other lost hikers? The notion was deeply unsettling.

He gave the shelves, loaded with supplies they hadn't fully explored, a closer scrutiny. "I know I just said we shouldn't dwell on it, but…what we're looking at in those jars is potentially proof of a crime. I think we have an obligation to see what else is down here."

Anya hunched her shoulders and wrinkled her nose. "I was afraid you'd say that…because it's what I was thinking, too." She paused a beat before adding, "Dang it."

"If you want to sit this one out, I can reconnoiter by myself."

She looked at him as if she wanted to accept his offer,

but after a moment she shook her head and dropped her arms to her sides with a deep breath. "No. I'm being a baby about this. I'm a trauma nurse. A trained SAR volunteer. A grown-up. I can face whatever horror he's got stashed down here. It was just the shock of finding that hand and knowing…"

Without finishing her sentence, she squared her shoulders and stuck her hand out for the phone. "My turn to go treasure hunting in the ghoul's storeroom."

"Anya, you don't have to—"

"It's all right. I can do this."

He handed her the phone but said, "*We'll* do it. To-gether."

Her smile reflected an appreciation and relief that she had someone with whom to share the ominous task. While she held the phone and poked warily at the boxes of rifle cartridges on a low shelf, he moved aside canned meats and condiments on another. "Nothing suspicious here. Unless you count the guy's clear obsession with canned fish of every kind."

"This shelf is just ammunition. Thank God. And who'd have thought I'd ever be glad to find a sniper's storage room full of rifle cartridges? But there it is."

"Yeah. Right?" He turned his attention to the top shelf. "Shine the light up here, will ya?"

She complied, and Brody stretched to access the top shelf. He swept away a lacy cobweb and a good bit of loose dirt, then slid several cans of soup and a coil of rope aside to search the back row of goods. A plastic storage box held a bag of rice, a bag of flour and a bag of cornmeal. Beside the plastic box sat a mousetrap with a dead mouse in the sprung clamp. He scooted a can of tomato soup in front of the trap and chose not to tell Anya about the dead mouse.

"Find anything?" she asked, as if reading his mind.

"Nothing worth mentioning."

"Nothing of note here, either," she muttered, motioning to the center shelves. She pivoted ninety degrees to face the next metal shelving unit. "Next up, canvas tarps and random steel cans and bowls." She exhaled with a little *whoo* sound of dread before whispering, "Please be empty. Please be empty."

While she checked the middle shelves, he crouched to push aside a five-gallon plastic gasoline can like the one he used to fuel up the riding mower and other lawn equipment the landscaping company used. The gas can slid easily, proving it was empty, and Brody was about to replace it and move on in his search when something lighter colored than the rich brown dirt surrounding them caught his attention. He got on his hands and knees for a better look. "Hey, shine the light down here."

Anya crouched beside him and aimed the beam from the phone where he pointed. "What is it?"

"There's a sheet of plywood back there, but it seems like it's embedded in the dirt, like making a wall or barrier of some sort."

"And you want to poke that hornet's nest, don't you?" she asked, her tone thick with sarcasm…and fear.

Brody chewed his lip. Weighed his choices. "Yeah. I do." He angled his head as he regarded her. "Aren't you even a little curious?"

"I don't know. At the moment, the old adage about ignorance being bliss sounds pretty good. Isn't it enough to be trapped down here with a hand, ears and a heart in jars?"

"It may be nothing, but I feel like we need to know. What if there's another way out of here? A passage to another door?"

She sighed. "You're right. The need to know outweighs my horror-movie logic that you don't want to know what's making that strange noise in the attic."

Brody gave a dry laugh. "Well, if it helps, you don't have to look. Help me move the shelf?"

Fortunately, this shelf wasn't burdened with so many jars and was reasonably easy to scoot away from the plywood panel. Brody knelt in front of the panel and examined it more closely, finding it had been screwed to metal brackets on a framework embedded in the dirt and rock wall. He pulled out his pocketknife again and used a small blade to loosen the screws. Once the screws were removed, he used a larger blade to pry the warped wood away from the frame. He set the panel aside and, flashing the phone's light inside, scanned the hole that had been hidden behind the wooden partition. The space was only big enough for a person to crawl in, though a short distance in, the tunnel seemed to narrow.

"Well?" Anya asked.

"Nothing immediately obvious, but there must have been a reason to dig this tunnel and go to the trouble of installing the frame and brackets for a panel to close it off."

"True."

He glanced over his shoulder at her, her face barely visible in the dim residual glow from the phone's flashlight. Even without much illumination, he saw the deep furrow of her brow as she bit her bottom lip.

"Stay here. I'll check it out and keep anything gruesome I find to myself."

She scoffed. "Are you crazy? Have you never watched a horror movie? Never, ever go alone into the creepy dark place."

"Well, horror movies aside, there's only room for one person to crawl through. At least at first. If I find a ladder to a second trapdoor, I promise to come back for you."

She didn't look convinced. "You better come back. You have our only light. I am *not* staying in this creepy hole with preserved body parts without some kind of light."

"It'll be all right," he promised her.

She nodded, and as he turned to head into the tight tunnel, she said, "Wait."

When he glanced back again, she caught his face between her hands and planted a kiss on his lips. His adrenaline kick of surprise was followed quickly by a wave of pleasure and the warmth of promise. When she broke the kiss and sat back on her heels, he slanted her a grin. "I'll definitely be back, if only to get more of that."

Facing the tunnel again, he squeezed in, crawling on his hands and knees as far as he could—only three or four feet—then dragging himself on his elbows and belly when the opening narrowed. He paused after belly-wiggling a couple feet to pull the phone from his pocket and shine it down the tunnel. A faint foul odor was detectable, and he considered that he might find a sceptic pit. He hadn't noticed what sort of plumbing the cabin had, and an outhouse didn't seem implausible based on the other primitive accouterments of the cabin.

His pulse skipped. An outhouse pit would be disgusting, true, but it might also mean a way out, a hole leading to the surface. He could make a *Shawshank*-style escape if he had to.

And if the potential second exit hadn't been buried under the landslide rubble, too.

"Brody?"

"Yeah?"

"Talk to me. Don't leave me hanging."

"So far so good." Aiming the light beam ahead again, he got the sense the tunnel widened ahead. He glimpsed a hint of something pale in the dirt. Likely rocks. "I think I see something ahead. Hang on."

Holding the phone up while he used his elbows and forearms to drag himself forward, Brody inched farther down the tunnel, which did, indeed, widen into a small cavern big enough to kneel in. As he pulled himself onto his knees, he used his hand to wipe dirt from the nearest partially covered white object, his heart drumming in his ears.

Until he realized what he was seeing, what he was revealing with each swipe of his hand. A skull. Jerking back, he swung the light around the small cavern, noting the other pale protrusions around him. More bones. More victims. Full skeletons. At least two, maybe... there was a third. His nerves jangled as he assessed the handiwork of a madman who kept human body parts in jars and hid the other remains of his victims in a pit below his remote cabin.

Shock rippled through him, and Brody's gut roiled.

Three victims, at least. And that was just the remains he could see without much digging. No way was he going to dig and uncover more of the sick secrets the sniper had stashed here. Brody had seen enough. The man had killed multiple people and concealed the proof in this underground bunker.

"Brody, do you see anything? Please tell me you found a way out of here." Anya's voice pulled him from the trance of horror that had gripped him.

"I'm...coming back out." Carefully turning in the tight chamber, trying not to disturb any of the bones, he reversed course and headed back to the cellar. His every nerve ending seemed hyper-charged as he shimmied back through the tunnel, every lump and rock that brushed his skin sending fresh jolts of shivers rippling through him. Had the victims been dead as the sniper moved them down this tunnel? Had he forced them into the tiny cavern and left them to die? His discovery was the stuff of nightmares, and he wouldn't soon get over the sight, the smell...the implications. As he struggled through the narrow, dark passage with only the phone light to guide him, another thought crashed through his brain.

What had happened to the sniper? After he'd come by the cabin wreckage and fired into the cellar at them, where had he gone? Was he lurking close by, waiting to ambush rescuers who came looking for Brody and Anya? Brody now knew why the hermit had been so determined to ensure that no one left his cabin alive. He had buried secrets. Literally.

Would the killer come back to his cabin to ensure his secret *stayed* hidden?

Chapter 10

Anya hadn't realized she was holding her breath until the bright beam of the phone light shone in her eyes, and, relief surging, she released the air in her lungs. Brody was back. The sides of the tunnel hadn't collapsed on him. He hadn't encountered any dangerous creatures or undetonated explosives or other forms of disaster her mind had conjured as she waited for his return. Thank goodness! Maybe she had an overactive imagination, or maybe the reality of seeing firsthand, in emergency room triage, the innumerable, unbelievable ways people could injure themselves was to blame.

But now that he was back, scrambling out of the creepy dark hole, she felt much better.

Until the phone's light illuminated his face, and she caught the stricken expression he wore.

She swallowed hard. "What?"

His gaze shifted to hers, but he said nothing.

"Brody? Did you find something? What was in there?"

"You don't want to know."

She shivered. Frowned.

And her mind kicked in again conjuring all forms of shadowy creatures and horror movie scenarios.

When he held the phone out to her, he added, "We should turn that off. The battery is down to thirty percent."

She didn't douse the light quite yet. Instead, she angled it a little to study the knit in his brow and glower in his eyes. "I may not want to know, but I'm getting the feeling I *should* know. If you don't tell me, I'll only go nuts imagining the worst."

He inhaled deeply and blew it out shakily as he scrubbed both hands over his face. His dirty palms left smudges of soil on his cheeks. "I don't want to freak you out."

She seized his wrist and clung. "Too late. You *are* freaking me out. Because *you* are clearly freaked out."

A muscle in his jaw twitched, and he looked away. "Let's just say I found evidence that whoever donated her hand and heart to those jars wasn't the sniper's only victim."

Air stuck in Anya's lungs. The bitter acid in her stomach rose to burn the back of her throat. As if of its own will, her gaze jerked to the dark opening that suddenly resembled a mouth, open wide in a scream.

Brody moved stiffly to the plywood board and jammed it back in place. When he'd finished, his shoulders sagged, and she swore she saw him shudder. Glancing back at her, he said quietly, "Help me move this shelf back in place?"

She nodded, getting the sense he was trying to place barriers between himself and whatever nightmare he'd found down the tunnel. *Evidence that whoever donated her hand and heart to those jars wasn't the sniper's only victim.*

Forget barricades. They'd found enough gruesome proof in this cellar of murder and/or torture to keep her thoroughly haunted until they were rescued from this horrid pit. Or more likely, for months, years to come.

Assuming they *were* rescued. Fresh waves of nausea sawed in her belly at the possibility they wouldn't be found.

When the shelf was in place again, she moved to the other side of the cellar. Lifting a finger to turn off the phone's light—she balked. Now, even more than before, she didn't want to be in the pitch black. Her heart clambered inside her as if trying to scamper up out from the cage of her ribs. "Brody, I—"

He eased closer, took the phone from her and wrapped her in a hug. As if reading her mind, he murmured, "I know. But you're not alone." He sat on the floor, tugging her down beside him and drawing her close before he tapped the screen to turn off the flashlight app. "Try not to think about it. Any of it."

She gave a scoffing laugh. "Yeah, right."

"Tell me more about… I don't know…say, your childhood. Did you have pets? A best friend? Birthday parties?"

She took several deep breaths, exhaling slowly and pressing her thumbs together to calm herself. Pets… "Yes, a dog, a cat and a hamster at various times." She swallowed hard. What else had he asked? Best friend… "Um, Hannah B-Burns was my best friend." Ragged exhale. Don't think about what's behind that wood panel. "Until she, um, started hanging out with Ginny Hemphill in…what? Tenth grade? Then she started ignoring me."

"Bummer. But who needs fickle, disloyal friends, right?"

"Yeah, it sucked." Even though the snub, Hannah's rejection was fifteen years in the past, the memory of it still stung. She fisted her hands and, suddenly feeling a cold that burrowed to her core, she scooted closer to Brody, wanting to feel the reassuring warmth of his body next to her. "Let's see. Did I have birthday parties? Uh, sort of. Mostly family parties when I was younger, then as a teenager I'd have a friend spend the night or a few of us would go to the movies. We didn't really do the whole balloons and games bit."

"But you had cake, right? I mean…cake's important."

"Yeah. I had cake." She twitched her lips. Brody was trying so hard to distract her. Bless him. She rubbed her hands on her pant legs and focused on recalling her last birthday cake instead of the horrors lurking in the dark with them. She shuddered.

"Chocolate?" He sounded hopeful, as if he were going to get a slice.

"No. I always got a vanilla cake with strawberry icing."

"Hmm. Chocolate on chocolate was always my favorite."

"Oh, vanilla with strawberry icing wasn't my favorite. I liked it okay, but when I was seven and in the middle of an everything-must-be-pink phase, I told my mom I had to have pink frosting. She apparently thought it was my favorite, and the tradition was born. My actual favorite cake is…" She paused to think about it. "Yellow cake with chocolate frosting, I guess. But honestly, I'd rather have ice cream than cake any day of the week. Salted caramel or rocky road."

"So noted." He was quiet a moment, and he bombarded her with dozens more trivial questions, clearly designed to keep her brain busy with something cheerful, anything banal or distracting.

His technique worked—to an extent. He managed to calm her and pass the time for an hour or three—or five minutes? It was so dang hard to tell in the blackness of the cellar. After a while, they snoozed again. Or he did. His breathing growing deep and even, lulling her into a light slumber.

"Anya?" His groggy voice roused her sometime later, and she shook off the cobwebs of sleep.

"Hmm?"

"Just curious…why didn't you tell your mom that vanilla cake with strawberry icing wasn't your favorite?"

She shrugged, then remembered he couldn't see the gesture. She thought about her answer for several seconds, shoving sleep further aside, in favor of old memories and childhood rationalization. "Because… I didn't care that much. And I didn't want to hurt her feelings. And it *was* my dad's favorite, so it made him happy."

"Are you generally a people pleaser, putting other people's wants over yours?"

His question caught her off guard. She'd never really thought about herself in those terms. Was she a people pleaser? She did strive to make others happy, but didn't everyone? She frowned. She had only to think of the variety of people she encountered through her job—both colleagues and patients, members of her own extended family, the grumpy lady last week at the grocery store who'd pushed past her in the checkout lane insisting her need to check out quickly took priority over any consideration of Anya's.

Furrowing her brow, Anya recalled how she'd quashed her impulse to scold the woman's rudeness because she didn't want to appear rude herself. She'd backed down. Given in without even a disgruntled look. Conceded as if the woman were right and Anya's needs didn't matter.

Why?

"I guess I am," she said finally, her tone filled with the surprise of her realization. "Geez."

"Hey, that's not necessarily a bad thing." He gave her a shoulder bump with his own. "It's good to be kind and thoughtful and want other people to be happy. Just don't discount your own needs and let people push you around. My sister Isla is something of a people pleaser, too. She had a boyfriend that messed with her head and made her believe she was being selfish to exert her will or preferences, while he always got his way. Thank God he's gone now."

Look, don't turn this into a fight, Anya. You can pick the movie next time. Tonight, we're going to see It.

The memory of Mark's insistence on seeing the horror movie, even though she'd told him repeatedly she hated horror movies, replayed in her mind. Along with instances of him choosing which restaurant they dined at and which TV shows they watched together.

She cringed knowing how often she relented rather than pressed for her choice.

"Been there," she said quietly.

"Really?"

"Mmm-hmm. My ex, Mark, got his way most of the time." *All of the time?*

"Well, then it's good he's an ex, I say. Relationships should be a give and take. Equals."

Although she heard his reply, Anya's brain had traveled further back, remembering her mother saying, "Your father is the head of the family. Whether we like it or not, the decision has been made. Don't cause trouble."

And so she'd gotten the kind of car her father chose for her, gone with her family to the vacation spots her father chose for the family—and had the flavor of birthday cake that her father preferred at her birthday every year. And when she'd started school, wanting to fit in with the other kids...

"I've been doing it all my life," she said aloud, more to herself than to Brody.

"What's that?"

"Just... I was realizing how often I do try to please others. I can remember wanting to make my friends happy as a kid."

"More than just being nice? How...?" He let his voice trail off.

"I'm saying I did it hoping they'd like me for it. I mean, when you already feel different from everyone else, you'll do whatever it takes to get people to like and accept you."

"Were you...*bullied* because you were South Asian?"

She thought about his question, shook her head. "Not exactly. Don't we all get teased at some point as kids? For me it was fragrant food at lunch, klutziness at volleyball..."

Anya sighed her regret when other memories surfaced, ones that shamed her now. Her embarrassment when her mother and grandmother would come to the school wearing their saris. She loved the beautiful clothes and the heritage they represented now, but when she was thirteen, her mother's clothes only highlighted the differences she was trying to hide. As if she could…

Look, it's been fun hanging out with you and all, but my family is pressuring me to settle down, and I just don't see myself married to you. You're not what I want in a wife.

In the days since Mark dumped her, she'd often replayed his words, trying to read between the lines. What was it about her that he didn't see as marriage material?

Like looking at the sun too long, staring too hard down that rabbit hole only caused pain, so she shoved it aside.

"Well, for what it's worth," Brody said, "I like you. I think you're nice. I think you're pretty. I think you're compassionate. I think you're a great kisser."

She chuckled. "Stop. I wasn't digging for compliments. I was only having an 'aha' moment about why and how I tried to make kids like me in school."

"Did you kiss me to make me like you?"

Hearing the teasing note in his voice, she laughed again. "No!"

"Because it worked. Before I thought you had cooties. Now I want to sit in a tree, k-i-s-s-i-n-g."

With a snort, she play-punched him, and he caught her hand, lacing his fingers with hers.

Her heart performed a giddy tuck-and-roll when he lifted her fingers to his lips to brush a kiss on her knuckles.

"Anya and Brody sittin' in a tree…" he whispered in a singsongy voice. "Kiss me."

She leaned toward him in the dark, their noses bumping as they fumbled to find each other's mouth. Then his other hand was in her hair, their tongues dueling, and thoughts of school days forgotten. The tantalizing way he slanted his lips on hers with gentle suction, the massage of his fingers on her scalp and the quiet sound of satisfaction in his sigh when he raised his head to take a breath were a potent combination.

"I like you, too," she whispered.

"Mmm. First comes love, then comes marriage," he chanted quietly. "Then comes... Oh, man. I don't remember the rest."

"A baby in a baby carriage," she supplied.

"Really? Wow. Presumptuous little nursery rhyme, huh? What if they both want careers first?"

"Brody?"

"What if they decide not to have kids?"

"Brody?"

"What?"

"Kiss me again."

And he did. Her lips, her neck, her breasts, and...

In the darkness, Anya allowed herself to be bold, allowed herself to pretend this was meant to be, allowed herself to believe that giving herself freely to Brody, to pleasure, didn't mean that tomorrow her heart wouldn't be at risk.

As their clothes were peeled off, as their dark-blind explorations of each other's bodies grew more heated and intimate, she ignored the doubts that tickled her conscience. She didn't want to second-guess Brody's intentions. Couldn't she just savor his attentions, his talented hands, his whispered seduction, taking it all at face value?

By unspoken accord, they pleasured each other in ways that needed no protection, something she'd been too embarrassed to do with Mark and a lighted bedroom. But Brody put her at ease, set her on fire, filled her with courage and desire and curiosity. For her, their lovemaking was not just a pastime. She was learning about herself, about Brody, and feeling things she'd never experienced—physically and, more frightening, emotionally.

She didn't want to form an attachment to Brody, but how could she not, when he was awakening her senses, showing her kindness and humor, protecting her. He'd expressed real interest in who she was, what she believed and wanted from life, and how she'd become the Anya Patel she was today. He asked questions even she hadn't asked herself. He made her think. He made her want to know *him* as deeply and introspectively.

He was making her fall in love. And that was as scary to her as what the sniper had hidden down here in his dungeon of horrors.

By late morning, Sol had wandered down the highway to the main street of the closest town, Pinehill.

He was hot. Tired. Determined to find some transportation. Walking everywhere sucked.

Weighing his options, he searched the signs lining the street ahead, looking for a used car dealership where he could test drive a vehicle and not return it. Or a minimart, where trusting souls in small towns left the keys in the ignition because they were just running inside for a second to get a soda and a lottery ticket. Or an old man he could swindle for a ride that would end badly for the obliging fella.

He'd made it several blocks into town when he found the bustling body shop with every garage bay full and customers waiting in line in the lobby to talk to the worker behind the counter. Sol strolled in, poking his hands in his pockets as if settling in to wait his turn in line. Instead, he observed. Calculated. Assessed.

The guy behind the counter—Walter, his shirt patch read—was explaining to a woman that the parts needed to fix her car were not readily available. They would have to search area salvage yards or online parts shops for the needed fender. "It could be a week, maybe two before we even locate the part, ma'am. Another week after that to do the repair."

The teenaged boy beside her shot Walter a look of dismay. "Three weeks? Prom is weekend after next, and I told my girlfriend I could drive us!"

"Sorry about that, pal. But I don't see how we can get it back to ya any sooner."

Sol glanced away as the spoiled teen griped some more about being inconvenienced for some time to come without a vehicle. *Boo-freaking-hoo, you mama's boy*, Sol thought, careful not to let his disdain show on his face. Shifting his attention to the other customers, he watched a sixty-something guy peek over the top of a newspaper, sigh and go back to reading. A guy with long hair pulled back in a ponytail leaned against the wall staring at his fingernails. A woman with a fussy baby sat in the chair closest to the door. She bounced the baby on her lap, repeating, "It's okay. Just another minute. It's okay, sweetie."

"Ernie, I need you up front!" Walter shouted from the front counter, startling everyone in the waiting room and sending the baby into a higher octave of wails.

A red-haired mechanic strolled in, scratching his shoulder. "What?"

Walter tossed him a key. "Move that Chevy out front around to the back, will ya?"

"And be careful with it!" the teenager added, frowning, before turning back to Walter with, "If it comes back with any extra scratches—"

"Now, Chad, I'm sure they'll take good care of it," the woman said, her expression conveying an unspoken threat.

Without turning his head, Sol tracked the red-haired mechanic as he returned to the garage, bouncing the key in his hand…and dropped it on the top of a toolbox by the bay door.

Sol's pulse skipped, and from his peripheral vision, he watched Ernie return through the door that read, "Employees Only."

The woman and teen left together, Chad casting a sullen look across the parking lot before following his mom to a tan SUV.

Walter turned his attention to the guy with the ponytail.

Ernie stayed in the back room.

The key to the Chevy continued to sit on the toolbox.

With a casual glance to confirm the frazzled mother, newspaper reading man and Walter were all still preoccupied, Sol eased into the garage, slipped the key in his pocket and strolled out to find the Chevy in question.

Only one Chevrolet was parked in the front lot. A Nova from approximately 1975 that had more rust than paint and a crumpled passenger-side fender.

Sol snorted, his steps faltering. *This* was the teenager's precious car he was so eager to get back? Worried would get scratched? How would he even tell if it got dinged?

Gritting his back teeth, Sol slid behind the wheel and cranked the engine. Stylish or not, if the car ran, it served his purpose. For now. Of course, he had to leave Pinehill pronto. No doubt everyone in town knew who owned that rusty Nova. He'd use the car for a few days, then dump it and find something else. The Nova purred as he backed it up and pulled onto the highway. Transportation—check.

Next—new lodging, far from town, where he and his projects wouldn't be disturbed.

Brody roused from his half sleep when Anya stirred beside him. The silky skin of her naked body slid sinuously against him, a reminder of the intimacies they'd share hours before. The memory of her hot mouth on him caused a fire to flash through his blood, and his skin tingled with anticipation of another round of carnal pleasure when she woke.

But then his conscience poked him, and his thoughts veered onto a new path. What did he want to happen if—when—they were rescued? Brody had never considered himself a one-night-stand kind of guy, but he was no stranger to casual sex, if it was what the woman wanted, too. He was attracted to Anya, no question. He liked everything he knew about her—her compassion and skill as a nurse, her intelligence and sense of humor, her dedication to her family and friends. But as much as he liked her, as much as he like talking with her and learning about her, was he confusing the shared bond from their mutual confinement with the kind of real affection and intimacy needed for a lasting relationship?

Was he imagining the feelings he had for Anya because of their unusual circumstances, because the horrors they'd discovered had stoked his protectiveness of her.

Her toes slid along his bare calf, and he groaned softly. How was he supposed to sort real feelings from situational emotions while her warm body was pressed against his? He cared enough about Anya to want what was best for both of them. He didn't want to lead her to believe he felt things he didn't. But even he couldn't get his head straight about where his emotions were, what he wanted. He didn't want to hurt Anya. He didn't want to give her false hope. He didn't want to make a mistake that would lead to heartache for either of them down the road.

Anya stretched lazily, and her hand moved to his cheek. "You awake?"

"Mmm-hmm."

"Were your dreams as sweet as mine?" Her tone was honeyed and arousing.

"Depends. What were you dreaming about?"

She gave a husky chuckle. "Oh, so coy. I think you know." She stretched to cover his mouth with hers, and he cupped her bottom as the kiss deepened.

And just like that, rational thought, his efforts to sort through his emotions and intentions, melted like ice cream in summer. He still had thinking and processing to do...but it could wait.

Chapter 11

Isla Cameron could usually manage her stress with a little yoga, some scented candles while she took a hot bath and sipped a cup of chamomile tea. *Usually* being the key word. But having her brother go missing and listed as presumed dead was a different level of stress, and no amount of yoga or tea would calm the anxiety twisting inside her or soothe the pain in her heart.

Brody had been missing for almost two days, and when the search teams had stopped looking last night due to darkness, the men digging through the mounds of tumbled earth and uprooted trees held little hope of finding her big brother alive. Isla had spent much of the last forty-four hours at her mother's side. Her mom had sat, uncharacteristically still and silent. Not eating. Not sleeping. Not even crying. And Isla worried what definitive news about Brody's fate might do to their mother.

Her sisters and their families had come and gone from their parents' house many times—bringing food, offering hugs, sharing tears and prayers. But, really, all any of them could do was wait.

To assist in that wait, Isla started a pot of coffee for the family and friends she knew would return today to continue the vigil. She glanced out her mother's kitchen window at the early morning light, casting its buttery rays on the herb garden where chipmunks romped and robins hunted worms and insects. She yawned and stretched, willing her thoughts to remain positive. The family needed all the positive energy they could muster.

Last night, Isla had slept on her parents' couch, a few feet from the chair where their mother had sat for much of the past two days. Mom clutched a well-worn oak prayer cross in one hand and a rock painted like a ladybug that Brody had made for her as a third grader in her other. Mom had refused to go to bed "in case there was news about her boy." She wouldn't listen to the reasoning that no news would come overnight, because the search had been suspended until daylight returned.

When the coffee maker beeped that the brew cycle was finished, Isla poured herself and her mother each a cup, sweetening her mother's with a level spoonful of sugar and a hefty splash of creamer and her own with just a small amount of cream. She was carrying the two mugs into the living room when her father appeared from down the hall, his hair rumpled and his eyes shadowed.

He offered Isla a wan smile. "Morning, sweetheart. Did I hear the coffee beep?"

She offered her cheek as her father greeted her with

a chaste kiss. "Just finished. I can fix it for you. Go on into the living room."

"How is she this morning?" he asked, not having to elaborate on who *she* was.

"About the same. I think she got a little sleep sometime after two—"

The backdoor burst open, and Isla's oldest sister, Emma, rushed in, her eyes bright. "They found Jerry Romano! He was alive!"

"Alive?" Isla set the mugs she held down with a thump that sloshed hot coffee on the counter.

"He was seriously injured, lots of broken bones, barely conscious and is in ICU now in a medically induced coma, but he is alive!"

Isla shared a look with her father and sister that spoke the hope they didn't dare speak aloud lest they jinx the situation. *If Jerry was found alive, maybe Brody will be, too.*

"Could he tell them anything before they induced the coma?"

Emma shrugged. "Not much. The officer who called me this morning said Jerry's jaw was broken. But he wrote one word that has the searchers and police perplexed."

"What word?"

"Pit."

Behind her, Isla heard a quiet sob, and she turned to find her mother clinging to the doorframe with wide hopeful eyes. "Who is alive? My Brody? Did they find my boy?"

Isla rushed to her mother and guided her to a kitchen chair. "Not Brody, Mom. His boss with the volunteer firefighters. Jerry was found alive."

Her mother's shoulders wilted, and she nodded as she dabbed her eyes. "Oh." She sighed. Nodded harder. "Good. That's good."

Retrieving the two coffee mugs from the counter, Isla set them on the table and pulled out the chair next to her mother. Scooting the hot brew closer to her mom, and Isla rubbed her mother's arm briskly. "It is good news. Encouraging news. It means we shouldn't abandon hope."

Her father took the seat on the other side of her mom. "Grace, you need to eat something. Let me fix you some toast, at least."

A chiming noise sounded across the kitchen, and Isla glanced to her sister. Emma pulled her phone from a back pocket and glanced at the screen. Frowned. Put the phone back in her pocket.

"What?" Isla mouthed.

"A text, but not from a number I know," Emma replied quietly, waving a dismissive hand.

"What did it say?" Isla asked.

"Didn't read it. Not even a local area code. Probably spam."

Isla rose from her chair and crossed the room to her sister. "You should read it. It could be someone with the search teams or law enforcement." She kept her voice low in deference to her parents, who were having their own discussion about whether or not her mom would eat an egg with her toast. "Until Brody is found, you should read every text and answer every call."

Emma twisted her mouth as if considering. "You're right, of course. But I've already had to fend off two TV stations this morning, and yesterday it was a talk radio reporter along with three different nosy neighbors looking for a scoop for gossip." Emma pulled out her phone and swiped the screen.

"Vultures," Isla said, her tone dark and low for her sister's ears only.

Once again Emma frowned as she studied her phone. "This can't... Is this a sick joke?"

Isla sidled close to her sister to read over Emma's shoulder.

Emma angled the phone so Isla could read.

Anya Patel and Brody Cameron are trapped in the underground cellar of sniper's cabin. Please send help!

Isla's gut swooped. "Oh, my God!"

Emma grabbed Isla's wrist. "Jerry's one word was 'pit.'"

Isla gasped and squeezed Emma's hand in return. "As in a cellar? A cellar could be a pit, right? Or am I making too much of this because I want it to be true?"

Emma shrugged, but her expression held the same desperate hope swirling through Isla.

"We have to tell someone! Call the police! Tell the rescue teams!"

Her sister was already tapping her phone screen. "Way ahead of you, Sis."

Chapter 12

Anya thought at first what she was hearing was the buzz of a noisy insect. A low droning noise that filtered down from the air hole they'd dug to the surface. But then voices reached her. Men calling back and forth to one another.

"Are you sure these coordinates are right?"

"Hey, over here!"

"My God, how could anyone still be alive under that?"

"Stan, bring the backhoe up here."

Anya jackknifed to a seated position and reached beside her to jostle Brody. "Wake up. Someone's out there!" She scrambled to her feet and stood directly below the ventilation hole. Cupping her hands around her mouth, she yelled, "In here! Below ground level. In the cellar. Help!"

"Hey! Down here!" Brody added his booming baritone voice to hers.

Fumbling her phone from her pocket, she woke the screen and turned on the flashlight app. Would the tiny beam of illumination help the searchers find them? Unlikely, but she was willing to do anything that improved their chances even an iota.

In the glow of the flashlight app, she cast her gaze to Brody—rumpled, dried blood on his forehead, covered in dirt stains and the handsomest thing she'd seen since he'd first been brought to her emergency room. He gave her a smile that tripped giddily through her, making her body hum from head to foot.

Reaching for her with fingers callused from creating their ventilation hole twice, he brushed her cheek tenderly. "I told you we'd get out of here. And when we get back to town, I want you to meet my family."

She pressed her hand over his, trapping his hand against her face. "Deal. I'd love to get to know them." Arching an eyebrow, she added, "But can I shower first? My grime has grime, and I'm positively itchy with dried sweat."

His groan was laced with longing. "Oh, yes. A shower! Long and hot with lots of soap. I can't wait!"

She laughed, then tipped her head, waggling her eyebrows suggestively. "What if we shared a shower? I'd scrub your back, if you scrubbed mine."

His eyes widened, blinked. He dropped his hand from her cheek. Brody opened his mouth as if to say something, then furrowed his forehead and mumbled, "Umm, Anya, I—uh…"

Humiliation and disappointment speared her, but she played off his reluctance, forcing a light note in her tone as she swatted at him. "Just kidding. Gosh, after spending a couple days in a dark cellar with a guy, you'd think they'd know when you were teasing."

She was spared further discussion of her faux pas, when more voices called from above them. "Hello? Brody? Anya? Where are you?"

"Down here! Look for our ventilation hole," Brody called back, framing his mouth with his hands.

Masking her heartache with a brave smile, Anya wondered about the relief on his face. Was it due to their imminent rescue or gratitude he was saved from continuing the awkward discussion of how he didn't want to continue a sexual relationship with her now that they were leaving the pit?

Sure, they'd had sex last night, comforting each other and breaking their boredom with a pleasurable activity. The dark made it easy to pretend, deny and simply embrace life when they weren't sure they'd survive this cramped and creepy pit. But now that searchers had found them, he no longer had need for her. Like Mark, it appeared Brody had only been passing time with her. Shoving aside the pain that arrowed to her core, Anya told herself she was lucky to have seen the truth before she got her heart in too deep with Brody.

"Brody Cameron?" a male voice called from right above them.

"Yes! And Anya Patel is with me."

"Hang tight, man. We're going to dig you out."

"Are you injured?" another voice asked. "Do you need water or food?"

"Surprisingly not. We had a supply of food and fluids." He gave Anya a quick look before adding, "You should summon the police, though, if they're not already here. Major crimes. Not just street patrol."

There was a beat of silence. "What?"

"Yeah, we, uh…found evidence that the sniper that fired on the rescue teams Saturday had kidnapped the missing hiker…and committed several other murders."

As the rescuers dug through the landslide debris and cleared the trapdoor to the cellar, Brody put an arm around Anya. But she remained stiff, her smiles stilted.

In a matter of a couple minutes, she'd gone from suggesting they shower together, a tantalizing offer that had both startled and intrigued Brody, to cool detachment and fake grins. What had changed? Was it the knowledge that they were being rescued and would be returning to their regular lives? Had she considered what a relationship with him might be like and had second thoughts?

He wanted to ask her about it, but not now. Not with the search team in earshot, listening through the vent hole to everything they said.

Crumbles of dirt pattered down from the air hole as the rescuers' shovels plowed through the muck and debris. For an instant, adrenaline blasted through him, a knee-jerk reaction to the prospect of their hard-earned ventilation tunnel collapsing again. Never again would Brody take air, freedom, life for granted again.

Then the heavy wooden door to the cellar was clear, and the men opened it, allowing a wide swath of light to stream into the pit that blinded Brody with its brightness after so many hours in the dark. Shielding his eyes, Brody gulped the fresh air that poured in carrying the scents of pine, grass and wildflowers. "Are we ever glad to see you guys!"

"I bet," a bearded man with a baseball cap said as he peered into the pit. "It's nothing short of a miracle you two are alive. This hole saved your asses, you know."

Beside him, Anya was also taking long deep inhalations and squinting up at their rescuers. "Saved ours but took others, I'm afraid."

Though his head was backlit, the man's frown was plain enough. "You have casualties with you?"

"Get us out of here, and we'll explain everything." Brody scrubbed a dirty hand on his cheek. "Do y'all have ropes or a ladder of any kind we can use to climb out?"

Twenty minutes later, Brody joined Anya above ground, and beaming his relief and gratitude to all the rescuers, he shook each one's hand. Facing Anya, he wrapped her in an impulsive hug and planted a kiss on her mouth.

Though she returned the kiss, she ended it quickly and backed out of his arms without looking at him. Brody would have dwelled on her odd, distant response had he not been surrounded by the rescue team and his first topside view of the devastation the landslide had caused. The entire side of the hilltop had been sheered away by the massive explosives and a field of debris the size of several football fields had replaced the peaceful woods and blossoming mountaintop meadow. Brody gaped at the raw earth, broken rock and snapped trees they'd been buried under and shivered despite the warm sun. It was a miracle they'd survived. But the carnage begged the question he'd carefully avoided before now, simply because he knew the likely truth was more than he wanted to deal with while he and Anya were trapped and trying to stay optimistic.

"We were with three other people when the explosions and landslide started," Brody said, accepting a bottle of cold water from one of the men. "My boss with the VFD, Jerry Romano, the missing hiker, who we found trapped in that pit, and another searcher named Frank. I don't recall Frank's last name, if I ever got it." He took a deep breath for courage. "Have they been found? Did they make it?"

The bearded man deferred to an older man next to him with a glance. The second man swiped perspiration from his brow with the back of his wrist and started haltingly, "Well, the news there is mixed. The hiker, Ms. Bane, was killed. Her body was found with Jerry Romano."

Brody's gut churned, and he braced for the news to come.

"Jerry was found alive but critical. He's in a coma in the ICU in Asheville."

Anya stepped closer to listen, her expression grave. "And Frank?"

"Hasn't been found yet." The second rescuer motioned to the debris field. "It's been slow going. Dogs led us to Jerry."

"And how'd you'd find us?" Anya asked, echoing the question on the tip of Brody's tongue.

"Your sister," the bearded man said, nodding toward Brody. "She called the state police and rescue headquarters this morning saying she'd gotten a text from Ms. Patel about your location."

Brody exchanged a startled look with Anya.

"One of my messages made it out?" A smile spread across her face as she pulled her phone out of her pocket and kissed it. "Good girl. Add that to the list of miracles along with all the other crazy circumstances that allowed us to survive unscathed." She flashed her dark screen to the rescuers. "My battery died just before you reached us. If that text hadn't gotten out when it did, we wouldn't have been able to keep trying."

"Hey, Chris?" another searcher called, and the second man, who appeared to be in charge, turned in response. "HQ wants to know if they're gonna need to be airlifted down the mountain or if they can walk."

Chris sent Anya and Brody a querying look. "Well?"

Brody stretched his arms over his head. "A walk will feel good after being cooped up down there for the last couple days."

Anya nodded her agreement. "I can walk...assuming—" She warily scanned the top of the ridge. "Any sign of the sniper since this started? I'm not keen on being used for target practice again."

Chris cut a side glanced to the rubble and beyond to the highest vantage point. "We haven't had any issues in the last forty-eight or so hours, but neither have we had reports the suspect has been apprehended."

Anya sidestepped closer to Brody, her expression reflecting her uneasiness. "I'm just...so ready to get home. Can we go now?"

"Sure." Chris spoke into his handheld radio. "We're all walking out. No significant injuries reported but have medical transport standing by. Over."

The hike down the mountain took a fraction of the time that climbing up had, both because going downhill was easier and because they weren't in the intentionally slow and scrutinizing search mode of their ascent. When they reached the road where the search teams had assembled, they were met by more than just the search coordinators, law enforcement and an ambulance. The media had come out.

A small cluster of reporters wielding microphones and shouldering cameras approached Brody and Anya as they arrived at the tents and tables of the makeshift search headquarters.

With a glance to Anya, whose hand went to her loose hair having clearly realized how dirty and disheveled they both looked for the cameras, Brody straightened his shoulders and met the barrage of questions with a stiff smile.

"How did you survive?"

"Was there a point you thought you might die?"

"Can you tell us about being attacked by the sniper?"

"Do you have a message for your families?"

Brody zeroed in on the woman who'd asked the last question, "My message to my family is, I'm safe. I'm coming home, and I love them. Oh, and I'm really craving my mom's cheesy chicken casserole. Mom, if you're listening, could you fix a big pan of that casserole for dinner?"

The reporters chuckled and shifted the microphones to Anya. "Do you have a message for your family?"

"Um… Yeah, I love them and will call as soon as I can get to a charged phone. I'm safe, thanks in large part to Brody—"

She flashed him a half grin, and he shifted his weight, uncomfortable with the credit. Their survival had been a joint endeavor. Luck. God. Fate. Cooperation.

When the cameras turned back to him, he waved off her assertion. "I didn't do anything extraordinary. We handled each crisis as it came up, together." He pinned a look on her that said, "Right?"

Another female voice piped up, drawing his attention. "People are already calling your surviving the sniper, the landslide, being trapped for days a miracle. Would you agree it's a miracle?"

"Who's calling it a miracle?" Anya asked. "We aren't even off the mountain yet?"

"Well," the woman reporter said, her tone hedging, "I, uh, heard one of the rescue team members say it."

Brody snorted. "Look, if you need a clever tagline for the story, then, sure. Call it a miracle. That's as good of a way to look at it as any. Now, if you'll excuse us, it's been a while since we showered or slept in a bed and we're eager to remedy both."

Brody placed an arm around Anya's waist and escorted her through the throng of media, hearing cameras click and hustling footsteps as the reporters rushed to be the first to air footage of their rescue.

He headed straight for the ambulance, knowing the value of having at least a minimal health check, even if they weren't suffering more than scrapes and bruises. One of the EMTs, a woman about Anya's age, greeted Anya with a hug and a broad smile. "Oh, my God! Anya, are you all right? When I heard it was you that was trapped, I flipped out!"

Returning the hug, Anya nodded. "I'm okay. Especially now that we're out!"

Click, click, click.

Brody angled his head to give the photographers a disgruntled look, yet resigned to the knowledge that for the next couple of days, he and Anya would have little privacy. Their rescue would be on everyone's tongue and

TV until the next big story hit. The media had hounded Emma and her husband, Jake, after they'd helped shut down the sex-trafficking ring several months back, and Emma still got stopped in the grocery store by people who recognized her.

Once the bay doors to the ambulance were closed, giving them at least a modicum of privacy, Brody leaned toward Anya, whispering, "If that footage airs, as I expect it to in the next half hour or so, you can bet my mom will have a vat of the world's best chicken casserole made by mid-afternoon. If you don't have other plans, why not join my family for a celebration dinner tonight?"

She turned her eyes from watching the sphygmomanometer readout while her blood pressure was checked. "Will your grandmother make me eat haggis?"

He was happy to see the spark of teasing in her eyes. Her mood shift as they'd been rescued still nagged at him. Why had she grown so somber and distant earlier?

"I promise you won't have to eat haggis." He gave her a conspiratorial wink, adding, "This time."

The check by the EMTs confirmed that they were in overall good health, and Brody and Anya were released to talk to the local sheriff's department about their experience with the sniper. Their discoveries in the root cellar.

He and Anya were separated for questioning, and she cast a worried glance toward him as she was led away to an interview room. He flashed a smile, hoping to calm her, encourage her, but his own gut somersaulted knowing his testimony could be key in the hunt for and conviction of a serial killer.

A tall, balding deputy escorted him into an office

and motioned for Brody to sit in an old office chair with a ripped vinyl seat. The deputy set a small voice recorder on his desk and turned it on, stating his name and asking Brody to state his.

When asked to do so, Brody recounted his story, from the time the sniper started shooting until they were rescued that morning, for the official record. The interviewer also took notes with pen and paper, commenting that writing things down helped him think and process information.

"Did you touch or disturb anything in this side chamber?" the deputy asked.

Brody shook his head. "Not intentionally. Once I realized what I'd found, I got outta there quick. If I disturbed something in my haste to backtrack, I'm unaware of it."

The deputy nodded and made a note with pen and paper.

"We handled the jars, though."

"Tell me about that."

"When we found the body parts in the canning jars, we were flabbergasted. I pulled it off the shelf to get a closer look, to figure out what we were seeing. It was so surreal, finding that heart in a jar, I just didn't think about the ramifications of touching the jar."

The deputy nodded as he scribbled. "We'll need a full set of fingerprints from you for the forensic team, in order to isolate your prints from any others found."

Brody winced, realizing his prints could have obscured those of the killer. "Yes, of course. Whatever you need."

"I don't need to tell you that this evidence of multiple murders is explosive stuff." The deputy paused, twisted his lips. "Sorry. Poor choice of words. The point is, we need to play this close to the vest. It's critical that you say nothing to anyone about your discovery or this investigation. We don't want the killer tipped off, and we don't want to jeopardize our ability to prosecute the case down the road."

"Understood. I, uh…already mentioned the bodies to the men that dug us out."

The deputy ducked his head once in a nod. "They've been briefed and warned to keep silent." Dropping his pen on his desk and shutting off the recording, the deputy stood and stuck his hand out to Brody. "We may need to ask you more questions later, but we're done for now. Thank you. Go home and get some rest."

Anya finished her interview within minutes of Brody. He'd lingered in the lobby of the sheriff's station, waiting for her. "Deputy Grigg has offered to drive us to pick up our vehicles. I left mine at the firehouse."

"Mine's at the high school. That's where our team met up to carpool to the mountain," she said, half to Brody and half to the young deputy who stood close by, squad car keys in hand.

As Brody had expected, a swarm of reporters was waiting outside the sheriff's office. He smiled to the cameras but didn't slow as he crossed the parking lot to Deputy Grigg's vehicle. "I'm grateful to be safe and going home," was all he said as a volley of questions came at him.

When Grigg reached the firehouse, Brody took Anya by the hand and met her eyes, saying, "The offer of dinner at my parents' house was sincere. Please come."

She tugged up a corner of her mouth. "Let me get a shower and some Tylenol, and I'll see how I feel tonight. But thank you. It's a tempting offer. Especially after hearing so much about your...*clan*."

He chuckled at her use of the Scottish term and her attempt at the accent. Taking the business card the lead investigator had given them each from his pocket, he borrowed a pen from Deputy Grigg and wrote his phone number on the back of his card and handed it to Anya. "Let me know what you decide."

Dipping his head, he kissed her scraped knuckles before closing the squad car door and heading toward his truck.

As Deputy Grigg waited for traffic to clear so he could pull onto the highway, Anya watched Brody climb into his truck. After spending so many hours with him in the dark, it was odd to watch his long-legged stride, the play of his muscled shoulders as he turned to wave goodbye, the flash of gold in his hair from the sunlight. He was certainly a fine-looking man, her ordeal companion, her new friend...*her lover*.

Anya sank back on the seat and exhaled a long, slow breath. So much had happened in just a few days, and somehow, for her personally, *that* was the headline. She'd had sex with Brody. And it had been great. But she had no idea what to expect now, what she wanted to happen, what it all meant, if anything, to him. Was she just one more in a string of one-night stands for him?

She'd thought things were going well between them, that maybe they'd been building a foundation of friendship for a deeper relationship. But when she'd made her comment about showering together, only half jesting, he'd tripped over his tongue, retreating as if she'd suggested cannibalism. The difference had been their imminent rescue, the prospect of continuing what had started between them out in the real world. His back-pedaling stung. Had she only been a plaything for the duration of their confinement? Had he been humoring her with his sweet words and gentle touches? Had she ignored clues, missed body language cues due to the darkness that would have tipped her to his real feelings? She'd been all too glad to have someone to cuddle with in the dark, someone to hold her hand and distract her with peppy conversation, a champion whose quick thinking, ingenuity and protectiveness had helped her survive the scariest days of her life. But was that all he'd been?

The last thing she wanted was any more pain or turmoil in the wake of Mark's cold breakup. She pinched the bridge of her nose. Too much. Too soon. Too painful. How did she sort through her feelings for Brody while she was still processing the horrific events of the past few days? How did she make a clearheaded deduction when her brain was muzzy and her body so tired?

Time. She needed time to figure out what her heart was telling her and make sure she didn't repeat the errors from her past.

Chapter 13

The house was perfect. He could hardly believe his luck.

Sol walked through the empty farmhouse, the scent of mold and disuse confirming his suspicion that the abandoned home hadn't been occupied for years. No power ran to the house, but he'd seen the old power lines outside and had no doubt he could rig a line to the house. He'd done that sort of work before with the military. When he turned on the faucet, the spigot shuddered and coughed before rusty water trickled out. He let it run while he did a bit more exploring of the grounds. He'd have to cover the windows. Didn't need light inside giving away his presence to locals who knew the house to be abandoned. He could cook on a camp stove if the gas stove didn't work. He'd done enough of that.

And the best part was, his nearest neighbor was at

least two miles down the highway. The new women could scream and scream, and no one would hear. Perfect.

He shut off the water that had cleared some after running through the rusted pipes but still had a slight pinkish tinge. Like washing away blood. His hands flexed and bunched. He hadn't gotten to enjoy the hiker the way he'd wanted. He still had that itch to hear a woman yell and beg for mercy and stare at him with terror in her eyes. Acting too soon would be a mistake. He needed to lie low, let the trail the cops were following from the mountain grow cold.

But how would he know when that was? He needed to know what the cops knew. He exhaled and scratched at the several days of beard that had sprouted since he'd left the mountain. He needed a shave. He needed supplies. But most importantly, he needed information.

Hours later, after a long shower, a restless nap and endless circular thoughts, Anya decided to go to Cameron Glen, to Brody's parents' home. She needed to see how he reacted to her, how he looked at her so she could get some perspective. And wouldn't he be his most natural, his truest, most transparent self with his family?

She could call it a test, an experiment to see if she'd imagined the attraction between them. Or she could call it by the other truth she'd discovered in the last few hours at home. She really didn't want to be alone tonight. Not while so many horrifying images, smells and memories were still so raw and looming. Chloe worked on Monday nights, and she hadn't made any other close friends in Valley Haven since she'd moved there eighteen months ago. Mark had occupied much of her free time for the first year and since then, she'd thrown herself in her work, taking extra hours to fill the empty spaces in her life.

Moving to her phone, which was still plugged in her wall socket charging, Anya dialed the number he'd given her on the sheriff investigator's business card. "Hi, it's me. I'll come. What can I bring?"

Anya drove slowly up the one-lane paved road that wove through the scenic property of Cameron Glen, admiring the beauty of the place where Brody had grown up. She marveled at the blooming azaleas, the lush green hillsides of Christmas trees, quiet ponds with geese waddling along the banks, and flower beds with a rainbow of blossoms and flitting butterflies. "Paradise," she murmured, while thinking of course a prince like Brody would come from a Camelot like Cameron Glen. Through the hardwoods populating much of the property, she glimpsed the cabins nestled in shady spots, each with a porch and rocking chairs and plenty of privacy. When she reached the side driveway Brody had told her to turn onto, she goosed her Civic to get it up the steep hill to the house at the top of the ridge. Before she had even turned off her engine and climbed from the driver's seat, Brody appeared on the front porch and trotted across the yard to greet her. A parade of smiling women, children and even an orange cat followed him.

"Welcome," Brody said, pulling her into a hug then waving a hand toward the gathering crowd. "Come meet the clan."

Anya wiped damp palms on her shorts before she extended her hand to the nearest woman.

"This is my youngest sister," Brody said, at the same time the strawberry blonde said, "Isla."

Isla gripped Anya's hand between her two small hands and beamed at her. "So nice to meet you."

"Same."

A girl of about five pushed her way to the front and tapped Anya's hip. "Are you Anna?"

"I'm *Anya*," she replied, bending at the waist to greet the girl. "And if I'm right, you're Lexi?"

The girl blinked. "How'd you know?"

"Brody told me all about you. Plus, I met you last summer at the hospital. I was your nurse after you fell in the river."

Lexi's expression turned awestruck. Instead of acknowledging or denying she remembered, Lexi bent to heft the orange tabby into her arms. "This is my cat, Pumpkin."

"Hi, Anya. I remember you." The woman behind Lexi offered her hand. "I'm Emma, Lexi's mom. So nice to see you again."

"An-ya," Lexi said as if testing the feel of the word on her tongue.

"Yep. Like in the princess in the movie *Anastasia*."

The girl wrinkled her nose and looked behind her. "Mommy, have I seen *Anastasia*?"

"Hmm, I don't think so," answered an attractive brunette with eyes the same sky blue as Brody's.

Anya lifted her brow as if in dismay and said, "Oh, my! We will have to fix this. I own a copy on DVD, and you can borrow it any time."

The girl nodded haltingly, and Brody leaned into whisper, "Ask her if she knows what a DVD is."

Anya whipped her head toward him then back to the girl's mother, the shock real now. "What, seriously? Oh, my God. How old am I?"

"I know what a DVD is! It's those things with Fenn's movies." Emma guided forward an attractive teenager girl with the same chestnut hair that her mother had. "My older daughter, Fenn."

"And this is my brother, Daryl. Did you meet him last summer?" Brody asked, giving the teenaged boy a light punch in the shoulder.

Daryl shook her hand and flashed an awkward smile. "Hi."

"I don't think I met you, but I heard all about you. You were the hero of the day, getting everyone help when Brody went down."

She detected a flush of pink beneath Daryl's dark complexion as he stuck his hands in his pockets and shuffled back to allow the next brunette woman with pale blue eyes to surge forward. "I'm Cait. We met at the hospital, in Brody's room."

Anya nodded. "I remember. How are you?"

"Much better now that my brother is safely home. And I believe we have you to thank for that?"

"Me?"

"Your text to me," Emma said. "That's what tipped the scales to help the searchers pinpoint you. They looked for cabin debris. They'd been digging through landslide rubble hundreds of feet away, where they found Jerry."

The squeak of the front screened door heralded the arrival of an older woman, who hustled down a wheel-chair ramp to the side of the porch steps and rushed up to Anya. "Anya dear, welcome!"

"Hello, Mrs. Cameron." Smiling, Anya held her hand out for the woman who was obviously Brody's mother to shake. Instead, she pulled Anya into an embrace.

"Oh, dear one. A handshake is too formal for someone who helped bring my boy back to me. As is Mrs. Cameron. Call me Grace. Please."

"I didn't really have anything to do with rescuing—"

"Nonsense. You were there for him, and he for you. That's not nothing." She held her at arm's length and gave her a teary smile. Then as if sobering, she cast her gaze around her family. "Why is everyone standing in the yard? You must be starving. Come in, come in! Nanna and my husband can't wait to meet you."

Grace linked her arm with Anya's and guided her inside the ranch-style house with rustic, homey accents. Grace took her straight into the living room where an older, white-haired woman in a wheelchair waited with a bright smile and his father pushed out of a recliner to greet her. Anya shook Neil Cameron's hand, and she exchanged the conventional pleasantries as she reintroduced herself to Emma's and Cait's husbands, both of whom she'd met briefly last summer at the hospital. Her head swam a bit as she tried to keep track of all the members of this big gracious family, and she wasn't done. She faced the elderly woman, patiently waiting her turn with sapphire-blue eyes sparkling.

"Oh, come here, ye bonnie lass." The older woman's outstretched arms said she expected a hug, and, crossing to her, Anya obliged, earning a dry kiss on the cheek, as well. She couldn't say Brody's family hadn't welcomed her warmly. They were already up that point on Mark's family.

Brody crouched beside his grandmother, a contented look on his face as he touched Anya's arm. "Nanna, this is Anya. She can't wait to try your haggis."

Anya shot Brody a startled, quelling look, and Nanna

laughed. "Don' fash yourself, dear. This one is a joker. There's no haggis today, but c'me back any time, and I'll have some ready. It's really no' as bad as it sounds."

"Hmm, maybe I'll take you up on that offer. Brody told me quite a bit about you and your family, and it's a pleasure to meet you."

Grace enlisted Brody and his father to finish setting the table while Emma helped Grace get the meal out of the oven. Brody's other sisters flanked Anya as they went to the table, asking her about her work, her family—much of the same information she'd shared with Brody over the past couple of days. Daryl pushed Nanna's wheelchair to the table next to the chair Anya had been given, and the white-haired woman reached for Anya's hand with fingers knotted with arthritis.

"How are you doing, lass?" Her tone and compassionate expression told Anya the question was not casually thrown out.

Still Anya put on a brave, polite face. "Fine. Thank you. I really appreciate the invitation to—"

"Posh," Nanna said, her brow dimpling with a frown. "So polite…" She waved Anya's answer aside. "You've had an ordeal, love. You're allowed to be a wee bit bothered. Or more than a wee bit. Has anybody held you since you were dug out of that hellscape and let you weep or scream or thrash your fists?"

Anya blinked at Brody's grandmother. "I, um…" She hadn't really allowed herself to think, to feel much of anything since the rescue. She hadn't wanted to. "There really hasn't been time," she hedged.

"Posh!" Nanna said again, her Scots brogue thick. "You've time now, and it's no' healthy to keep your spleen inside." She turned to Isla and said, "Am I right, dear?"

"You're right, Nanna."

Anya glanced around the table where Brody's family was gathering, and chuckled awkwardly. "Well, now's not the best ti—"

But before she knew what was happening, Nanna had angled her wheelchair, seized Anya by the arms and was tugging her close. Rather than fight the older woman, Anya let Brody's grandmother pull her against her breast, wrap her in frail arms and stroke her back. "There you are, *a cahird*. Empty your weary soul. Let go of your fear. You are safe now." As if the older woman had kicked down a wall, opening a floodgate of dammed emotion, Anya hiccupped, and moisture filled her eyes. Stifled pain burst in her chest like a bubble, and suddenly sobs were wrenching from her chest and she was soaking Nanna's shoulder with her tears.

Nanna held her and crooned words Anya didn't understand, but took comfort from all the same. Her voice was kind, warm and tender. A motherly balm she hadn't realized she needed.

"What the.? Nanna, what happened?" she heard Brody say.

"She'll be fine in a moment. Don't worry, *a bhobain*," Nanna said.

"An emotional purge," Isla said, "Very healthy."

Embarrassed by her outburst, Anya raised her head and swiped at her cheeks. "I'm so sorry. I don't know why—"

Nanna's surprisingly strong hand cupped the back of her head and tugged her close again. "Don'na stopper it. Let it all go free."

Anya sniffled and sank back into the hug Nanna offered unreservedly. She hadn't realized how much she missed her own mother and grandmother, how frightened she'd been while trapped that she might not ever see her family again. The maternal embrace, the permission to feel and express the tangled emotions she'd suppressed for days, was exactly what she needed. How had Nanna known that more than a meal, more than sleep, more than a shower, she'd needed...this? Family. Connection.

After a couple moments, during which she was keenly aware the entire Cameron family was watching, Anya felt she'd exhausted the tears she'd needed to release and pulled free of Nanna's embrace. She dried her eyes then blew her nose on the paper napkin at her place setting.

"All better?" Nanna asked.

Anya bobbed her head. "Yes. I— Thank you."

Isla sent her an encouraging nod and smile. "Perfect."

"Daryl dear, will you get Anya a new napkin?" Grace said.

Brody's younger brother glanced up from his cell phone. "Sure."

As he left the table, his mother added, "And leave your phone in the kitchen. You know the rule about devices at the dinner table."

"So," Neil said, reaching for the hands of the people to his right and left, Cait and Brody. "This is a day to celebrate!"

Daryl returned with extra napkins, handed one to Anya and slid back into his chair. Beside her, Nanna took Anya's hand and Brody took her other, as the rest of the family joined hands. The gesture spoke so eloquently and simply of the unity and familial love she'd just been admiring that a fresh lump of emotion lodged in Anya's throat.

"Not only is Brody home safely," Neil continued, "we have a new friend with us, *and* my whole family is around my table. As our lives get busier and my children grow older, I do not take that for granted."

Around her, the Camerons replied with "Oh, aye," and "Hear, hear," and "True that!"

Neil closed his eyes and bowed his head, prompting the rest of the family to do likewise.

"Heavenly Father, we thank You for our many blessings..." Brody's father began.

Anya dipped her head slightly but used the moment to steal a glance around her at Brody's big, loving family. Extra chairs had been squeezed around the large table and family members sat so close they bumped elbows. *A good problem*, she could remember her own grandmother saying about situations like this. As her gaze moved from one face to another, she met Lexi's curious eyes and gave the girl a wink. Lexi's smile spread, and with a giggle, the five-year-old squeezed her eyes shut.

When Neil finished the prayer, everyone passed their plate to the person on their left. Anya followed suit. What happened next was a display of coordination and cooperation that amazed her. Plates were passed, comments overlapped and each person served the food that was in front of them or was the official plate holder. Somehow, everyone seemed able to keep track of where their plate was as it made the circuit around the table, receiving a scoop of each dish.

"Green beans, Anya?" Isla asked, while Brody queried, "Lexi, you like sliced tomatoes. Right?"

"More, please."

"Another biscuit, Jake?"

"That's plenty, thanks."

"Green peas, Anya?"

Anya passed the plate that was handed to her and glanced across the table to Cait. "A few. Thank you."

When her own plate returned to her, laden with chicken casserole, biscuits, vegetables and fruit salad, Anya chuckled. "Wow! Y'all could teach the hospital a thing or two about team coordination and efficiency."

"Yeah, well, we discovered quickly, it was either coordination or chaos," Cait said.

Brody leaned close with an impish grin. "I voted for chaos. You just can't beat a good food fight."

Daryl silently offered Brody a fist bump.

"But," Brody continued, giving his sisters a significant glance, "I was overruled."

"Everything is delicious as usual," Jake said.

"I helped with the fruit, Daddy!" Lexi said.

Jake sent his daughter a bright-eyed look. "I thought I tasted some of your magic in there! Well done, Kitten."

"So, Anya," Isla said, "We all know you're an ER nurse, but not much else. How long have you lived in Valley Haven?"

Anya cast a side glance to Brody, and he met her look with a crooked smile, as if he read her mind. *We've just had this same conversation over the past two days.*

But Anya cheerfully answered Isla's question and the dozens more that other members of the family peppered her with. Brody made sure the family told Anya a bit about themselves, as well, and she appreciated having the spotlight off her briefly.

Emma's husband, Jake, owned a construction company. Cait managed the rental cabins for Cameron Glen, while her husband, Matt, wrote true crime and action novels. Grace had recently donated a quilt she'd made to the organization Emma and Jake had founded to fight sex trafficking, and the quilt had raised a whopping six thousand dollars at auction.

"That's amazing!" Anya smiled at Brody's mother. "And kudos on founding a group to fight sex trafficking," she added, turning to Jake and Emma.

"Well, after what happened last year with Fenn, we had to do something to save other girls—and boys—from the same."

Brody leaned close to whisper, "She was kidnapped for sex trafficking."

Anya blinked as she replayed Brody's comment in her head. "Wait...what? Fenn was—" She cut her gaze to the teenage girl across the table from her who'd been mostly quiet—except for whispering and chuckling with Daryl.

Fenn looked up and gave a grimacing nod. "I was. Lucky for me, my parents are badasses, and they rescued me."

Lexi gasped and cut a wide-eyed look to her mother. "Umm! Fenn said a bad word!"

Emma flashed a smirking grin. "Yeah, but I think we can let it pass this time. I mean, we are kinda badasses. Right, hon?"

Jake nodded without glancing up from his plate. "Definitely. Hundred percent."

"Oh, I need to hear this story," Anya said, dividing a look between Emma and Fenn.

"See, last spring, I ran away. Stupid right?" Fenn began. "Well, I made it as far as the mini-mart in town…"

Anya listened in awe, as Emma and Fenn took turns explaining how Fenn was kidnapped and summarized how Jake and Emma had recovered her. Fenn and her parents were all in family therapy to help her process and deal with the events in a healthy way.

"That's…" Anya goggled, searching for a word, "… incredible!"

"Matt and Cait caught a murderer and embezzler last year, too," Daryl added as he bit off half of a biscuit in one bite.

Anya's eyes opened wider. "What!"

That story was told, as well, which prompted Grace to flatten her hands on the table and declare, "Frankly, I've had quite enough of my children being kidnapped and shot at and buried alive, thank you." She gave each person around the table a stern look. "Would you all please go back to safe, humdrum lives now?"

Anya joined the Camerons in a chuckle when Brody lifted his iced tea glass. "To humdrum lives!"

Other glasses lifted, but Nanna countered with, "Not humdrum! Adventure and soul-stirring love matches are the spice of life!" She raised her glass and made her own toast. "To adventure, true love and spice in your life—all done safely, of course."

Glasses were raised again, and when Brody sent Anya a steamy look, heat rose in her cheeks. She caught the knowing glances his sisters shared and knew an even deeper flush must be coloring her face. So Brody was not against letting his family believe they had a more-than-platonic relationship. She paused with a biscuit halfway to her mouth when she realized he could mean this dinner to be *that* meal. The one where he introduced his new love interest to the family. Anya's pulse tripped, and she set the biscuit back down while mulling that notion. He'd invited her, calling it a celebration of their rescue, a good meal featuring his mother's cooking after two days of odds-and-ends provisions. But was more going on here? Did she want more?

She had only to think of the comfort Brody had offered her during their confinement, the way he kept her distracted, her mood boosted, the sweet sensations he'd stirred in her when they'd been intimate to know Brody was everything she wanted. His family was a happy bonus.

With fresh interest in getting to know the Camerons, Anya focused her strayed attention on what Brody's father was saying. "…plan to pick up the truck from the body shop in Pinehill tomorrow. It'll be nice to have it when we pick up the sod for the Juniper cabin this weekend." Neil looked at Brody. "You going to be available to help lay sod this Saturday, son?"

"I'll make time for it," Brody answered.

"I can help, too," Matt said.

Anya asked Emma about her interior design business, and by the end of the meal, she'd also learned that Isla, a graduate student at the Western Carolina University, had pet goats. Daryl was a straight A student hoping to major in computer programming, while Fenn loved to read and was active in her parents' organization to end sex trafficking. Cait's husband had served in the military, had a prosthetic leg and had a new military thriller releasing in a month.

"Will you do a book signing?" Anya asked. "My father would love a signed book for his birthday. Of course, I'll need a copy, too."

"I'm looking into signings," Matt said. "But regardless of official signings, I'll make sure you get as many signed copies as you need." He added a wink, and Anya couldn't help but smile as she thought how much she liked Brody's eclectic, loving family.

Oh, yes. She wanted this, wanted Brody in her life. But on the heels of that recognition, her heart squeezed and a small voice in her brain threw up caution flags. Falling for this charming family would only make it harder, more painful for her if a few weeks into a relationship with her, Brody changed his mind. She'd be crazy to invest herself in these people, no matter how kind and welcoming they were, until she figured out what she felt for Brody…and he for her. Yet when Isla invited her to join her, Emma and Cait for a sisters' night on the town later that week, Anya heard herself saying, "I'd love that!"

Chapter 14

As Brody and Anya reached her car after the family meal, he wiggled his finger in a circle. "Turn for me?"

Anya crinkled her face in query. "What?"

Again he motioned for her to turn. When she did, she asked, "Why am I turning?"

"Checking that you're still in one piece after my family's interrogation and—let's face it—rather odd and pushy behavior."

She laughed and gave his shoulder a light push. "Yes, I'm in one piece. I like your family. A lot."

"Still," he said, scratching an eyebrow as he reflected on the events and conversations during the meal, "I know they came on pretty strong. Especially Nanna and Isla."

While glad to know she liked his family, he couldn't quiet a strange niggling inside him that had started soon after they'd been rescued. A feeling of being off-balance with Anya. A deeply seated uneasiness over the intimacies they'd shared tumbled through him. Had he taken advantage of her? She'd been frightened, restless, needing comfort and reassurance, and he'd let his attraction to her blind him to the realities of their situation. He never took a woman to bed so early in a relationship. He wanted to know there was true affection and understanding between him and his girlfriends before things became so...serious.

He barely knew Anya...in many ways. In other ways, he felt he knew her better than any woman he'd ever dated. He didn't like the confusion and ambiguity. He liked order. Intention. Clarity.

"I'm sorry about that whole bit where they pressured you to cry, and then Isla putting you on the spot about going out with my sisters and all the questions about—"

She clapped a hand over his mouth, her dark eyes sparkling with mirth. *She's even more beautiful than I remembered. The cell phone light didn't do her justice.*

"It's okay," she said. "I *did* need a good cry to release some tension, and I *want* to have a girls' night with your sisters, if only to learn more about their brother." She flashed a teasing grin.

"Okay," he said and shifted his weight, his gaze lifting to the tree branches as if he could find answers there. "It's just that we aren't even really a couple. We're not dating or... I mean, we were thrown together by chance and tragedy, and they're acting like... I don't know. Like I brought you here to introduce my future wife."

When he returned his gaze to Anya's, her face had grown somber. "Yeah. Well..."

His heart jolted. God, he didn't want to hurt her, but

replaying his fumbled words just now, he knew everything had come out wrong. Sighing, Brody dragged a hand over his face and tried again. "I mean, I like you. I do. Obviously…" He gave her an awkward smile before rushing on. "We just need to sort things out. We started under unusual circumstances. We should back up and think about what we want."

Anya drew a trembling breath and stared at him for long, silent seconds before asking, "And what do you want, Brody?"

"I want to see where this will go," he said, brushing his knuckles along her cheek. "I like you, but we've moved too fast, too soon, I think. And maybe we should pull back a bit and see if this is really right for us."

She inhaled deeply. Nodded. Opened the driver's door of her Civic. "Of course. You're right."

"Are you okay?" he asked, because he was getting a weird vibe from her.

She returned a tight smile and shrugged. "Just tired, you know? A lot has happened today."

"True that." He pressed a quick kiss to her forehead before she could slip inside the car. He should have felt better, having put a few of his cards on the table with Anya. But somehow, he felt worse. Like he'd lost something valuable. Like he'd made matters worse. Good grief, he needed a manual on relationships with women. Somehow, no matter how hard he tried to do the right thing, he seemed to keep screwing things up.

At her boss's insistence, Anya took two days off to decompress and get fully rested before going back to work. An ER nurse couldn't afford to be mentally or physically exhausted when patients' lives were literally in their hands.

But mental and physical rest were hard to come by. If Brody's withdrawal and "let's think about this" speech weren't enough to preoccupy her thoughts, her cell was constantly chiming incoming texts from friends asking how she was or buzzing with calls from radio stations seeking comments. Her doorbell rang often as news reporters from around the state showed up on her doorstep wanting on-camera interviews. She was recognized in the grocery store and at the McDonald's drive-through. Being in the spotlight was mentally taxing. At the end of the day, when she needed sleep, her brain recycled the conversation with Brody after his family dinner.

We've moved too fast...

We should pull back...

While Brody examined if she was "really right" for him, she berated herself for falling so easily for another man. Hadn't Mark taught her anything? Why hadn't she been more cautious with her heart?

And while Brody backed away, her parents tried to claw back her independence. Her parents asked for Zoom meetings each night, as if to reassure her mother she was, in fact, safe and in one piece.

Turn for me?

"You need to come home, Anya. It's not safe for you to live alone," her mother said each night.

"I'm fine, Mom. Really. The whole incident on the mountain was a fluke event." She didn't dare tell her mother the whole truth about the sniper, being shot at and what she and Brody had discovered in the cretin's cellar. Her parents would be at her door in hours, dragging her back to Charlotte if they knew the whole story.

"You need to quit the search team then," her mother pressed. "It's too dangerous."

Guilt bit Anya. She'd always obeyed her parents' wishes in the past. But having lived on her own, started a career she loved and forging her own path for the past several years, she had discovered an independence she wasn't ready to abandon. Surviving the lair of a killer had taught her life was too short for regrets.

And Brody... Anya conjured treasured memories of his kisses, his encouragement in the cellar, his heart-stopping smile. If not a future relationship, he'd at least given her the courage to believe she could pursue what *she* wanted from life.

I want to see where this will go.

She clung to his assertion when doubt demons raged. She wasn't ready to give him up, either. But she'd be careful. Much more careful with her heart...

"I'm not leaving the search team, Mom. I promise I'll be all right. You don't have to worry. The search team does good work. I love it. Everything that happened last week was...an anomaly, I swear."

"Tell her," her mother said to her father. "Tell her to come home!"

Anya held her breath. Her father was so hard to say "no" to. But he just gave her a stern look through the computer camera and said, "Be careful out there, Anya-bug. We're proud of all you're doing in Valley Haven, but your mother and I worry about you. You're too trusting."

Too trusting? Her father's words poked her like a a prickly ball that continued to pain her as she rolled it in her thoughts that night.

By the third day, when she returned to the ER, her

celebrity status had reached the hospital. Not only did her coworkers want to hear every detail of the search-gone-wrong, being trapped and her rescue, but patients recognized her from the unending media coverage. She wore the unearned fame like an itchy homemade sweater from her favorite aunt. She was grateful for the reason behind her recognition—her and Brody's fortunate rescue—but the attention also reminded her of those that didn't survive, of the horrid truth she and Brody had been compelled to keep silent, and the fact that she hadn't actually *done* anything to earn the accolades. The rescue teams that searched relentlessly from sunrise to sunset, done the backbreaking digging and the tedious sifting through debris were the heroes. But each time a patient did a doubletake or another hospital employee stopped by the ER to shake her hand and hear her retell her story, Anya gave gracious answers and patiently repeated highlights of her tale. Because she was grateful to be alive and understood the human fascination with surviving disasters.

She used her break to sneak upstairs to the ICU and visit Jerry. Though he was still in a medically induced coma, his body in numerous casts and hooked to machines, she wanted to lay eyes on him and whisper in his ear that she was rooting for him, that recovery was possible and he had a host of friends, old and new, in his corner. Jerry's wife greeted Anya with a warm hug, even though they'd never met, simply because of the tragedy that linked them.

After telling Jerry to keep fighting and thanking him for his leadership with the volunteer firefighters, Anya gave Carol Romano another encouraging embrace. "Don't wear yourself out. Take time to go home and sleep in your bed, get a shower, eat something that didn't come from a vending machine. Jerry would want you to take care of *you*."

The older woman gave Anya a tired smile. "You're not the first person to tell me that. And I hear you. I will. Soon. But until he turns the corner, I can't... I can't leave him."

Anya called Brody on her way back down to the ER and reported on her visit. They'd texted once or twice, but this was the first time since she'd left his parents' house that she'd heard his voice. And she realized how much she'd missed it. She'd missed the comforting tones in the darkness, the humored lilt as they'd passed the time and the lusty, baritone rasp when they'd been intimate. She'd missed...him.

"So...how are you?" he asked after getting the recap on Jerry's condition.

"Back at work, throwing myself into helping vomiting children and banged up car accident survivors to keep my mind off of...other things." Like you. "What's up in Brodyville?"

"Weeds. In the First National Bank's flower bed and Mrs. Higginbotham's yard. And a new client, who signed me after seeing me on the news and wanting to support the local hero. His term, not mine. Honestly, this semicelebrity status is just weird business. People who see me working around town will stop and want to shake my hand, hear a recounting of what happened on the mountain."

"Same here. The mother of the aforementioned vomiting child was so enamored with meeting me, she couldn't give me a medical history on her poor boy until I gave her a bullet point summary of our rescue. Crazy!"

As she pushed through the doors from the main corridor into the emergency department, Anya heard a page for assistance in one of the exam rooms. "Brody, I gotta go. Duty calls."

"Of course. Go save lives!"

She hesitated a beat, waiting, hoping he'd add something about calling her later or asking if she was free this weekend or…something. But he didn't. And she didn't. And with a pang of disappointment in her chest, she said, "Bye, Brody." And disconnected as she rushed in to assist the new nursing student in starting an IV for a patient with rolling veins.

"Was that Anya?" Isla asked as Brody ended his call.

He raised a suspicious eyebrow. "Why?"

Townspeople weren't the only ones stopping him and wanting to hear his story. His family had been especially attentive and wanting slices of his time since his return. His brush with death had scared them, he knew. The extra attention, lunch invitations, drop-in visits after he got home from work and stream of texts were understandable. Considering how often, while trapped under the landslide, he'd wondered if he'd ever see his family again, he took the attention in stride, even savored the time with his family.

Today was Isla's turn to take him to lunch at Ma's Mountain Kitchen. The diner was a hot spot for country cooking at its best and one of Brody's favorite places to eat. Isla, who preferred a vegetarian diet and steamed veggies over anything fried, had few choices on Ma's menu, but she had obviously picked the diner for her brother.

"So it was Anya?" Her smile was calculating as she

stole a french fry from his plate and popped it in her mouth.

"I didn't say that. And if you want french fries, next time order your own."

"I only want a couple, and your face answered for you. So...what's the story with you two?" Before he could answer, his sister added, "She's very pretty. Smart. Friendly. I like her. I get a good vibe from her."

Brody chuckled and lifted his iced tea for a sip. "I like her, too."

"So what's the problem?" his sister asked as she tucked a wisp of her strawberry blond hair behind her ear.

"Who said there's a problem?"

"I'm not sure. That call ended rather quickly."

"She was at work. Had to go."

"Are you going to ask her out? Follow up on 'I like her, too'?"

"Maybe." He got a kick out of being intentionally vague with his nosey sister. It drove her up the wall. And what else were brothers for than to give their sisters fits?

Isla poked at her salad. "You're hopeless."

"Thank you."

"You know she's been hurt before, right?"

Brody snapped his head up. "She told you that?"

"She didn't have to. I could tell."

He gave her a skeptical look, well-familiar with his sister's sometimes leftfield observations and beliefs. "Really? You could read her mind?"

"Not read her mind so much as her body language, the emotions I sensed in her, what I read in her facial expressions."

Brody leveled an unblinking stare at Isla. "Uh-huh,

and what am I thinking right now? Can you read my feelings?"

Isla set her fork down and met his gaze. "I can, as a matter of fact. You're irritated with me for poking at your love life, but you're withholding your snarkiest comments because you know I'm buying lunch. And… wait…" She narrowed her eyes slightly as if having difficulty with the last portion. "And you know I have your best interests at heart, so you're going to hear me out."

He snorted and arched his eyebrow. "Ok. I'll give you that last one."

"Seriously, though, Brody. At dinner the other night, if you paid attention, whenever Anya looked at you, she had what I could only call a *wistful* look in her eyes. I sensed a shadow, some suppressed pain holding her back. She wanted you, but she was afraid."

"You're sure she wasn't worried you and Nanna were going to make her cry in front of strangers again? That was…pretty awkward, wouldn't you say?"

"No. I'd say it was cathartic. And telling. That her tears were that near the surface only backs up my impression that she had a recent pain or hurt."

"Oh? Like, I don't know, *being shot at and trapped in an underground pit for two days*?"

She gave a shrug. "That was part of it, sure. But not all. You said she was dating someone last summer when you met her, when she turned down your drug-addled proposal?"

Brody sighed, both because this dive into his personal life was drawing out longer than he wanted and because Isla was cutting close to the truth. Anya *had* been hurt by her ex. She'd admitted that in their pit conversations. But how deep were her scars? What had Isla picked up on that he had missed?

He'd never admit it to her, but he admired his sister's innate empathy and ability to understand and sympathize with people. She cared deeply, felt deeply…sensed things many people missed. Her intuition about people was something he lacked, and she was rarely wrong.

"So what are you telling me, Isla? I should avoid Anya?"

She rolled her eyes and shook her head. "I'm not saying that at all! I like Anya, and I'm pretty sure she likes you. I'm just cluing you in. With relationships, you're not always the sharpest tool in the shed—" Brody pressed his mouth flat as he shot his sister a scowl. "Don't look at me like that. When it comes to women, you know it's true. I told you Nancy was a gold digger, but would you listen to me?"

"Go on. You were saying about Anya?"

"Be careful. That's all I'm saying. Don't give her false hope if all you want is a fling. Consider her feelings. Know what you want. Tread lightly. Look before you leap."

"A stitch in time saves nine."

Isla wrinkled her freckled nose. "What?"

"Oh, I thought we were all spouting clichéd sayings now."

Her mouth clamped in a thin line, then flapped a hand at him. "Okay, be that way. I tried. If you end up hurting her, let it be on your conscience until the end of time."

"I won't hurt Anya." Brody wiped his mouth on his napkin and put it on his plate as he glanced out the front window of the restaurant. Gray clouds were building in the north, and the wind was picking up. Rain was coming.

"Not intentionally. You're too good-hearted for that. But unintentionally…you could bungle this if you're not careful. I don't want that for either of you."

Brody scratched his cheek. "Look, I gotta get the grass mowed at the high school soccer pitch before it rains, but thank you for lunch. Thank you, I think, for the warning about Anya." He pushed his chair back and walked to Isla's chair. He bent to give her a hug and whispered, "I hear you. I'll be careful. Now, no more meddling in my love life."

"I'm not meddling!" she countered as he strolled toward the door, then called, "Love you, brother!"

He turned to aim a finger at her in a "back atcha" gesture. As he strode to his truck, the scent of ozone was already in the air. The rain was closer than he'd realized. But the rain was forgotten as he settled in the driver's seat and headed toward the high school. What did he want with Anya? How did he avoid breaking her heart? Wasn't it kinda presumptuous to think he could break her heart? That implied a level of love and commitment they were nowhere near, didn't it?

Yeah, he liked Anya. A lot. And they'd shared some rather personal moments while trapped. Not just physical intimacy, but painful reminiscences, deeply held convictions. And the hardships and terrors they experienced together were a unique sort of bond. So where did that leave them? Maybe he'd been too quick to dismiss Isla's expertise in people and relationships. Isla might not be in a relationship at the moment, but that didn't mean she wasn't an excellent resource on human nature, the female brain and emotional gobbledygook Brody had trouble sorting out.

He'd told Anya they needed to go slow, figure out where they were. Wasn't that protecting Anya from pain? But after three and a half days of thinking about nothing but Anya, Brody's head was still muddled.

Yeah, he shouldn't have been so quick to dismiss Isla's advice. He needed clarity.

As the fat raindrops slapped against his windshield, he wondered where Anya's head was after a few days apart, a few days to figure out what she wanted. The past three and a half days had felt like months, but he'd wanted to give her space.

Her call, while all business—Jerry, the media, work—only fueled his need to see her, talk to her. If he wanted to know where her head was, he needed to go to the source. Tonight.

"There you are!" Isla said brightly that Thursday, giving her a warm hug.

"Am I late?" Anya checked her watch. "We did say seven, didn't we?"

Cait put down the frothy concoction she'd been sipping and shook her head. "You're not late. We were early. Emma is on her way."

"Come! Sit!" Isla patted the barstool next to her then waved the woman behind the bar over. "Name your poison. First round is on me."

"Oh, thanks! White wine would be nice," Anya told the barkeeper. "Nothing too sweet."

"I was just telling Isla about the little brewery in Asheville Matt and I visited last month," Cait said.

"Great variety from dark stouts and fruity seasonals to hoppy IPAs. If you like beer, you should check it out."

"Oh, yes!" Isla's face brightened with excitement. "Brody loves trying different beers. That'd make a fun day trip for you two. I can suggest a great restaurant with seating along the French Broad River for dinner in the evening, too."

Cait gave Isla a *look*, the kind that said, *Ixnay on the atchmay akingmay.*

"What?" Isla gave an innocent shrug. Turning to Anya with a wince, she said, "Y'all are a couple now, right? I mean, when he brought you to dinner the other night, I thought…well, you just seemed so happy together. Cozy. Into each other."

"I, um…don't know. I mean, I like your brother. He's great. I just don't know if…how he feels…" Anya's drink arrived, and she used the wine as an excuse to sort out her thoughts. She took a sip buying time before she said, "We haven't really discussed a relationship per se."

"Oh, he likes you. That is obvious to me," Isla said, touching Anya's arm and smiling with confidence.

"Isla, geez! Way to pressure the poor girl and put her on the spot!" Cait gave Anya an apologetic grimace. "Can't take her anywhere!"

Anya chuckled and wiped condensation from the base of her wineglass. "Moving fast and high expectations runs in your family it seems. Brody proposed to me the day we met."

Isla and Cait both sent her stunned looks.

"Last summer? When he ended up in the ER with the thing in his leg?"

Cait's face brightened. "Oh, that's right! How could

I have forgotten Brody's proposal?" She gave a hearty laugh.

"Well, I think it's romantic! What a great story!" Isla said, practically cooing.

A strange warmth filled Anya as she recalled her first meeting with Brody and his family at the hospital.

Cait snorted. "Romantic? Which part is romantic? The rod in his leg? The painkillers?"

Isla lifted her nose and gave a small sniff. "I'm just saying, if they do start dating and fall in love—"

Cait rolled her eyes and mouthed to Anya, "Sorry."

"—they'll have a great meet-cute to tell their kids about."

Anya sputtered as she sipped her wine then laughed. "Oh, my God. Now you have us married with children?"

Emma hurried up to them, pausing to give her sisters hugs before flashing Anya a smile. "Sorry I'm late! Got stuck on a call with a client. What did I miss?"

"Isla's been planning Anya and Brody's wedding, marriage and future family," Cait said with a sardonic grin.

Emma's eyes widened as she swung to face Anya. "Really? I didn't realize you two were that serious."

Lifting a shoulder, Anya said, "We're not. We haven't even been on a date."

Emma nodded knowingly. "Oh, I see." She cast Isla a patient glance. "You do love a fairy-tale ending, don't you?"

Again Isla dismissed them all with an innocent look and a shrug. "So sue me. I have a feeling about you Anya. You're good for Brody. I want my brother to be happy, and I saw how happy he was at dinner the other night with Anya."

"You and your 'feelings.' Maybe he was happy to have been rescued? To be safe and with his family?" Cait suggested.

"Cynic," Isla muttered. "You know my instincts are usually right."

Cait gave an acquiescent nod. "Yeah, I know. Well, now that we're all here, I'll go ask about getting a table."

As Cait headed toward the hostess stand, Anya watched the interaction between the sisters and silently mused how great it would be to be part of Brody's big, loving family. She had a good relationship with her sister, but rarely saw Pasha since she'd married.

"For what it's worth," she said, meeting Isla's gaze, "I hope you're right. I think Brody is sweet and handsome and kind, and I'd love to go out with him, see where it leads."

"I knew it!" Isla's eyes danced. "Can I tell him that?"

"No!" Emma said. "No meddling in our brother's love life."

"You're a party pooper," Isla said with a scowl. "Clearly my Prince Charming got lost on the way to the castle. Can't I have a little fun playing matchmaker?"

Emma flagged the bartender with a little wave. "Can I get a margarita on the rocks?"

"Sure." The woman did a double take. "Hey, aren't you the one who was trapped on the mountain last week?"

Anya cut an awkward glance to Brody's sisters before nodding. "Yep. That was me."

"I thought I recognized you. You've been all over the news lately." The bartender started mixing Emma's drink saying, "I'm sure glad they found you when they did."

"That makes two of us," Anya said with a chuckle. She lifted her wine to take a sip and was overcome by a prickling sense of being watched. With a quick scan of the bar, she noticed a thin man with graying black hair at the other end of the bar. The man was staring at her with dark brown eyes that narrowed when she met his gaze. She didn't know him, but he continued staring, his attention unsettling, until she turned her back to him and focused again on the conversation between Brody's sisters.

Sol sat with his hands wrapped around his gin and tonic, staring at the wood grain of the bar, his ear tuned to the television set above the bar, waiting for the evening news. He'd been at some bar, somewhere at the dinner hour the past several nights, waiting for the local channel to update him on the rescue of searchers from the mountain. The hovel he'd found outside of town was no more than a temporary refuge. It had no TV, no access to news. Not that he had many needs. He preferred living off the grid, a minimalist lifestyle. But he had to know what was happening, what the cops knew, so he could stay one step ahead. He'd made a point of being somewhere that wasn't a sports bar—where they only wanted to tune their TVs to whatever basketball or soccer game was being played somewhere in the world—in order to watch the evening broadcast every night. Earlier in the week, the rescue of the Indian woman and blond dude had been dubbed "The Miracle on the Mountain."

A miracle? He snorted to himself. The real miracle was that nothing had been said yet about his secret stash being found. Was he actually going to make a clean escape? It was too soon to assume as much.

"Hey, aren't you the one who was trapped on the mountain last week?" he heard the bartender say, and his heart jolted. He jerked his head up, certain he'd been recognized.

But how? No one on the mountain that day had seen his face. Well...no one that lived to tell about it. The little hiker had been killed by the landslide, even if the man with her had been pulled from the wreckage and was still breathing. Lucky bastard. Now *that* was a miracle. One he'd have to monitor. What had the lady hiker told her rescuers before the mountain came down on them?

But, no, the bartender wasn't talking to him. Her question had been for the dark-haired woman at the other end of the bar. Sol squinted in the dim light to make out the woman's face. Recognition dawned, even as he heard the bartender say, "I thought I recognized you. You've been all over the news lately."

Sol pinned a hard stare on the woman down the bar. As if she felt his eyes on her, she angled her head, met his gaze. Froze. Did she recognize him? He didn't think that was possible, but...now was a good chance to test that theory. And if she gave even a hint she knew who he was, well... Wouldn't it be interesting to start his new collection with the Indian beauty?

"Five more minutes," Cait announced as she returned from speaking with the hostess.

"So, Anya, where did you grow up?" Emma asked. "Not locally, obviously, or we'd have met. Valley Haven High is small enough that everyone knows everyone."

"That's what my friend Chloe says. She went to Valley Haven."

"Chloe Masters?" Cait asked, and Anya nodded confirmation. "She was in my class! We were cheerleaders together."

"That's Chloe. She's still a cheerleader in all the best ways. My biggest advocate and mood booster when things get tough at the hospital." Anya turned back to Emma. "And to answer your original question, I'm from Charlotte. My parents are still there."

"Hey, look!" The bartender tapped Anya's arm then grabbed the TV remote and raised the volume. "There you are again!"

Sure enough, Anya watched the same footage that had been played over and again for the last week, aired again, this time with a voice-over from a reporter. The caption at the bottom of the screen read, "Miracle on the Mountain takes gruesome turn."

Anya stilled, holding her breath as the male reporter's voice announced, "Sources close to law enforcement confirm that the remains of four women were discovered in an underground chamber connected to the root cellar where Anya Patel and Brody Cameron were trapped for two days. Investigators believe the women were murdered and their bodies buried in the underground chamber over the course of as many as ten to twelve years."

Anya's stomach churned with the reminder of the severed hand and preserved organs, Brody's description of the remains he'd discovered, the terror of the hiker who been in the cellar when they'd found her. From the corner of her eye, she saw Brody's sisters all focus their gazes on her. She swallowed hard as she met their dismayed looks.

"Did you know this?" Isla asked, her face pale.

Anya nodded weakly. "We were told not to say anything. The police didn't want the news getting out before they'd had a chance to analyze the situation, see if they could get any forensic evidence to connect the killer to the remains. Connect the killer to the sniper." She pressed one hand to the cool wood of the bar top and lifted her wine for a deep sip with the other.

"Officials with the state police had no comment when contacted, but we will, of course, be following up on this tragic twist to the events on Kiper Mountain."

"Holy moley!" Isla gasped. "How awful!"

"As if being trapped in the dark for two days weren't bad enough," Emma said with a visible shiver.

Anya nodded then raised a hand to ward off further questions, as the newscaster continued. "In happier news, Jerry Romano, who had been in ICU since being rescued earlier this week, has regained consciousness and been moved to a regular room. Romano is said to be helping investigators piece together events leading up to the landslide that buried him alive."

"That's great to hear, Betsy. We all wish Mr. Romano a speedy recovery," the newsman beside the first reporter said as the broadcast went to commercial.

"So there were more victims besides Sophie Bane?" Isla asked. "How could you and Brody fail to mention that to us?"

"Because we were asked not to. Told not to. Can we please talk about something else? It's bad enough those bodies have been giving me nightmares all week."

"Yes," Emma said firmly. "I know all too well how

tricky it can be to put horrible stuff behind you when that's all anyone else wants to talk about."

Anya cocked her head. "Do you mean when Fenn was kidnapped? That had to have been so stressful!"

Emma nodded. "No kidding."

"The good news is the story has a happy ending," Isla added, giving her sister a side hug.

"Anya?"

Hearing her name, Anya turned to the bartender, bracing to dismiss questions from the curious woman, as well. Instead, the barkeeper slid a dark red drink toward her and hitched her head to the end of the bar.

"The guy down there sent this to you. I told him the wine you were drinking, but he insisted I make you a Bloody Mary."

The drink was pushed closer, and Anya caught a whiff of the tomato juice. Instantly she was back in the black pit in the aftermath of being shot at by the sniper. The scent of jarred tomatoes, the splash of red that covered the ground and Brody like blood, the ringing in her ears from the gun blasts.

She swallowed the bitter taste of bile and wine as her gorge rose, and she battled it back down. Shaking her head, Anya shoved the drink back across the bar. "No. I can't. I… I don't want it."

She cut her eyes toward the man who continued to stare at her, filling her with icy discomfort. He arched one wiry eyebrow and sipped his drink without breaking his eye contact. Anya's pulse spiked. In light of the media coverage since last week she shouldn't be surprised she had attracted this guy's attention, but his stare sent chills to her core. Not to mention his drink choice. Was it some kind of sick joke? A Bloody Mary? How oddly specific and hinting of gore.

"This way, ladies." The hostess's chipper voice was a welcome distraction, a well-timed excuse to flee the man's unsettling glare.

Anya followed Brody's sisters to a corner booth where they enjoyed their meal, good conversation and plenty of laughter. But throughout dinner, Anya glanced frequently toward the bar. The guy remained at his stool, drinking, loitering and studying Anya.

When it was time to leave the restaurant, Anya walked out to her car with Brody's sisters. Cait and Isla were in the same vehicle, headed back to different houses within walking distance of each other in Cameron Glen. Emma's house was also on the Cameron Glen property, but she was in her husband's truck.

Anya turned the opposite direction, toward her townhouse, but noticed a pair of headlights followed her from the parking lot. Followed her even as she made one turn, then another. Slowed in front of her home as she parked in her driveway and got out of her car. She caught a glimpse of the driver before the dilapidated sedan sped away. A thin man with wiry eyebrows and graying hair. The creepy guy from the bar had followed her home.

Chapter 15

Fear balled in Anya's gut like ice. Hard and cold. Heavy.

"Hey! How was dinner?"

Anya screamed when a man appeared from the shadows of her yard and touched her elbow.

"Whoa." Brody raised both palms, wincing. "Sorry. I thought you saw me."

Anya clapped a hand over her galloping heart. "No. Geez, you scared the crap outta me."

He touched her arm gently. "Obviously. Again, sorry."

"I…" She shook her head. "It's just I was already jumpy. Did you see that car that was behind me when I got here?"

"Saw there was one but didn't pay particular attention to it." He frowned. "Why?"

"The driver was at the restaurant bar all night. He kept staring at me, then followed me home."

The crease in Brody's forehead deepened, and he looked down the street in the direction the rusty sedan had disappeared. "Did he threaten you?"

"No. In fact, he sent a drink to me at the bar, like he wanted to pick me up."

A slight grin lifted a corner of Brody's mouth. "Can't blame him. You probably were the prettiest lady there. With apologies to my sisters." As if he sensed her mood was still grim, he placed a hand on her shoulder while his other hand stroked her cheek and tangled in the hair at her nape. "What?"

"The drink he sent over…was a Bloody Mary."

Brody screwed his face in a moue of confusion. "Odd choice."

"Right?" She sighed and leaned into him, burying her face at his neck. "Brody, the smell of that tomato juice….God. It took me back to the jar of tomatoes that the sniper shot up. It looked like blood, and I—"

When she trembled, he drew her closer, hugging her, holding her. "It's okay. You're safe now."

She tipped her head back and met his blue gaze. "News of the bodies we found has leaked. It was on the local news tonight."

"I saw. That's one of the reasons I came over and waited for you." He cupped her cheek, and she savored the contact.

"News this important will be picked up by bigger outlets, maybe national media," she said. "If we thought the press hounded us when we were rescued, we should brace ourselves for a full assault in the next few days."

Brody swatted at a mosquito that buzzed in their faces, and she hitched her head. "Come on inside. We can talk in there without getting eaten alive." She'd made the comment casually enough, one she'd probably said dozens of times in the past. One did not live in the humid southeastern United States without dealing year-round with mosquitoes. But now a shiver ran through her, remembering the hand she'd found in a canning jar. Just how sick and depraved was the sniper? Her dinner and wine roiled in her gut, and she cast another uneasy glance down the road in the direction the creepy guy from the bar had driven. She'd had her fill of disturbing encounters with questionable men in the last several days.

Brody touched her elbow. "You all right?"

She gave a shimmy as if shaking off the heebie-jeebies that had assailed her and bobbed a nod. "Just thinking about that weirdo that followed me home."

"You're sure it was the same guy from the restaurant?" he asked as they climbed her porch steps.

"Positive. He was behind me all the way from the parking lot as I drove home."

Anya unlocked and pushed open her front door. Whiskers trotted in from the living room, tail high, meowing her greeting. Stooping, Anya picked up her cat and buried her nose in soft, warm fur. Comfort. Unconditional love. The quiet rumble of a purr.

"I can spend the night, if you want," Brody said as he closed the door behind them.

She lifted a surprised gaze, her body flushing hot at the implication. Did he assume, because they'd had sex while trapped, that it was now something they'd do whenever they had an itch to scratch?

He must have read something in her expression, because he waved a hand, adding, "On your couch, to make sure the guy doesn't bother you if he comes back around."

Anya's heart stumbled. "You think he might come back?"

Brody shrugged. "I don't know. But considering we've been in the news, considering he followed you home, considering—" He scrubbed a hand on his face as he grimaced. "Considering they haven't tracked down the sniper yet…"

Anya hugged Whiskers tighter—so tightly that the feline chirped a protest and wiggled free. Whiskers might offer emotional support, but she would be worthless if the creep from the bar or the sniper showed up at Anya's door later.

A dizzying tingle swept through her, as if all the blood had drained from her head.

"Hey, I didn't mean to scare you." Brody crossed the foyer and slid a hand along her jaw, under her hair to cradle the side of her face. "I just thought you might sleep better knowing you weren't alone in the house."

Covering his hand with hers, she whispered, "I would…if you don't mind."

"Do you have Oreos for midnight snacking?" he said, clearly trying to lighten the mood.

She smiled, grateful for his efforts to calm and distract her. "I do. But why wait for midnight? How about dessert?"

Ten minutes later, they were curled up on her couch, Oreos on the coffee table, Whiskers making herself at home on Brody's lap, and a mindless, prime-time game show glowing on her small, wall-mounted TV screen.

They passed the hours much as they had in the root cellar, talking, teasing lightly and leaning against each other. Without the specter of endless confinement, rancid blackness and uncertainty hovering over them, Anya could be more present in the moment and found herself enjoying Brody's company, savoring the brush of his hand on her knee and the crinkle of humor at the corner of his blue, blue eyes. The pull of attraction she felt was as real, as strong as when they were trapped, she realized. Stronger, even, knowing he was with her voluntarily, not because they'd been buried together. She could well imagine spending every night here with Brody, sharing kisses and—

Stop it. The rebuke came from the recesses of her brain, slapping her with a stinging reminder of how quickly Brody had retreated when she made her suggestive offer to shower together, his request for distance after his family dinner, how he'd quickly corrected any perception that he was here tonight to sleep *with* her. His reluctance to even commit to getting a *dog*.

The prime-time television line-up ended, and a local newscaster appeared on the screen to plug the upcoming broadcast. The well-coifed man announced the top story—the leaked evidence of the murders she and Brody had found—with a grim expression.

Beside her, Brody tensed. "Remember, we were told not to comment on the case. I haven't been called yet, but apparently this news broke late. You can bet we'll get calls in the morning."

She nodded. "Right. No comment. Refer them back to the police." Remembering she had a shift to work starting at three in the afternoon tomorrow, Anya groaned. "And I know every Tom, Dick and Harry I treat in the ER tomorrow will think they're owed a scoop."

"Yeah?"

She nodded, dejection weighting her shoulders. "Guaranteed. I've already been recognized and cross-examined every shift since I got back. And that's just us being rescued, before you factor in the mass murderer headline."

Putting an arm around her, he hauled her closer. "There are advantages to working with plants and trees. They really aren't the gossipy sort. Well, except roses. Man, those roses are a chatty bunch."

She gave him a side glance and a humored snort... which sent them both into peals of laughter. Bless him. Even now, after their rescue, he was trying to keep her distracted, buoyed, optimistic. Her heart pinched with gratitude and something more she didn't dare name. She couldn't, wouldn't fall for Brody Cameron.

But even as she thought the warning, Brody dipped his head and caught her lips with his. The kiss startled her, and she jerked away. For several beats, she only blinked at him while her head spun, and her pulse roared in her ears.

Brody's expression shifted, regretful for a moment, then schooling to an even, detached look. "I had an early morning...well, all of my mornings are early, trying to beat the heat of the day, so..." He stood and stretched his back. "If you'll point me toward your linen closet, I'll get a blanket for the couch and a towel for after my shower in the morning."

"Brody, I'm sorry. I—" Why had she balked? "You just surprised me. I mean, after what you said at your parents' house—"

"No," he interrupted waving a hand. "You're right. I said we should take a step back and know where we wanted to go. We haven't had that conversation yet, so it was wrong of me to assume..."

We could have that conversation now, she wanted to say. Instead, she heard herself say, "The linen closet is to the left at the top of the stairs."

Brody stared at her with guilty eyes for a moment before he nodded, turned and disappeared up the steps.

Anya sank back down on the couch with a sigh. She'd had her chance to tell him she wanted him, wanted to pursue a relationship with him, wanted the joy and warmth and encouragement he'd brought into her life every day, not just once in a while. And she'd swallowed the words. Because she was scared to hear what he had to say. As long as they didn't hash things out, they could have nights like tonight. Companionship and laughter. Could she be satisfied with just a little bit of Brody? Should she risk everything by telling him she was falling for him? Falling hard.

Forget the unsettling guy from the bar, her real fear was putting her feelings for Brody on the line and having him decide she'd been a lark, a divergence with which he'd grown bored. She knew the tender feelings they'd shared were born under unusual circumstances. Stress and death had surrounded them from all sides, and they'd clung to each other for hope and affirmation of life. Brody was smart to be reassessing.

But his kiss tonight had felt genuine, but then he'd given her that look of regret, of guilt. She pinched the bridge of her nose and groaned as her thoughts circled again.

Go slow. Tell him the truth. Maybe it's too soon. He's everything you want. He can't commit.

Enough stalling.

Brody gathered the linens he thought he needed for one night along with his determination to have the talk he'd come to have. Their rapport tonight, the chemistry he'd sensed crackling between them had led him to kiss her. And everything had turned on a dime. Her confusion and hesitation were obvious.

Ask her what she wants. The only way he'd know how to move forward was to lay it out. As Isla had so bluntly put it, when it came to women, he was not always the sharpest tool in the shed.

Brody returned downstairs to find Anya with her head bowed, nose scrunched and fingers pressed at the inside corner of her eyes. The posture was heartbreakingly pained, conflicted, broken. His resolve crumbled.

"Headache?"

Her gaze snapped up at the sound of his voice. "Uh, sort of."

The last thing he wanted was to inflict more hurt or turmoil on her. As he strolled back into the living room, he mentally set aside the question of what she wanted from him, what would happen next for them. "Can I get you anything? Tylenol or…"

She shoved to her feet, pasting on an obviously forced smile. "Naw. I'm gonna head up to bed. Sleep well, Brody." She paused at the foot of the stairs to lift Whiskers into her arms. "And thanks for, well…"

"No problem."

Something like regret or longing tugged at his chest as he spread out a sheet on the couch. But why? There was no hourglass spilling sand on them. They could take things slow for days, weeks. Let the brouhaha of the media and fresh traumas of the mountain subside.

Could he really say he had everything sorted out himself? No.

He inhaled deeply as he settled in to sleep, and the

light floral scent of Anya that lingered in the air filled his nose…like she filled his dreams.

Four nights later, Anya got off her shift at three in the morning, and as she headed to her car in the employee parking lot, a man approached her. "Aren't you Anya Patel?"

Alarm streaked through her, not only for being approached by a man in a dark parking lot, but because this man knew her name. Her scalp tingled, and without answering him, she quickened her step.

"If I could just have a minute. I'm with the *Piedmont Mountain Herald*. I've been waiting out here since ten o'clock for a chance to talk to you. Security threw me out when I asked to talk to you inside."

She kept walking, her keys clutched in her fist and poking through her fingers like metal claws. If he came any closer…

"The police are not being very forthcoming about what's going on up at the Kiper Mountain site. It stands to reason that since you were their key witness to what happened up there, that'd you know more than you're saying, as well."

She cut a glance to the man, and a flash went off in her eyes. "Hey! Don't do that!"

"We know there were human remains found, know the cops are looking for the man who captured and killed the missing women, but I'm looking for a person angle. A firsthand account as it were. Care to comment?"

"No."

"Ms. Patel, I've waited for *hours* out here. I'm not going home with nothing."

She grunted her disgust with the presumptuous reporter and clicked her fob to unlock her car. "I have no comment."

"Did the cops tell you to say that?"

Her heart thundered as the reporter caught up with her before she could slide inside the front seat and close her door. "Get lost, all right? Ambushing a woman in a dark parking lot after she's finished a twelve-hour shift is not the best way to get an interview."

"Police cover-up, yes or no?"

"No comment." She climbed behind the steering wheel and slammed her door. Hit the lock button. Still trembling inside, she started the ignition. She backed out, resisting the urge to drive over the reporter who had the temerity to click a couple more pictures with his phone as she left her parking space. "Good grief."

She pulled to the exit, checking her rearview mirror to watch the man slowly stroll toward the visitors' parking area. Was this how it would be for the foreseeable future? Recognized, questioned, followed when she was in public? Had the police found evidence of more extensive crimes? She and Brody were already material witnesses against a serial killer. They'd have to testify at trial...assuming the sniper could be found, caught.

Geez. She pressed a hand to her belly as the renewed fear swirled through her. She gave the parking lot a final glance in her mirror, discovering another car had pulled up behind her at the exit. "Sorry," she muttered to the other driver and pulled onto the road.

The other driver pulled out right behind her and stayed close enough to her back bumper that their headlights glared in her mirrors. Already irritated and rattled by the reporter, she was having none of this driver's tailgating. She pumped her brakes telling the car be-

hind her to back off, but the other car stayed close behind. She made a right turn, sooner than she normally
would so that the other car could pass. But the tailgater
also turned.

Next she turned left. The other car stayed right behind her.

Anya grumbled a bad word and with a series of right
turns, returned to the main road. Every time the tailgater's headlights followed her in the turns, her pulse
revved higher. At one point, thanks to a streetlight and
a sharp turn that meant the bright headlights weren't
blinding her, she was able to catch a glimpse of the
vehicle. An old sedan. Lots of rust. Like the vehicle
of the man who'd followed her home from the bar last
Thursday.

A chill puddled in her core as irritation morphed to
cold terror. This was no coincidence. The man who'd
recognized her had discovered where she worked, had
waited for her, was following her home.

No. Not home. She wouldn't go home, where she'd
be alone. But where did she go? She thought of Brody
first, the protection he'd provided on the mountain, the
comfort he'd offered last Thursday…

But if she drove to Brody's house, she'd be telling
the man where Brody lived. If this sicko was following
her because of the events on the mountain, Brody could
easily become his next victim. She wouldn't, couldn't
take any potential danger to him. Nor could she go
to Chloe's. Or Cameron Glen. As much as the idea of
being surrounded by family and friends appealed to
her right now.

So where?

If only a cop would drive by right now, she thought. *I'd signal him and—*

"Of course!" she whispered aloud—and headed for the police department. Valley Haven being small, she was at the police department in three minutes. No sooner had she pulled in the parking lot, than the rusted sedan sped away. She tried to get the license plate number of the car, but there was no tag.

She considered just going home. She was so tired and wanted nothing more than a glass of wine and a hot bath. But being followed twice by the same guy was serious. It deserved attention. And so with a groan, she headed inside to file a report.

While she waited for the officer on duty to write up her complaint, she called Brody, knowing she would wake him, but needing desperately to hear his voice. And to warn him, she told herself. When his groggy, worried, "Anya? What time is it? What's wrong?" greeted her, tears pricked her eyes.

"Brody, I…" She cleared her throat. "Can you meet me at my place in a little while? I…don't want to be alone tonight."

Having only recently gotten back to sleep, Brody roused when his regular six o'clock alarm chimed on his cell phone. Both Anya, who'd fallen asleep next to him on her couch, and Whiskers, who slept on her lap, bolted upright at the jingling sound. Whiskers jumped to the floor with an unhappy mew for being disturbed.

Still in her hospital scrubs, Anya raked her thick hair back from her face and cast a confused glance around her living room before her gaze settled on him.

"Sorry," he said, reaching for his phone on the coffee table to silence the alarm. "I forgot to cancel that earlier."

She sank back against the sofa cushions with a weary sigh. "So last night wasn't just a bad dream? That creepy guy followed me again?"

"Apparently so." He squeezed her shoulder. "You okay?"

She rubbed her face and let her head fall back against the couch. "I…yeah." Turning her face toward him, she gave him a sleepy smile. "Thanks for coming. I was pretty freaked out last night."

"Last night? You mean two hours ago?"

Her brow dented. "Huh? What time is it?"

"Six. I typically get up now to beat the heat of the day, get most of my jobs done before two."

She seemed to process that, though she was clearly still groggy. "So…you're getting off work about the time I go in for the late shift."

"And I get up for work shortly after you go to bed."

Her expression darkened. "So you need to go." A statement. He heard her reluctance, the disappointment that weighted her words.

"Not if you want me to stay. With a few calls, I can reschedule today's clients and—"

"No." She shook her head vehemently. "I don't want to be an inconvenience."

He framed her face with his hands. "You're not an inconvenience. You're—" *My world.* He caught the words before they tumbled out. But the truth behind the sentiment was like being doused with sobering cold water. Of course she was his world. He was falling in love with her. "Anya, I—"

His phone rang with an incoming call, and he frowned

at the interruption. But when he saw Isla's name on the caller ID, his heart leaped. For Isla to be calling at this hour…well, it couldn't be good.

"Sorry, I should answer…" he said even as he reached for his cell. "Isla? Hey. What's up?"

His sister's voice sounded grim as she said, "I guess you haven't turned on the news this morning, then?"

His chest tightened, and he motioned for Anya to turn on her TV. "No, what's happened?"

"Oh, Brody. I hate to be the one to tell you. I know he was your friend."

Anya clicked on her television, and Brody gritted his teeth impatiently as the television cycled through seemingly endless startup screens.

"Just tell me, Isla."

"Jerry Romano is dead."

Grief washed over him like a tidal wave. "But…he was recovering. I thought—"

"Brody, it was intentional. Someone got into his hospital room last night and suffocated him."

Brody's ears buzzed as he tried to process the news. "No…but—"

"Brody, he was murdered. They think it was connected to what happened on Kiper Mountain," Isla said, her voice cracking. "Please, please be careful. I don't want you to be next."

Anya watched the local news recap with ice settling in the pit of her stomach. She'd been at the hospital last night when the man, whose face had been hidden from security cameras, had stolen into Jerry's room and—

A shudder raced through her. Then, just moments later, someone had followed her home.

"I should go see Carol," Brody said, sounding stunned, heartbroken. "She's got to be devastated."

Anya's pulse slowed, remembering her conversation with Jerry's wife just days earlier. "Brody, I… I encouraged her to go home at night. To rest. To take care of herself. But if she'd been there, with Jerry—"

Brody's gaze sharpened. "Don't." He shook his head, and his nostrils flared. "Do not play 'what if' or blame yourself or…" He huffed his fatigue and grief. "If she'd been there, she might have been killed, too."

Fresh chills swept through her considering that possibility. "It's him, isn't it?"

She didn't have to say who *him* was. She saw understanding flash in Brody's eyes.

The sniper. The serial killer who'd maimed, killed and hidden women beneath his remote mountain hideaway. And, she was coming rapidly to believe, the man who'd been following her.

"Do you own a gun?"

She scowled. "No. I could never shoot someone."

He dragged a hand down his face. "Do you have any other way to protect yourself until I can get back here later today?"

"I took self-defense before I moved here. I have pepper spray on my key chain."

Brody twisted his mouth. "That's better than nothing but… I don't want to leave you here alone."

She didn't want to be alone, either. But she couldn't ask Brody to put his life on hold and babysit her for however many days, weeks or—God forbid—months it took the police to catch Jerry's killer. She wouldn't cower at home or ask Brody to give up his livelihood to be her bodyguard. So she mustered a look of confidence she wanted to feel and said, "I'll be fine. I always lock my doors. I'll keep my keys and phone close by. You can go. Tell Carol I'm sorry for her loss and that I'll be by later. I'll take her a meal. Not that she'll feel like eating, but…" she shrugged "It's what we do in the South. Feed people in their grief."

Brody nodded and pulled Anya into a hug. "Yeah. I'll tell her." When he backed out of her arms, his expression was still dubious. "I can have Jake or my father or Matt—"

"I'll be fine." She forced another smile. "I'm going to sleep. Shower. Stress eat." She tugged a quick grin. "Oreos to the rescue."

With one hand rubbing the back of his neck, Brody grunted, still clearly unconvinced.

"I won't be alone. I have Whiskers." His frown told her the joke fell flat. "And I'll call Chloe to come over for a while later this morning."

"Okay," he said, his tone grudging. "Until then, I'm just a call away if you need—"

"I'll be fine." She took his hand and walked him to the foyer. As he headed out the door, an impulse, a sudden fear or flash of premonition seized her. "Brody?"

When he faced her, she rose on her toes and kissed his mouth. Deeply. "You be careful, too."

He stared at her as if startled by her kiss, and those damned doubt demons that had plagued her for days bit hard. Especially when he narrowed his eyes on her and said softly, gravely, "Anya, I can't… Just know, no matter what happens, I want what's best for you, even if that's not me."

Chapter 16

Even if that's not me.

Anya tossed in bed, her covers getting more and more twisted around her legs. Brody's parting salvo was a giant spoon stirring a witch's brew of troubled emotions inside her. Kissing him that way, when he'd said they needed to pull back and assess, had been stupid. Reckless. If she could take it back…

When sleep continued to prove elusive, Anya called Chloe to help her pass the afternoon hours. She filled Chloe in on Jerry's death, the reporter in the parking lot, the car that had followed her home.

"And Brody?" Chloe asked, perceptive as always. "Isn't he the real reason you asked me to come over?"

"What do I do? I… I think I really messed up this morning. I pushed when he asked for time, and now…"

"And now?" Chloe prompted when Anya fell silent.

"What if I've scared him off? What if by calling him last night, kissing him that way this morning, I came off as needy or desperate, and he's trying even now to figure out how to get away from me before I drag him down."

Chloe ached a manicured eyebrow. "Really? If he'll run so easily, if he spooks at the first sign of trouble, you don't want him. Mark ran. Mark was a user. Mark left you gun-shy." Chloe reached across the table and pressed Anya's hands between hers. "But, sweetie, you can't let Mark ruin your chance to be happy with Brody. Talk to Brody. Hear him out. If he's half the guy I think he is, you'll work things out with him. If he's a big chicken like Mark—"

Anya sputtered a laugh. "Chloe!"

"If he's a chicken," Chloe started again, "I will personally kick his feathered ass and be here with all the Oreos, ice cream and Pinot Noir you need to put him behind you." Chloe gave her a sympathetic grin. "I got your back, girlfriend."

Anya leaned across the couch to give her best friend a hug, whispering, "I really need to find another outlet for stress and disappointment or I'm gonna need bigger scrubs soon."

Chloe laughed. "Gail swears by jogging, but honestly, all that sweat is so—" she pulled a face "—sweaty."

Anya chuckled and nodded. "Sweat is sweaty. Noted." Then plucking at her shirt, she added, "Which reminds me. I haven't showered since I got off work."

Chloe stood. "And I need to get to an appointment. I lost a filling in a back tooth over the weekend, and Dr. Lambruth is squeezing me in at the end of his regular workday." Chloe tipped her head toward the foyer. "Lock the door behind me. Yeah?"

She did, checking the bolt twice before picking Whiskers up and climbing the stairs to her bedroom. Her phone rang before she could get to the shower and seeing Brody's number on caller ID, twin sensations of pleasure and anxiety twisted inside her. She answered with a chipper voice, but his tone held a note of something grim.

"What's wrong?" she asked. "Something besides Jerry's death?"

"I…no. It's rough seeing someone you care about hurt so much. Carol's a wreck. And I… Well, I've spent a lot of time today thinking."

No need to ask what he'd been thinking about. She'd been thinking about the same thing. But along the same lines? She tried to swallow, her mouth suddenly dry. "Yeah. Me, too."

"I just…well, can I come over? I feel like we need to talk."

Anya's heart plummeted to her toes. *Here it is. The reckoning she'd predicted.* She'd felt it coming. Warned herself. Tried, however ineffectively, to fight her growing attraction and affection for Brody. And now the jig was up. Working to keep her tone casual and light, she said, "Yeah. We can talk." She knew she'd be a mess the moment she looked into his beautiful eyes, and she added, "Why not talk now? I was just about to shower, but—"

"This deserves to be face-to-face. Besides, when I went to your place, I forgot to charge my phone this morning, and all the calls to the funeral home and family today for Carol have drained my battery. It could die at any moment."

She scoffed lightly. "Didn't our ordeal on the mountain teach you the value of keeping a good charge on your phone? *Always*."

"Apparently not. So can I come?"

She closed her eyes, took a few slow breaths to quiet the stir of jitters at her core. "Give me about thirty minutes to get my shower."

"Works for me. Can I bring something in for dinner?"

Again struggling to keep her timbre teasing, Anya said, "Am I going to have an appetite after we have the discussion you have planned?"

"I hope so."

She grabbed the small encouragement and held on to it with both hands. "Then sure. Nothing too spicy or garlicy. I work the second shift and don't like to breathe my dinner on patients."

"Oh, you have work? Maybe another night—"

"It's fine. I don't have to go in until three a.m."

"Okay. I'll see you in thirty minutes or so with non-garlic—"

"Brody?" Silence. "Brody?"

Clearly his battery had died, dropping the call. Anya rolled her eyes, hung up and headed to the bathroom. She climbed into the shower, trying to distract herself from the upcoming conversation. Her throat tightened painfully as she fought tears. She cared deeply for Brody—and his family—and didn't want to see their budding romance end. But neither did she want to play the fool again, hang on in a dead-end relationship, pour more of her soul into something that could tear her apart down the road.

Anya rolled her shoulders under the massaging fingers of hot water. Relax. Don't assume the worst.

But she couldn't help remembering the times Brody seemed reticent to commit to a long-term relationship. He couldn't even commit to getting a dog, for Pete's sake! Guess she'd learn soon enough how he felt, because even if Brody's point in coming was unrelated to their relationship, she needed answers, needed some hope or guidance going forward. Break it off now or ask him to give her some believable reassurances.

Anya cut off the water, stepped out of the shower to dry off and was in her room dressing when she heard sounds from downstairs. Whiskers scurried into the bedroom looking frazzled, and Anya frowned. "What is it, girl? What's going on down there?"

Taking the towel with her to continue tousle-drying her thick hair, Anya stepped to the head of the stairs. "Brody, that you?"

He didn't have a key, but it was possible, however unlikely, that he'd found a back door open and let himself in. But…no. She'd been vigilant about keeping her doors locked in recent days, even above and beyond her normal single-woman carefulness. But when she a heard a bump and the scrape of a kitchen chair, she was sure someone was downstairs. "Brody?"

She crept down the stairs, pausing in the foyer long enough to take her umbrella from the stand by the coatrack. *Don't do this*, a part of her brain whispered, *go back upstairs and call 911*. But a warring, defensive part of her bristled at the thought of a home invader. Was it nosey-invasive media? Considering the area wildlife, it could even be a bear that busted in her back door. She'd just take a cautious peek to see who or what was there.

Brody would arrive soon, if the noise wasn't him. Clutching the umbrella tightly, she eased forward, her back to the wall as she approached the kitchen area where she'd heard the scraping chair. Holding her breath, she stole a glance around the corner from the living room.

A man sat at her table, chair turned, watching the living room door. But not just any man. The wiry-framed creep from the bar. The lowlife that had followed her. Twice.

Ice sluiced through her, freezing her for a precious second.

Only when the man's dark eyes narrowed and he lunged from the chair toward her did her flight response kick in. Whirling, she scrambled for the stairs, stumbling when she stubbed her bare toe on the bottom step.

The brief hesitation as she righted herself gave him the time to catch up. He seized a handful of her long hair and yanked her head back. Threw her off balance.

As she toppled backward, unable to grab the handrail quickly enough because of the umbrella still clutched in her hand, the man caught her around the waist. Although he wasn't a large man, he was deceptively strong. She dropped the umbrella and clawed at his arm. Kicked. Struggled. Screamed. *Brody, help!*

Her captor dragged her backward, into the living room where he flung her onto the couch. Immediately, she sprang up to attempt an escape, but he blocked her path, landed a blow to her cheek that made her head snap back and her ears ring.

"Hello, Anya Patel." From under his shirt, the man produced a terrifying-looking handgun. Black, shiny and aimed right at her temple. "I thought it was time we got to know each other better."

Holding her stinging cheek, she glared at him. "How do you know my name?"

He snorted. "Who doesn't? You and your boyfriend have been quite the news item lately after your astonishing escape from the mountain."

Of course, she though balefully. *Thanks, media.* She wouldn't kick herself for asking. When a strange man breaks in your home and knows your name, it's kinda the first question you instinctively ask.

But then he added, "I was surprised when I heard you and your friend survived my cellar."

Anya tensed. His cellar? If she'd needed any more proof of who he was, she had it now.

"I really thought if I hadn't finished you when I unloaded my rifle into the pit that you'd have suffocated before help arrived."

Waves of cold washed through her even as adrenaline spiked her heartbeat. Good Lord, he was the serial killer. A murderer. The sicko who kept body parts in jars. Here. In. Her. House.

"I got sloppy," he said with a frown and waved the gun closer to her. "But I'm here to correct that mistake."

Chapter 17

Anya battled down the swell of panic that clambered inside her. She needed to draw on her practiced modes of staying calm and focused in an emergency, as she did so often in the ER. She'd dealt with her share of drunk, hurting, enraged and irrational patients—though usually with the assistance of orderlies and sedatives. Taking a restorative breath, she lifted her chin. If she acted cool and collected, maybe she could trick her head into believing it. "So you know my name. I think it's only fair then that you tell me yours."

"Fair?" he sputtered. "Was it fair that you and your people trespassed on my mountain and started the chain of events that destroyed my home, my refuge, my whole damned life!"

Now it was Anya's turn to goggle. "Your mountain? That mountain is public land. And you're the one who opened fire on the search team, started the landslide with your explosives—!"

He lunged toward her, sticking his face inches from hers. The cold metal of the gun kissed her cheek. She could feel the spray of his spittle as he shouted, "'Cause you invaded my home! Trespassed on my land! You gave me no choice!"

Anya fisted a hand, struggling to keep her face impassive. She took a beat so that her tone, hopefully, would not betray the quiver at her core. "We put your secret hobby at risk. You didn't want anyone to know what you did up there alone on that mountain."

He gave a callus shrug. "Wasn't nobody's business."

His blasé attitude shouldn't have galled her. But then this man had the heartlessness and savagery to kill and dismember innocent people. "It was very much other people's business. By your own admission, you were killing people—"

"Trespassers. I only killed the folks who came on my land. I have a right to defend my property, my home."

She opened her mouth to remind him that the mountain wasn't his property. It was public land, and he was a squatter. But she changed her mind. She knew better than to argue with a wall. This man's belief system would not be changed by anything she could say. Instead, she needed to gather as much information as she could before Brody arrived. The dynamic would change when Brody arrived—*please, Brody, hurry!*—and she wanted something, anything, that might sway things in their favor. Was it possible she could negotiate with this madman? Buy time until the police arrived?

The police. Oh, God! She needed to call 911, or get some signal out that she needed help. And she had to warn Brody, so that he didn't stumble blindly into a bullet! Maybe if she got the man talking, venting his complains, she could use his distraction long enough to grab her phone—damn, it was upstairs! Could she make a run for the back door?

She tipped her head and asked, "For someone who's so opposed to trespassing, you don't seem bothered by breaking into my home, Mr.—I'm sorry. I didn't get your name."

He gave her a cold smile. "Sure. Why not. Not like you're going to live long enough to tell anybody." He tapped the muzzle against her temple again, and a chill shimmied through her, her gut roiling with acid. "Sol Guidry's the name. Former Army Ranger," he paused before grunting and adding, "which also means former US government pawn in Afghanistan."

Sol Guidry. She repeated the name in her head, committing it to memory, while a dozen other questions zinged through her head. "You're ex-military? Is that where you learned to set explosives?"

He shrugged. "Maybe. And maybe I taught myself anything I thought I should know. Plenty of information out there on the interwebs."

She blinked. "You use the internet?"

Sol frowned. "That surprises you?"

"Well…yeah. You're clearly someone who prefers to live off the grid."

"Off the grid doesn't mean I'm ignorant of technology or how to use it." He sounded irritated, offended by her assumption. "In fact, I'd say my knowledge of how Big Brother is watching every aspect of technology available today is why I choose not to use tech. But there are ways around Big Brother. If you're smart."

Okay, she already knew he was not right in the head. Anyone who could kill and torture another human was mentally sick, but she factored in this evidence he was paranoid, as well. Again, arguing with him about his convictions wouldn't help get her out of this mess, but playing into them might.

"Why are you here?" she asked, squaring her shoulders and doing her best to appear calm and unintimidated, despite the furious flap of hummingbird wings in her chest. She mustered a bit of the ire his past tactic had stirred, channeling her fear into anger. "Why have you been following me?"

He pulled a face that said he was disappointed. "Aw, come on, Anya. You know why?"

"Because you believe I…*trespassed* on your mountain?"

He ducked his head once in assent, then held up a finger. "But more importantly…you didn't die like you should have. You came down from the mountain and started blabbing to the cops." He leaned close to her, his dark eyes narrowed. "Didn't your mama teach you that it wasn't nice to tell other people's secrets?"

"Didn't your mother teach you it's not nice to hold people hostage? Or murder innocent women? Or save their body parts in canning jars!" she snarled back.

His hand whipped toward her, and she flinched. But instead of striking her, he wrapped his fingers in her long hair and tugged hard, angling her head back. "You have a sharp tongue, Anya. Maybe I should cut it out. Hmm? What do you think?"

Anya swallowed, a quiver gripping her belly.

A floorboard creaked, and when Sol jerked his gaze behind him, Brody's angry voice growled, "I think if you don't let go of her immediately, I will cut out something more vital than your tongue!"

Brody wielded his folding buck knife, his only weapon, as he stepped closer to the middle-aged man holding Anya's hair and bending her head back. He wasn't sure how he'd defend himself against the man's gun—he was taking this as it came, without any time to plan—but he'd be damned if he'd let this cretin manhandle Anya the way he was without doing *something*.

When he'd arrived, he'd parked his car a couple houses down the street, the best spot he could find, and had been walking back to her townhouse when he'd noticed tire tracks left in the neighbors' sod. Because of the recent rain, the ground was soft and vulnerable, and as a landscaper, he was aggravated on the homeowner's behalf for the ruined yard. Shielding his eyes from the sun that sat low on the horizon about to slip behind the mountains for the night, he gawked in the backyard. Taking in the extent of the damage, he mentally calculated an estimate should the homeowner want help repairing the lawn. He followed the track of the ruts from the neighbor's yard into Anya's, determining what vehicle had done the damage to the expensive grass and—

He froze when he recognized the old model sedan with rust spots parked at the end of the tire tracks. The car that had followed Anya, twice.

Spinning away and dropping the bag of chicken sandwiches and fries he'd brought, he hurried to Anya's house on full alert. Instead of ringing her doorbell, he snuck around to the back where he found the broken glass pane in her porch door. With his heart in his throat and moving as quietly as he could, he eased along her back wall to peek in the kitchen and living room windows—and saw the man with Anya. The gun. The man's aggressive demeanor.

Brody dug his phone out of his pocket, and silently cursed when he saw the low battery message and the screen blinked to black. Dead. Gritting his back teeth, he enacted a hastily devised plan to sneak in the porch door to the kitchen, move up behind the man, unseen and tackle the creep. But then the floor had squeaked, giving him away, and leaving Brody improvising again.

"Let go of her. Now!" Brody growled, inching closer, wielding his knife—as if the blade were a defense against the man's bullets. Damn!

"Well, look who's joined us," the cretin said, angling the muzzle of his weapon toward Brody. "This couldn't have worked out better if I'd planned it." The man's face darkened, and he motioned with the gun. "Drop the knife, or Anya takes a bullet."

Brody hesitated. The man knew Anya's name. How? Why was he here? What did he want?

When Brody didn't comply, the intruder twisted harder on Anya's hair, wrenching her neck to a sharper angle, and she yelped in pain.

"Stop!" Brody shouted, holding up a hand and letting the knife clatter to the floor. "Stop. Just…let her go."

"Now kick it to me."

"Let. Her. Go."

He scowled. "Oh, I can't do that, friend. I have plans for her. She's going to help me start my new collection."

When Anya whimpered, a chill slid through Brody. Like the shadows growing in the room as the sun sank outside, black suspicions took form in Brody's soul.

"Collection? What collection? What are you talking about?"

"It's him, Brody," Anya rasped, angling a terrified look at him despite the grip the man had on her hair. "The sniper. The killer from the moun—"

The man jerked hard on her hair, snarling. "Shut up. The men are talking."

The sniper? Fresh waves of horror and understanding pooled acid in Brody's gut.

Anya's expression hardened, clearly not happy with being told to be silent or yield to the men. "His name is Sol Guidry."

"I said shut up!" The creep thrust Anya onto the floor and pointed the gun at her.

Brody's thoughts were scrambling, trying to keep up as the level of danger, the information Anya was feeding him, the changing dynamic all clicked quickly into place.

Sniper. Serial killer. Collection. *Holy hell...*

He had to get the man's focus off Anya. Get the weapon trained on her aimed somewhere else. Or, better, out of Guidry's possession.

"Hey!" Brody barked. "You want the knife?"

As Guidry cut a glance toward him, Brody snatched the buck knife off the floor at his feet and hurled it toward the intruder.

Guidry flinched, but the blade still stuck in his shoulder near his collarbone. He roared in fury and pain, grabbing for the blade to remove it. And Brody lunged.

He tackled Guidry, shoving him away from Anya as he charged. Bent at the waist, Brody kept his center of gravity low, the way he'd learned when he played high school football. The two stumbled together until they hit the couch. Brody battled Guidry's hands, fought for possession of the gun made slick as Guidry's blood spread. A loud blast echoed in Brody's ears. Then another.

"Brody!" Anya screamed.

He kept battling, knowing even if he'd been shot, adrenaline could mask the pain for several minutes. But with a stunning tactical move, one that didn't rely on size as much as leverage, Guidry wrenched free. With a foot planted in Brody's chest, the killer shoved Brody away, raised the gun. Fired.

This time Brody did feel it. The impact of the bullet hitting his torso knocked him back a few steps. He tripped over something, his legs buckling, and he toppled toward the floor. His head hit with a thwack. Air left his lungs in a whoosh. His side stung. His vision dimmed. And his world went black.

Chapter 18

Brody didn't get up, didn't move. Anya scrambled toward him, her own breathing shallow and fast, panicked. "Brody!"

Before she could reach him, Sol seized the back of her shirt and stopped her.

"You and I are going to take a little ride."

Even as Sol hoisted her to her feet, Anya stared in horror at Brody's still, bleeding form, willing him to gasp for air or moan or...*something* to tell her he was alive.

Sol's arm snaked around her waist, and he hauled her toward the back door.

"No! Noooo!" She screamed, clawing at his arms, wrenching this way and that, trying to free herself from his steely grasp.

Between her fighting and his force, she stumbled, and without her legs under her, her full weight shifted to his arms, breaking his hold on her.

Ignoring the pain of crashing to her hardwood floor, Anya scrambled on her hands and knees, praying to get away. But his fist tangled in her long hair again, bringing her up short. She loosed another scream, of pain, of frustration, of fear. If she was loud enough, would one of her neighbors hear? Call the police?

With a hard jerk that caused a thousand fiery needle-pricks on her scalp, Sol yanked her hair to regain his control of her. Her glared down at her with fury in his dark eyes. "Clearly the only way to capture and transfer a wild tiger to captivity is a tranquilizer dart. Lacking that, this will have to do."

He raised the gun in his hand, and Anya gasped as she saw it arcing down. The first blow reverberated through her skull like a lightning strike. The second blow knocked her out.

Sol grunted his discontent when Anya slumped to the floor. He hated that he'd had to knock her out. Part of the fun for him was hearing the women's pleas for mercy, seeing the fear in their faces as they anticipated what he had planned, smelling the literal stink of terror on them. The more his women cowered, the more he savored his control over them.

But to get her into his car and out to his new hideout, he couldn't have her screaming and fighting and attracting the neighbors' attention. He pressed a hand to the stab wound on his shoulder. Warm blood seeped from the wound and the slice in his skin stung like hell. He shot a glower toward the blond boyfriend, Brody Cameron, the news reports said, and huffed his disgust. If the knife weren't enough insult, the hotshot had spoiled Sol's plans with Anya, beaten the odds by surviving the carnage on the mountain, and was giving the cops information about Sol's work at the cabin. Cameron deserved whatever Sol did to him.

Sol brooded over his choices as he stumbled to Anya's kitchen and found hand sanitizer to disinfect the wound, clean dish towels to staunch the bleeding and plastic wrap that, when wound around and under his armpit, would hold the folded towel tightly in place. Once finished with the on-the-fly first aid, he moved to stand over Cameron. Blood stained the right side of the hotshot's shirt.

He wasn't moving, but Sol found a steady pulse at his neck. So…shoot him and be rid of his interference? Dismember him and strew his body parts from here to Asheville?

Sol grunted. Enjoyable as that would be, he wanted Cameron to suffer. He'd been a key reason why Sol was having to start over. Cameron had taken so much from him, and he wanted the interfering buck to know real anguish. That'd be easy enough, knowing where he lived, where his family lived.

Anya stirred, and he thought about the obvious feelings Cameron had for the pretty nurse. Knowing she was with Sol and unable to stop him from torturing her would be emotional hell for the blond Romeo. With a satisfied grin, Sol kicked Cameron in the ribs where the bloodstain was growing. Hard. Once, twice, three times for good measure, chuckling to himself when an agonized groan rumbled from the jerk. *Buddy, you don't know pain yet, but you will.*

Cameron opened one eye and croaked, "Anya…"

Sticking his face the in would-be hero's, Sol gloated, "Anya is coming with me. We're gonna have a little fun, us two. But you're not invited. Not yet. But your turn is coming."

Sol hurried outside and retrieved the teenager's rusty Chevy. He parked right on Anya's back porch by her door. After keying open the trunk, he went back in for Anya.

He draped her over his uninjured shoulder, grimacing at the pain that shot up and down his arm when he moved the other shoulder, and lugged her out. He rolled her into the trunk and slammed the lid closed, his breath sawing from him. She hadn't been that heavy, but he'd lost a decent amount of blood. Grumbling a curse, he climbed in the driver's seat and sped away.

A hard smack to his side dragged Brody from the blackness. A moan slipped from him as his mind slowly processed what was happening, where he was, why his ribs hurt so—

Thwack! Another strike sent sharp waves of pain through him. And his thoughts focused, blurred.

Anya…

Someone hissed a threat in his face, the words garbled in his ears, but the tone was dark and chilling. More clarity returned… The serial killer. *Guidry.* A gun.

He seemed to drift in and out of consciousness, and he battled the darkness that sucked at him, pulled him down.

Anya…

Could he do anything to slow this creep down? Help Anya? Turn the tide?

The man jostled him, letting Brody's head thunk to the ground.

The next time he roused, the man no longer hovered over him. Where had he gone?

Anya...

The persistent drumbeat of her name called to him. A warning. An alarm. A catalyst.

Brody gritted his teeth and blinked hard. Stay awake. Stay here. Stay—

A noise across the room drew his attention. Guidry. Lifting Anya's limp form. Carrying her...out. Away...

Anya is coming with me. We're gonna have a little fun, us two. The sibilant whisper scratched at his brain. His imagination? Or had—

A car engine roared outside, and a blast of adrenaline pumped through him.

Anya!

He raised his head, his gaze searching frantically for her. Gone! Carried away...

Rolling to his side, he mustered enough strength to climb to his knees, to drag himself to a stuffed living room chair. To his feet. Stumbling, he crossed the floor to the back door.

The rusted Nova was pulling away onto the street. Turned left.

Panic shot reinforcing adrenaline coursing through Brody. Guidry had Anya...

She's going to help me start my new collection.

A different kind of pain sliced through Brody and filled his gut with acid. Guidry planned to torture Anya! Kill her!

Fists of anguish squeezed his heart. An image of the severed hand in the canning jar they'd found in Guidry's hellhole flashed in his brain. *No, no, no! Not Anya. Please God, not Anya!*

He reached for his back pocket where he carried his phone, only to remember the battery was dead. Hell! He bit out a foul word, picturing his phone's charging cord plugged in the wall at home. He couldn't even call for help, call the police. He was losing time. He had to follow Guidry or lose Anya forever.

Fueled by the punch of panic, Brody staggered outside, toward his truck. He focused his strength on putting one foot in front of the other. Ignore the pain. Rescue Anya—

His head swam, and fiery bolts streaked from his ribs as he pushed himself to an awkward lope. Fisting his hand and steeling his resolve, Brody battled through the waves of pain. He *would not* let anything keep him from following Guidry. Anya needed him and whatever it took, he had to save her from the madman that had taken her.

Anya woke as the hard surface she lay on jolted and shimmied. Her head bounced, bumping hard, throbbing harder. She blinked groggily, rubbed her temple... only to be bounced again. She tried to sit up in the dark space, only to bump her head from above.

Finally, the rumble of an engine and scent of exhaust filtered through her daze. A car. Confinement. A trunk?

Her heart revved when she remembered the moments before losing consciousness. Brody knocked out. Injured.

Sol Guidry, the serial killer, *in her home*...taunting her. Striking her—

The surface beneath her rattled and jarred her again, reviving the pain under her skull. And the swell of terror spinning through her brain.

Guidry was taking her somewhere. That much was clear.

I have plans for her. Bile rose in her throat when Guidry's words echoed in her head. She gagged, but managed to swallow, to catch her breath, to fight back the panic that threatened to overwhelm her. She had to stay calm in order to think. To process. To devise a strategy for escape.

She wasn't bound. A plus.

Sol was stronger than her. A minus.

She had the element of surprise when he opened the trunk. A plus.

Sol was armed. A huge minus.

And she had no idea where he was taking her...other than somewhere isolated.

Once again, a choking anxiety sat on her, stealing her breath.

When they'd been trapped in Guidry's cellar together, Brody had found ways to distract her, calm her, encourage her. She missed that voice of reason and comfort now. Missed Brody.

Brody... Brutally attacked. Lying so still. Oh, please, please, please let him be all right!

A whimper of grief squeaked from her throat. If she were ever granted the chance to see Brody again, she would tell him how much he meant to her. He might not want her, he might have been on his way to her house to let her down, break things off between them, but he would always be dear to her. She'd always be grateful for the way he helped her survive the terrifying days trapped on the mountain. She'd always—a fresh bolt of panic washed through her. *Always* for her could only be a few hours...minutes. Was she going to die tonight? If she couldn't get away from Guidry, would she end up in jars in this man's basement?

Panting and battling this new wave of fear, Anya sent a darting gaze around the dark car trunk. Dim light seeped in from rust holes and a small gap where the trunk lid wasn't well seated. Could she unlatch the trunk from inside? She knew more recent cars were built with that ability, but this car was old…

Maybe she could punch out a taillight and signal for help?

Turning as best she could in the close quarters, she smacked at the taillight with the flat of her hand. She quickly realized she didn't have the strength of leverage to knock the taillight glass out that way and tried to wedge a foot in position…

But as she twisted her body, the car slowed, made a turn. She heard gravel crunch beneath the tires. The car bumped over a large pot hole—then stopped. The engine cut off. A door squeaked on ancient hinges.

Terror swooped through Anya. Her time to strategize was up.

He had blood on his hands.

Brody stared at the red stains on his fingers, his shirt, and his heart sank. The flood of adrenaline in his veins had numbed him to the gunshot wound, but as he clutched his side and stumbled the last few feet to his truck, he remembered the hot sting, the impact that knocked him reeling. Blood loss would hamper his ability to catch up to Guidry and Anya. He had no phone to call for police backup, for an ambulance.

He glanced toward Anya's neighbors. Could one of them help? Could he borrow a phone? Night was descending quickly, yet the windows in her neighbors' homes were all dark. Not even a TV screen flickered through the front windows. Rather than waste time pounding on the doors of houses where no one was home, Brody climbed behind the wheel of his truck and cranked the engine. After taking a shallow, painful breath, he paused. He had to stem the bleeding or risk passing out as he drove.

He made his way to the toolbox in the bed of his truck and dug around until he found a roll of duct tape. Then, wadding his shirt over the gash in his side, he unwound the tape, wrapping it around his torso to hold the makeshift bandage in place. Every movement hurt like hell, but he gritted his teeth and powered through.

Anya...

He'd walk through fire for her. The ache in his ribs was nothing compared to the possibility of losing Anya, the agony of knowing what she could be suffering even now. Sliding behind the steering wheel again, he shifted into gear and headed out. He turned left as Guidry had, his only clue where the killer was headed. Brody squeezed the wheel and tried to reason out his next move.

If I were a serial killer who'd spent the last several years living off the grid on a remote mountain, where would I go with my next victim?

Away from town. Away from witnesses. Away from the interference of law enforcement.

One state highway ran through town, connecting Valley Haven with the interstate to Asheville to the east and rural farmland, rolling foothills and isolation to the west.

When he reached the highway, Brody headed west.

Within moments of setting out on his search, the sun sank behind the ridge of mountains, leaving everything bathed in a deep, unbroken darkness. The two-lane highway wound a curvy path through the countryside, and Brody split his attention between the ever-darkening road and the farmhouses and abandoned businesses that were spaced farther and farther apart the farther he drove from Valley Haven. Insects darted in and out of the twin beams of his headlights, and the objects in the yards he passed became more and more difficult to distinguish. How the hell was he supposed to find Guidry if he couldn't see beyond the pool of his headlights?

Fear for Anya and frustration for the growing difficulty seeing his surroundings spiked in his chest, tightening his lungs. His already shallow inhalations—in deference to the pain from his ribs—came quicker as his agitation rose. When his head spun, he recognized that he was going to pass out if he didn't calm his breathing and manage his rage and terror. Anya needed him to stay in control, focused, alert.

A car passed him, its headlights bright in his eyes as it rounded a curve in the road ahead of him. The first car he'd passed since leaving Valley Haven. He squinted as the vehicle passed. Not a rusty Nova. Of course not. That'd be too easy.

Finding Anya, saving Anya was not going to be easy. But he would not give up.

Anya followed the sound of footsteps in gravel as they approached the trunk, and prepared herself. She'd have one chance to catch Sol off guard, to spring at him, to launch an attack—

The trunk squeaked as the lid was raised, and Anya

lunged up, her fingers curled and tensed. With a howl of rage, she swiped at Sol, lashed out at him, raking her fingernails across his cheek and the arm he raised to block her attack. He fell back a step, cursing her, and she used the opportunity to tumble out of the trunk onto the gravel. She yelped as gravel bit her knees, but she quickly scrambled to her feet, swinging at him, clawing. She fought...until he arced his arm up and backhanded her chin.

The blow knocked her head back and made her ears ring. Her legs buckled, and she went to her knees again. The sting of gravel scraping her legs paled versus the fire of her scalp as he grabbed her hair again and dragged her away from the car. If she'd had scissors, she'd have cut her own hair at the root, just to stop him from using her tresses as a weapon against her.

"Get up!" he barked. "On your feet, bitch!"

If only to stop the pain needling her head, she staggered to her feet and angled her head to meet his cold stare. Long red streaks marked his cheek, and blood beaded in spots where she'd raked him with her fingernails.

With his free hand, he swiped at his face, and finding his blood on his palm, he glowered. "You'll pay for that."

He grabbed for her arm, and she twisted away, even though the move caused his grip to tug harder on her hair. With his second attempt to seize her, he caught her wrist and bent her arm behind her at a painful position. Still she fought, despite the excruciating fire streaking from her abused arm. She could fight—or die. Because she had no doubt that was her fate if she didn't get away from him...somehow. Even if she had to rip every hair from her head, dislocate her arm, chew her leg off like a wolf in a trap, anything was better than being the killer's newest victim. The start of his new *collection*.

With every ounce of strength she possessed, Anya battled. She swung and slapped with her free hand, kicked, twisted, screamed.

"Enough!" Sol shouted. Something hard struck her temple, and as fresh waves of pain reverberated under her skull, the edges of her vision dimmed. And her knees gave out.

Chapter 19

Brody had been driving for thirty minutes, finding no hint of Guidry, the rusted Chevy or Anya. Despair and frustration tangled in his gut, but he pushed on. His side throbbed and his head pounded, but he pushed on. The odds against him loomed grimly and the country road grew darker, but he pushed on.

Anya...

Just a little farther, he thought. Then he'd turn around and search the other end of the highway, east of town.

The phrase *needle in a haystack* came to mind, and he pushed the discouraging thought aside. Damn it, he would find that needle if it took going through every stalk of hay. The alternative was untenable.

Anya...

He needed help. Back up. More eyes out searching. Regret crawled through him that he hadn't driven straight to the police station, hadn't done more to find a phone to call for help instead of racing out of town following Guidry alone. He could only blame hubris. Panic and pain-clouded reasoning. Tunnel vision.

It's not too late to turn around and go to the cops.

His chest hurt thinking of abandoning his search. He had an itchy feeling he was close, so close to finding Anya...if only—

A pair of headlight beams pierced the night ahead of him. A car coming from the other direction. And he knew he couldn't miss this opportunity. Immediately he started flashing his own headlights to signal the approaching car. The car flashed its lights once, but didn't seem to be slowing. Damn!

At the last moment, Brody angled his truck across the lane for oncoming traffic and stopped. Flashed his lights again. The oncoming car slammed on its brakes, and after a few seconds, the driver climbed out.

The other driver, a portly man of about his father's age stormed up to Brody's window, shouting and waving his arms in irritation.

Brody rolled down his window as the man neared, yelling, "What the hell? Are you insane? You could have killed—"

"I need your help," Brody interrupted.

The other man must have seen something concerning, because his expression of outrage morphed to one of puzzlement and then alarm. "You're bleeding. Son, you need a doctor!"

When the other driver tried to open the truck door, Brody waved him off. "I'll be all right. I need you...to call the police. Tell them... Anya Patel was...kidnapped.

Guidry... Sol Guidry is...the serial killer from—"
Damn! Why was he so winded?

"Who was kidnapped? Boy, are you high on something?"

"No! I have to...find Anya. Please...just...call the police. Tell them to look for Sol Guidry. He took Anya...."

The other driver squinted, using his phone light to illuminate Brody's face. "Hey, aren't you that guy that was rescued from—"

"Yes!" Brody shifted gears to back his truck up. "Call. The. Police! The killer has Anya!"

Cutting his wheels hard to return to the proper lane, Brody watched the man's stunned expression move to action. He tapped his screen then lifted the cell phone to his ear, and Brody could only pray that he was doing as asked and summoning the authorities.

Okay, at least someone else knew what was happening. The police would soon know what was happening and head out this direction. But what if Guidry went the other way? What if Guidry went east and all the attention was focused here, west of town? Brody gritted his back teeth, debating, trying to reason out the best way forward. Prayed for discernment, for a miracle.

Slapping his hand on the steering wheel, he barked out a bitter curse word. Even when they'd been trapped in the root cellar, unsure if they'd be rescued, Brody hadn't felt this helpless, this overwhelmed. He was desperate to find Anya before it was too late.

Too late... He swallowed the sour taste that rose in his throat. Please, *please*, let him find Anya before it was too late! Not waiting for a side road or driveway to turn around, Brody cut is wheels hard and executed a three-point turn in the middle of the highway. If the cops were headed this way, he could expand the search parameters by driving east. Which only left north and south and a mind-boggling zillion other places that Guidry could have Anya by now.

The futility of what he was attempting sucked at him, despair and desperation rising like a tide. And like a drowning man, he felt as if he couldn't breathe. Anya was the woman he'd been looking for his whole life. The one he wanted to grow old with. He'd just found her. And now he stood to lose her in the cruelest of ways because he hadn't protected her. He'd let her down. He'd—

His heart jolted as his headlights glanced off of a vehicle parked in the side yard of an old farmhouse. Brody braked hard and threw the truck in reverse. He backed down the highway until the car in question was once again in the spotlight of his high beams. A rusted Chevy.

His heartbeat roared in his ears. He'd missed the Chevy earlier because of the dark, because he'd been too much in his head, because it had only been the curve of the road that momentarily angled his headlights enough to catch the vehicle parked next to the derelict clapboard house.

He'd prayed for a miracle—and it had been granted. He'd found the needle in the haystack. But…now what?

Anya came to on the dusty floor in an empty room. She blinked and raised a hand to her head where it ached. A pair of boots shuffled into her field of vision, and her precarious situation crashed through her brain like a locomotive. She sat up so fast her head spun and she had to brace herself as the floor seemed to shift below her.

Sol knelt in front of her, and her gut swooped. Her head told her to try again to run, to get away from him, but she couldn't make her legs cooperate. He grabbed her arms and wrapped something stiff around her wrists. Zip ties. Tears pricked her eyes, knowing he'd gained the upper hand. Knowing that with bound hands, she'd be so much more vulnerable to whatever evil he had planned for her.

Sol drew the plastic strips at her wrists tight, then dragged her to her feet. Her legs wobbled, and her head felt thick, muzzy, as if under water.

"Once upon a time," he began in a flat tone, "when I was a little kid, my father taught me not to trust any woman. From the days of Eve, he'd say, women have been deceitful and unworthy of respect. He kept my mother in line when he was home, but when he was gone for work or out of town on business, it was my job to be the man of the house and keep order."

Something deep inside Anya shriveled, knowing just how deeply rooted that meant Sol's disdain for women and history of abuse were.

He dug an S-hook from his pocket and hung it from something above her. She let her head flop back to see what was happening. A small, simple chandelier with bare bulbs hung from the center of the ceiling, and Sol had hung half of the S-hook from one brass arm. With a glance around her, she placed herself inside an empty house. The dining room based on the chandelier. All the windows she could see in this room and adjoining ones had been covered with blankets.

"But my mother, well…she had no real respect for

my authority when Dad was gone. She tried to boss me. When I stood up to her, put her in her place, she'd slap my face." Sol tugged Anya's arms over her head attempting to put the zip tie over the other end of the S-hook. Missed. He grimaced in pain and rolled his injured shoulder. Then meeting her eyes with a narrowed gaze, he growled, "I hated being slapped by that bitch."

The venom in his tone sent shivers to her core.

"I—I'm s-sorry that she d-did that to you," Anya rasped. And she was sorry. No child deserved to be abused, and Sol clearly was both physically and mentally abused. She wanted to make him see she wasn't his enemy, wasn't going to hurt or betray him, that he needed to let her go. But how did she reach him through the scars left by years of pain and mistreatment?

"Oh, and she was sorry for it, too," he smirked, "After I got finished with her."

Anya gasped. "What do you m-mean?"

"Well, I figured she couldn't slap me if she had no hands. So—" He yanked harder on her hands, stretching higher, higher…until Anya had to stand on her toes to keep the plastic strips from digging into her wrists. He frowned and clutched a hand to the wound at his shoulder. Finally, using his good hand to lead, he slipped the plastic zip ties over the end of the S-hook, and no amount of tiptoes kept the zip ties from cutting off Anya's blood circulation to her hands or slicing into her tender skin. She gave a cry of pain and fear when he left her in the agonizing position.

"One of the women who spent time with me on the mountain slapped me once. She thought she was being brave, fighting back. But she was just stupid." He stepped back, his breathing winded as he added, "I cut her hand off, too. Saved it to show other bitches who came my way as a lesson in what happened to women who step out of line." He mentioned the amputation casually, as if discussing the weather. "I loved the look of horror they gave me after that. They knew my power over them then."

Through the haze of her pain, Anya flashed to the gruesome discovery of the hand in a jar and her stomach rebelled. "Please…" she begged, not even knowing what she was begging for.

He aimed a finger to the bleeding scratches on his face. "This displeases me, Anya. You have to pay for what you did."

Her eyes widened in horror, and blood pumped past her ears in a panicked rhythm. "No. No, please…no."

Sol pulled a face, shook his head. "Oh, not your whole hand, I think. You'd bleed out before I'd have enough time with you. I learned that from my mother, too. She bled out before my dad got home, and we had to bury her body under the house."

Sol stepped back and rolled his shoulders. "I have to get my tools. But don't worry, Anya. I'll be right back."

He disappeared into the next room, the kitchen from what she could see through the open door, and she heard clinking, thumps.

Despite being strung from the chandelier like a pi-ñata, Anya tried to clear her mind, think of something, anything she could do to relieve the throbbing pain that streaked from her hands to her toes. Or to change Sol's mind about hurting her. Or to free herself from her deranged captor.

With a sinking heart, she realized her only chance was if Brody had survived Sol's attack and called for help. When she pictured Brody, bleeding and unmoving on her floor, an ache like jagged glass cut her to her core. Even if she survived Sol's torture—which was looking less likely by the minute—what would her life be like without the man she'd fallen in love with? Fresh tears spilled on her cheek, as much for the knowledge that she loved Brody as that she'd never get the chance to tell him. Show him. Share her life with him.

Sol returned, bringing a dilapidated wooden chair with him. He placed the chair near her, and she scrabbled to put her feet on it, to relieve some of the tension on her hands. Sol slapped her feet away, climbed on the chair and pulled a pair of needle-nose pliers from his pocket.

Anya's pulse kicked and new spasms of panic twisted inside her. "What are you doing?"

"Making sure you can't scratch me with these claws again," he said matter-of-factly, snapping the pliers in front of her nose.

Anya's gut roiled. "God, no! Please don't!"

She tried to curl her fingers defiantly into her palms, but Sol grabbed one hand and forced her pinky to straighten. Gripping her fingernail with the pliers, he yanked.

Anya cried out as the fingernail tore from her hand. Dots swam in front of her eyes, and she fought to stay conscious. Or did she want to faint? Succumb to the darkness to escape the pain?

Flicking the fingernail to the floor, Sol said, "Shall I do the rest now or…let you think about what's to come?" He chuckled darkly. "I do love to watch a woman squirm and fret." He patted Anya's cheek and climbed down from the chair. "Yeah. I'll let you think about what you've done, why you're being punished for a while."

"Wh-what?" Anya asked, her question caught on a strangled breath.

"Scratching me was only the latest. Everything that's happened since you trespassed on my mountain and told the police about my collection has to be punished. It's the only way to restore the proper order of things."

Her arms, her wrists, her pinkie all hurt too much to make sense of his rambling. Her heart ached too much for Brody…dear Brody, who was probably dead. It was the anguish over losing Brody that brought the feral cry from the black pit of her soul. She let her head fall back and filled the empty house with a shattering scream.

The new surge of adrenaline that poured through Brody upon finding Guidry's car helped dull the pain in Brody side and fuel his muscles. He backed even farther down the highway, not wanting to alert Guidry with extended illumination from his headlights. If the older man had called the police, they should be headed this way soon.

But Brody couldn't wait on that possibility. And how could he signal the police and direct them to this remote farmhouse? Sure, he could sit here in his truck and wait for the cops, but how could he do that when Anya was suffering who knew what at the sick man's hands even now?

Angling his truck to block the highway had worked before to signal help. It would…it *had* to work again. He parked his truck far enough down the road that he hoped his activity would go unnoticed by Guidry. Then leaving his driver's door open, his hazard lights blinking,

Brody pillaged his glove box and scribbled a note on the back of a take-out menu from an Asheville pizza shop.

Kidnapping in progress. Send police to white house 1/4 mile east.

Then, in case he didn't survive to convey the fact to the cops in person, he added, *Kiper Mountain serial killer = Sol Guidry.*

Brody slapped the note under his windshield wiper and took a breath. He turned to stare down the road toward the farmhouse. His impulse was to run all the way and burst through the door to save Anya.

Yeah, you see how well that worked last time.

Holding a hand over his aching side, he ran a mental checklist of options. Guidry was armed. Brody'd need to disarm him.

Brody was hampered by his injuries. He needed a simple way to overpower Guidry.

The police were coming—he hoped. He'd need to bind Guidry in some way so he couldn't escape.

"Yeah. Right." Brody scoffed a despondent laugh. "So glad I brought my crime-fighting kit and magic tool belt."

Puffing out a breath, he shoved aside the useless bemoaning of what he *didn't* have. What *did* he have? Because he sure as hell would not go rushing in unprepared this time.

Circling to the bed of his truck, he opened his toolbox and dug out a flashlight. Sweeping the beam over his landscaping equipment and the supplies he kept on hand for odd jobs, he made a mental list of his options.

A trowel, a Weed eater, a hoe, a tarp. An extension cord, a partially used bag of mulch, a can of bug spray, a pair of heavy-duty work gloves. Steel-toed boots. Fertilizer spikes.

He raked his fingers through his hair trying to find that *something* that would give him the upper hand... when he heard a woman scream.

Anya!

He made his choices quickly and set off toward the farmhouse with his heart in his throat.

Chapter 20

Brody hurried toward the farmhouse with a shovel in one hand, which he used as a cane or hiking stick at times when his side throbbed and he thought his legs might buckle from the pain, and a plastic grocery sack of random items in his other hand—wasp spray, a coil of replacement string for his Weed eater, the rest of the duct tape and the steel file he used to sharpen his mower blade.

He tried to stay out of direct view of any of the farmhouse windows as he approached, an exercise that proved less important when he discovered the front window had been blocked with some type of sheet or blanket. Light peeked around the edges of the window covering, but Brody couldn't find a wide enough gap that afforded him a glimpse inside.

But he heard voices. A man's. And a woman's—Anya's—choked with pain and emotion.

"Don't…please!"

"I love it when you beg. It's so satisfying to know I have your attention."

Brody shoved away from the front wall of the house and moved to the side yard. No doors or windows there. He moved on to the back.

Brighter light seeped from the edges of the rear windows, telling Brody these rooms were the source of the light. He tried again to peer inside, assess the situation and make a plan.

The first room he found was the kitchen. Empty but for a broken table and a wooden chair on its side. And a small pile of odds and ends on the floor that made his blood freeze. Cords. Small saws. Brown bottles of unknown liquids. His stomach rolled, and he didn't take the time to figure out what else he was seeing. He knew enough about what the odd collection was for.

Moving to the next window, he found a gap where the blanket used to block the window had a tear. He peeked inside…and his heart lurched.

Anya was strung up by her hands like a side of beef, and her face reflected the agony she was in. Guidry stood before her, his expression gloating. He held some sort of tool in his hand as he climbed on a chair to reach her hands.

The panic and dread that swamped Anya's face was all Brody needed to know he had to move fast to stop whatever was about to happen. He hustled to the back door, opened it quietly and moved inside, keeping his back to the wall. Setting the sack on the floor, he took the wasp spray from the plastic bag and shook the can.

Moving swiftly, he rounded the edge of the doorway to the next room, the pesticide can held aloft and the shovel in his other hand. Anya saw him first, and, her eyes widening, she gasped.

Guidry, seeing her reaction, spun toward Brody.

Brody blasted the stream of wasp spray in Guidry's face. Although he raised an arm to shield his face, Brody was certain he'd gotten a large amount in the jerk's eyes. His target. Unfortunately, there was no way to prevent Anya from catching some side splatter of the wasp spray. As Guidry shouted curses, choking and swiping at his face, he stumbled off the chair and went down on his knees briefly.

Anya yelped and coughed, and though Brody desperately wanted to rush to her, he had to deal with Guidry first. Guidry, who was even now reaching for the small of his back to bring out his pistol. With his eyes still blinking and tearing from the bug spray, Guidry aimed in Brody's general direction and squeezed off a shot that struck the spade of the shovel Brody used as a shield.

Brody returned fire with another stream of wasp spray. Blinded by the insecticide, Guidry fired wildly, sending rounds into the floor and walls. Brody darted behind the kitchen wall, crouching to make himself a smaller target, his hand still tight around the handle of the shovel.

As expected, Guidry pursued him. The second the creep appeared in the entry to the kitchen, Brody surged to full height, swinging the shovel at the other man's head. A solid *thunk* sounded in the empty kitchen, and the impact vibrated up Brody's arms, screamed through his ribs.

Guidry swayed and slumped to his knees. Brody swung again, knocking his opponent to the floor. The gun clattered to the floor, and the older man didn't get up from where he landed, facedown.

Brody moved quickly to kick the gun out of Guidry's reach, then, arms shaking, he held the shovel over his head, ready to strike again. But Guidry was eerily still.

He could go on swinging, Brody knew, smashing the shovel blade against the killer's skull until the horrid man was unquestionably dead. His breath sawing from his aching lungs, Brody hovered over Guidry, watching for movement, considering the chance he had to rid the earth of Guidry's evil once and for all.

But by killing a man, already knocked unconscious, Brody would sink to Guidry's level. He was no murderer. And Brody knew killing the man now would no longer be self-defense.

"Brody!" Anya cried, pulling him from his moral deliberation. He hurried to her.

"Anya! Where are you hurt? What did he do?" He set the wooden chair back on its legs and climbed up to reach the S-hook keeping her suspended.

"I'll be—" she coughed and squeezed her watering eyes closed "—all right. H-how did you find me?"

"Time for that story later," he said. His fingers scrabbled at the plastic strip binding her hands. When he took a beat to assess the situation, the S-hook, he shifted tactics and looped the arm on his uninjured side around her waist. Grunting and working through the fiery pain in his midsection, he lifted her an inch, then two, so she could wiggle her bound hands off the S-hook. He gritted his teeth, as she struggled, until she finally wiggled her constrained hands off the hook.

When Anya's feet touched the floor, he released her.

Her legs wobbled, and he had to catch her when she swayed.

"Can you walk?" He panted for a breath, holding his throbbing side. "We have to get out—"

"Brody, he's getting up!"

Setting her away from him, he pivoted to face Guidry, who'd made it to his knees and was staggering to his feet. Brody's head swam as he bent to grab the shovel from the floor.

Guidry reached him before he could straighten, tackling him with a growl. The impact, when the two men hit the floor, sent shockwaves of pain from Brody's ribs through his torso. He grappled with Guidry, twisting and fighting to get the man's weight off him.

His opponent grabbed a handful of Brody's hair and used the leverage to smack Brody's head against the floor. Brody groaned as spots swam in his vision. Then, for no apparent reason, Guidry was gone, rolling off Brody and scrambling away. He heard Anya yelp, and his chest squeezed. Struggling to his knees, he raised his head in time to see Guidry snatch the pistol from the floor in the corner of the room.

Anya!

Focused only on protecting Anya, Brody shoved to his feet and dashed to throw himself between Anya and the gun.

Brody lunged toward her, and in the next heartbeat, Guidry's gun fired. The blast reverberated in the small room, and percussive waves echoed in Anya's chest. When she and Brody tumbled to the floor, the impact of their landing stole her breath.

With her hands still bound, she struggled to right herself, to scramble for cover. But Brody's weight pinned her down, and her heartbeat thumped in her still ringing ears. She heard a scuffling sound and jerked her gaze up. Guidry stood over them, but each time he squeezed of the trigger, the gun gave only an impotent click.

Relief swept through her. When Brody rolled away and clambered to his feet, Guidry tossed the gun aside and charged toward Brody. Brody met Guidry's attack with fierce determination blazing in his eyes, but Anya could see the toll the hand-to-hand combat was taking on him. She had to do something to help Brody. But how? Her hands were still bound and—

Remembering what she'd learned from her self-defense class about breaking zip ties, Anya mustered all her strength and scooted across the floor. Using the wall to help brace her as she shinnied to her feet, she fisted her hands and raised her bound wrists in front of her. Clenching her back teeth, she drew her arms toward her gut in a quick motion, her wrists stiff. The move did nothing but send fresh pain arcing up her arms. Frustrated, she tried again twice more with no luck.

Her gaze flicked to Brody who was locked in a wrestler's hold with Guidry, neither man yielding. Guidry's arm was choking Brody, and anger flashed through Anya. Two could play that cruel game. She stumbled across the room and swung her bound arms over Guidry's head from behind and pulled the zip tie of her bound wrists taut over the serial killer's throat.

Guidry jerked in surprise, releasing Brody as he grabbed with scrambling fingers to loosen her hold on his neck, to relieve the crushing pressure on his windpipe. As Guidry gasped and struggled, Brody crawled out of the other man's reach, coughing and sucking air into his own starved lungs. Anya's wrists stung from the thin plastic digging deeper into her skin. But she didn't care. Until Guidry was incapacitated, until she knew Brody was safe, her pain meant nothing.

But Guidry was strong, and her limbs were numb after being strung up to the chandelier. When he grabbed her wrists and twisted hard to the left, he was able to jerk her off balance. She stumbled and landed on the floor with an "Oof." With her arms still tangled around his neck, Guidry fell with her. In seconds he'd freed himself from the loop of her bound arm and rolled to straddle her. His hands clamped on her throat as rage colored his face a mottled crimson. Anya wheezed, and her lungs burned, needing air.

She heard a roar, and from her peripheral vision, a blur of motion.

Chapter 21

Brody swung the shovel at Guidry with all his strength, a primal howl of rage ripping from his throat. Guidry glanced from Anya to Brody just as the spade arced down and smashed into his face. Blood spurted from Guidry's nose, which sat at an odd angle now, clearly broken. Guidry's eyes rolled back, and he slumped sideways.

Anya gulped oxygen when Guidry's hands fell from her throat, and Brody took precious seconds to go to her. He stroked the hair back from her face and whispered hoarsely, "I'll be with you soon, sweetheart. I have to tie him first."

"Brod—" she rasped, "I lo—"

Not waiting to hear her out—even now Guidry was groaning and cradling his face—Brody kissed Anya's temple. Shoving his hands under her arms, he dragged her to the kitchen as much out of harm's way as he had time for. "Get up, if you can!" he told her, scurrying over to the plastic sack he'd ditched on the floor earlier. "Get out of the house! Run!"

She shook her head, and his heart sank. Was she being stubborn or was she that badly hurt? He didn't have time to argue. Grabbing the roll of duct tape, he pulled off a strip...four-inches long. The end of the roll. Growling his frustration, he wadded the tape and scrounged in the sack for the replacement Weed eater string, then raced back into the front room.

Shaking from the inside out, Anya sat numbly staring after Brody, regaining a little more strength and focus with each breath she sucked into her lungs. She glanced down at her still-bound hands and moaned softly. The damn things had to come off! She was nearly useless to Brody until her hands were freed. Climbing awkwardly to her feet, she assumed the stiff-wrist position with her arms bent at the elbow again. Pouring all her fear, anger and frustration into the motion, she jerked her arms toward her body...and the plastic zip tie snapped.

Her hand felt as if they were on fire as blood rushed back into them and numb nerves woke. She sagged against the kitchen counter until she heard the sound of a struggle in the next room. Limping to the dining room door, she found Brody once again contending, hand-to-hand with Sol. Searching around her, she dug in the same grocery sack and found only a metal file. A file and a plastic bag. Not much but maybe...

She was weary to the bone, her wrists bleeding from the zip ties, and her head and pinkie throbbing from Sol's abuse, but she squared her shoulders and marched into the breech again. Brody needed help, and she would not give up the fight until Guidry was vanquished— or she was.

Like a wild animal that found strength to fight with the mortal wounds, Guidry fought Brody's attempts to bind his hands. Brody tried sitting on the man's back, Guidry face down, only to be bucked off. Guidry, his face bloodied, flipped over and spat at Brody. When Brody tried to restrain the killer again, Guidry bit Brody's arm. Despite the savage pain, Brody refused to release his prey.

And then Anya was there. Brody's heart lurched, and he shouted, "No, Anya! Get out of here! Get somewhere safe!"

She ignored him, and ripping the grocery sack she'd brought from the kitchen, she sat on Guidry's thrashing legs. Once his legs were pinned by her body weight, she wrapped the plastic bag around his ankles and cinched a knot.

She looked up at him triumphantly and asked, "Now what?"

Brody twitched a brief grin. "Help me turn him, then hold his arms."

Together they rolled Sol back onto his stomach, and she helped Brody wrench the struggling killer's arms behind his back. She held his shoulders down while Brody used the entire coil of plastic Weed eater string to bind Guidry's arms.

When he was finished, Brody raised his gaze to Anya's. He had so much he wanted to say to her, so much he wanted to promise her. But he couldn't...not yet.

* * *

Anya had expected a grin of victory or relief, a profession of love or questions about her injuries. Instead, Brody said, "It's not enough. Find something else to tie him with. Something strong we can use to secure him to until help arrives."

She wanted to wilt in exhaustion and nurse her raw wrist and her aching body. But one look at the black glower on Sol's bashed and bloodied face sent a chill through her. That face would appear in her nightmares for years to come.

While Brody held Guidry down, Anya stumbled through the empty house, wondering what she could use to more securely tie their captive. The man who'd once made her and other women his captive. *His collection.*

She shivered realizing how close she'd come to being his next victim.

Shaking off the morbid thought, her attention flew to the sheets and shabby blankets covering all the windows. Raising weak arms, she yanked down the thick blanket on the dining room window, and where a tear had started, she tugged, gritting her teeth until the frayed fabric ripped into strips.

Together, she and Brody tied Sol from one end to the other. They weren't taking any chances of the serial killer getting loose before the police arrived. When the last strip of cloth had been knotted at Guidry's ankles, she slumped onto the floor and let tears of relief pool in her eyes.

Lifting her ravaged hand, she stared through the blur of moisture at the raw nail bed of her pinkie. The fingernail would grow back, she knew. She told herself to be glad a fingernail was all she lost. Sol could have cut off her hand. Killed her. Killed Brody.

She shuddered and wrapped her arms around herself at the thought. But she couldn't stop shaking—too much adrenaline left in her system. She needed to clean the wounds on her wrists, as well, check Brody's injuries... but in the wake of the past hours' terror and constant vigilance, mustering the wherewithal to administer first aid seemed a Herculean effort.

Brody moved to the window and stared out as if searching for...something.

"If the cops don't come soon... I'll go—" He winced, and holding his side, he hobbled over to her and lowered himself awkwardly beside her. "You're safe now, sweetheart." He lifted one of her hands to his lips, then seemed to see her raw wrists for the first time. He frowned and angled his head to meet her eyes. "You're hurt." His chest rose and fell as his gaze sparked with anger. "What else did the son of a bitch do to you?"

She shook her head, not even wanting to think about the past several hours.

When he twisted to face her, he sucked in a sharp breath and clutched his side again.

His breathing was rapid and shallow, and somehow, through her brain fog, she recognized the problem his abnormal breathing posed. "You're going to...pass out if you don't...stop that. Slow breaths. Deeper, Brody."

He grimaced. "It hurts too much to breathe any deeper."

Finally, it clicked, and her nurse training clawed its way past her shock and fatigue. The memories she'd been trying to hold at bay rolled like a film in her mind's eye. Brody arriving at her house like an avenging angel, a struggle. Gun shots. Brody lying still…

"You were shot," she rasped.

He ducked his chin in a nod. "Grazed. I'll be okay."

Heart thundering, she shifted to her knees and dropped her gaze to the bloody, makeshift bandage taped to his side. "I need to check it. I have to—"

He caught her hands. "It'll keep until we get to the ER."

"But I—"

He leaned in, kissed her gently and hissed through his teeth. "I was so scared I would be too late."

Tears leaked onto her cheeks. "I thought you were dead."

He shook his head, thumbing away the moisture on her cheeks. "Anya, I—"

Brody stopped, glanced behind him to where Guidry glared at the two of them. Facing her again, he sighed and kissed her nose. "Later. When we have privacy."

Hours passed before Brody had a moment alone with Anya. The cops and EMTs arrived at the old farmhouse within minutes of Brody tying off the last strip around Guidry's feet. Two different calls had come into the Valley Haven police department within moments of each other—one from a man saying he'd been asked to call the police by a man who'd then driven away and the second from a woman who reported finding Brody's truck blocking the highway and the note he'd left. Brody smiled to himself, silently thanking the strangers who'd come through for him.

After identifying themselves and Guidry for the police, Brody and Anya gave a quick recap of recent events, the key moments of Guidry's terror campaign that evening. All three of them were transported to the local hospital, Guidry under police guard and Anya in the same ambulance as Brody.

Brody held Anya's hand all the way to the hospital, refusing to let go, even when the EMTs were treating his gunshot wound or her savaged wrists and pinkie. He blamed himself for not doing more to protect her when he'd known Guidry was out there, had been following her and was a threat. He'd never forgive himself for his failure, but he prayed Anya could.

Brody stared at the ceiling above his ER exam room bed. He hadn't called anyone from his family…yet. There would be time for that later. He was safe, his injuries relatively minor—a shallow gunshot wound and two cracked ribs being primary. In time, he'd heal. No biggie. No need to bother the clan in the middle of the night. He'd already caused them so much worry in recent days.

Right now, he could only think of Anya. When he closed his eyes, he saw her huddling over the searcher who had been shot, risking her own life to render aid to a fallen colleague. And standing on a rickety chair with a shovel handle, working until her hands were raw to ensure they had a ventilation hole. And giggling over Oreos and lame jokes on her couch. And kissing him yesterday while her whole heart shone in her eyes.

Compassion, dedication, conviction, humor, passion, beauty. How could he have doubted she was everything he wanted in a woman…and more?

Isla had warned him not to hurt Anya because she knew the truth about him. He'd spent too many years uncommitted to anything or anyone, living a carefree bachelor life. Even before leaving home, he'd had three sisters, a doting mother and an indulgent Nanna who'd spoiled and catered to him. He hadn't had to sacrifice or compromise often in his life.

But when he'd seen Anya with her hands bound over her head, strung up like prey for Guidry to torture, something primal had shifted inside Brody, and he'd known he'd give anything, even his own life to save her. His world would be bleak, black, empty without Anya. The bachelor who'd had the world at his feet for years only wanted to lay the world at the feet of the woman who'd spent her life wanting to fit in, be included, be seen for the amazing woman she was.

He wanted Anya, and he didn't want to wait another moment for a doctor to discharge him or allow him into her exam room. "Family only" be damned. Anya was more than family to him. She was his life, his world.

After unclipping and detaching all the IVs and monitors hooked up to him, he swung his feet to the floor and headed out of his exam room. Brody stepped into the hallway and looked left, right. He spotted the policeman posted outside Guidry's room and gave the man a nod. "Any idea which room Anya's in?"

The man raised one eyebrow, clearly suspicious.

Before the officer had a chance to voice his reluctance to provide any information, someone opened the door across the hall from him. A nurse came out, her eyes red from crying, and she paused in the door to say to her patient, "I'm just so, so glad you're okay. What a nightmare you've been through! I'll tell the pharmacy to put a rush on those pain meds. Okay, sweetie?"

He heard a soft familiar voice say, "Thanks, Angie."

The nurse gave Brody a grin as she closed Anya's door and hustled back toward the nurses' desk.

Drawing a hand over his mouth, he held his hospital gown closed in back and stepped across the hall. He gave a quick knock and without waiting for permission, he ducked inside.

Anya blinked groggily at him and sat up on her bed.

"Brody? What's wrong? Why—"

"Nothing's wrong. I just…wanted to check on you."

She gave him a tired smile. "I'll be all right. My co-workers are falling over themselves to help me, get me anything and everything I could want." She pointed to the bedside tray full of drinks, snacks and magazines. "Want anything?"

You. I want you. He almost said it aloud but caught it before it slipped from his tongue. He wanted to be more eloquent. Wanted to explain his earlier hesitancy, apologize for the mixed messages he'd probably given her. He wanted her to be certain of how he felt before he proposed—

He blinked hard when he thought about where they were, how he'd met Anya in this same ER eight months ago and been instantly smitten with her. Proposed to her…

His head swam a little, and he sat heavily in the chair beside her bed.

"Brody? Are you okay?" Anya asked, swinging her feet to the floor, ready to help him if he fell out. "Should I call for Angie?"

"No…no. I… I had a shot of…something…for pain. It's got me a little woozy but—" He saw the events play out in his mind like last summer, and it just seemed… perfect. Full circle. Fate.

He took her hand in his and met her look of concern with a sappy grin. "Anya Patel, will you marry me?"

Her eyes widened, and for an instant, he thought he saw a smile ghost over her lips. But then her brow dented. Her face darkened, and she shook her head. "No."

Chapter 22

"No?" Nanna repeated in shock. "How could the lass say no to ye?"

Brody shrugged. "Guess I misread her. I thought we had something...more than..."

"Well, didna you ask her why 'no'?"

"Nah. After she said no, I didn't see much reason to stick around. Her nurse came back in and I...took off." He waved his hand vaguely, then let his voice fall silent. "If it's all the same to you, I'd...rather not talk about it right now, either. Is Dad here?"

"No, I'm afraid not, *mo laochain*. He took your mother to the farmers market to arrange her booth for this summer."

Brody nodded, then asked, "*Mo laochain*? I don't know that one."

"My little hero."

He snorted. "Some hero. I let the woman I love get

kidnapped by a serial killer. No wonder she said no. How could she ever trust me in the small things if I failed so grandly in the most important thing—keeping her safe?"

Nanna sat back in her wheelchair as if shoved, her brow beetling. "Are ye daft?"

Brody frowned. "What?"

"Did ye hit your *heid*?"

He goggled at his grandmother, confused by her scolding tone. "I, uh…"

Leaning toward him again, Nanna seized both his hands and nailed a stern, narrow-eyed look on him that he'd never seen from his kindly grandmother before. "See here, Brody Cameron. That young lady is alive today because ye took extraordinary measures to find her, to rescue her! Not keep her safe? Pfft!"

"But if I'd—"

"Furthermore," Nanna continued, "ye helped get that jackal of a man off the streets! Ye made the world safer for the women he would have gone on to kidnap and torture. Heaven only knows how many lives ye and Anya saved by stopping that man's reign of terror! So when I call ye my little hero, don' ye snort at me! Ye have done well, dear Brody. I am *verra* proud of ye."

Love and gratitude for his grandmother's encouraging words swelled in his chest, but even Nanna's reassurances couldn't fill the hole Anya left when she'd refused his offer of marriage. Clearly he'd misunderstood her feelings for him and made a fool of himself for a second time, blurting his proposal. He'd been grateful when Angie had entered the room with a prescription for Anya. The distraction gave him the opportunity to slip out of the room and lick his wounds.

Anya had said no—again. No further discussion needed.

Except his family, especially Nanna, had wanted to talk about nothing else. *How's Anya? When are you bringing her by for dinner again? What do you mean it's over between you?*

Now, Brody squeezed Nanna's frail hands and forced a smile for her. "Thank you. But it doesn't change the fact that Anya doesn't see things the same way. She turned me down. I—"

"Haven't given her a chance to explain," Nanna interrupted. "The woman who ate dinner with us the night of your rescue was in love with ye. I saw it in the way she looked at ye. She could barely look at anyone else for staring at ye with her heart in her eyes."

Brody clenched his back teeth and swallowed the knot of wistfulness that clogged his throat. "That's a nice idea for fairy tales, but real life isn't as simple as starry-eyed looks, Nanna. We were already on rocky ground. I was headed to her house to work things out when the whole scene with Guidry blew up in our faces."

"Well," Nanna jerked a nod and squared her shoulders, "then it sounds to me like ye owe her a proper conversation."

"Nanna, she said no. Twice."

"Your grandda proposed to me five times before I said yes. I couldn't see marrying a man from America and leaving my homeland, even if he did have Scottish blood. But doin' so was the best choice of my life."

Brody rubbed a hand on his face, deliberating. Wishing. Wanting.

"Go to my room and get me the wooden box at the

bottom of my top dresser drawer. Aye?" Nanna said, patting his knee.

He gave his grandmother a curious look then nodded and did as she'd asked. Holding the box on her lap, she told him more about her courtship with his grandfather. Then, opening the box, she showed him the treasures she kept inside and said firmly, "Anya is worth pursuing. Talk to her, Brody. Then ask her again."

"He left?" Chloe asked, her eyes wide with dismay. "He asked you to marry him then walked out without so much as a goodbye?"

Anya nodded to her best friend and wiped condensation from her soda can with her thumb. "As if I needed more proof that he's too...unpredictable, too unsure of his feelings and... I don't know. Uncommitted?"

Chloe twisted her mouth. "But...he proposed. Isn't that evidence he's willing to commit?"

"You'd think so, but all I could think when he blurted out the question was how he'd done the same thing last summer, right there in the ER the day we met. He didn't really mean it then, and... I just couldn't believe he meant it last week, either. He'd just said he was woozy from pain meds. How could I believe he—"

A knock from her front door interrupted her, and her pulse jolted. She was still jumpy after having her home broken into, being kidnapped and tortured. She'd had no peace since coming home, what with the media hounding her and the police asking her to relive the horror in order to detail for them what had transpired in that remote farmhouse.

"Expecting someone?" Chloe asked.

"No."

"Want me to get it for you?" Chloe rose from her

chair, ready to suit action to her words. "I can send whoever it is away."

Anya nodded. "Thanks."

While her friend went to her door, Anya propped her elbows on the table and leaned her forehead against her palms. Why couldn't the world leave her alone? She was tired. Sore. Heartbroken.

She didn't want to give another interview. Didn't want accolades for her "heroic actions" or flowers from admirers. She didn't want to talk to the police, her neighbors or the women's auxiliary group anymore. She didn't want to talk to anyone. Except...

"Brody!" Chloe said down the hall, as if speaking Anya's thoughts.

Anya yanked her head up, her heart tripping, when she heard the warm male voice that had filled her dreams for the past weeks. Her balm in the darkness. Her companion and comfort. Her heart.

"She doesn't want to talk to you. Or anyone. I'm supposed to send people away so she can have some peace."

Anya lurched out of her chair and hurried to the foyer. "Actually..."

Chloe turned, a question denting her brow, and Brody seized the chance to push past her guard dog into her house. "Five minutes, Anya. Give me just five minutes to say what I have to say, then I'll leave you alone."

Leave you alone...

"Leave her alone?" Chloe repeated, picking up on the same sentiment that lanced Anya's heart. "If your plan is to leave her, don't make it worse with excuses and justifications—"

"Five minutes," Anya said, silencing Chloe.

"Are you sure?" Chloe asked, her concern written in her expression.

Anya nodded. "We can talk on the steps."

Brody exhaled heavily, as if he'd been holding his breath, prepared to be turned down. A smile flickered at the corner of his mouth, and he motioned to her to lead the way out to her yard.

She stepped out into the late spring evening, the scent of wild honeysuckle and her neighbors' gardenias perfuming the air. She usually savored the scents, but today they felt cloying, suffocating. Or maybe that was her own fault. She worked to release the tension in her chest, breath normally, not hold it in...

"Okay," she sat down on the top step and drew her knees close, hugging them with her arms as if to hold herself together. "So talk."

"Well, I uh...wanted to apologize."

"Apologize? For what?"

"I swore I wouldn't hurt you, but it seems I have. And I am so sorry. If I could take back whatever I did—" He huffed, and when he dropped heavily on the step beside her, she noticed the wooden box about the size of a book, in his hands. "Hell, I don't even know what I did wrong...specifically. I know I didn't protect you the way I promised I would, and I'll have to live with that failure the rest of my—"

"Brody, stop. Do you really think that's why I'm upset? You saved my life! I've no doubt I'd be dead now if you hadn't come after us."

"Then why..." His hand fisted, reflecting his frustration. "Why did you say *no* to my proposal?"

"Because...we hadn't talked. Because I didn't know..." She stopped and swallowed hard when a painful knot of emotion clogged her throat. "I wasn't sure, wasn't really sure how you felt about me."

"Weren't sure? I asked you to marry me!" His eyes

widened, and his eyebrows lifted. "Isn't that proof of how I feel?"

"No! You've asked me before, and it was joke."

"But this time was different. This time it was real."

"But how am I supposed to believe it's what you really want?" She threw up her hands. "The other day you were telling me you can't even commit to getting a dog! How am I supposed to believe you're really interested in committing to a girlfriend? To a *wife*?"

"Anya…"

She put a hand on his chest when he scooted closer. "How do I know you won't change your mind or wake up in a year or so having decided I'm an…*encumbrance*, like you called a dog, or…simply not the kind of girl a guy marries after all."

He pulled a face. "I called a dog an encumbrance?"

"You did."

"Well, I didn't mean—wait, not the kind of girl I'd marry?"

Tears welled and she blinked, fighting them back. "That's how Mark put it."

"Mark? Your ex?" He stiffened, and his eyes snapped with blue fire. "Wait a minute. Are you pushing me away because of what Mark did?" He screwed up his face and shook his head. "Anya, I'm…you can't… I know he hurt you, but—"

"But nothing, Brody. I can't repeat the same mistake I made—"

"Am I a mistake? Is that how you see me?" he asked, seizing her arms. "'Cause if I am that to you—a mistake—then I'll walk away now and not bother you again. It will kill me, but I'd rather suffer then cause you any pain."

Anya caught her breath. "I don't...want you to be a mistake. But how do I know...how do I trust..."

"Me? How do you trust me?" he supplied, his voice revealing his hurt.

"Not you. How do I trust myself? I misjudged Mark's feelings for me. Before I let myself love you, I have to be sure I'm not making another mistake."

"Are you saying..." Brody took a deep breath as if fighting to keep his composure or finding the strength for a terrible task. "Does that mean you don't love me?"

Anya opened her mouth to say "I can't" but snapped her teeth closed, trapping the lie. She owed him the truth. "Maybe that's the problem. I already do, and... I'm scared."

A tender compassion filled his eyes. "Honestly? Me, too, but—" He stroked his knuckles along her jaw. "You know that dog I didn't want to get? That I couldn't commit to?"

She nodded.

"I said I wanted to be free to go places, explore the world without worrying about a dog, but I never do go anywhere on a lark. Without someone to share it with, travel seems...lonely. As much as I hated being trapped on that mountain for two days, I look back now and think how wonderful it was to have you there with me. My house, my *life* feels empty without you beside me, Anya. And nearly losing you to Guidry showed me that I don't want just anyone to share my days—I want you."

A sweet stab of relief pierced her chest, and she rasped, "Brody..."

He raised a hand, stopping her. "Look, I know I've asked you to marry me...several times. So I'm not going to ask you again."

Anya's heart squeezed. Had she lost the best thing

in her life because she'd been too scared of rejection to reach for real love? "Brody, I—"

"Not without giving you proof first of how I feel. I want you to know, one hundred percent, I'm not under the influence of any pain medicine. I mean what I'm saying here, today."

She thumbed moisture from her eyes and nodded.

"But first, I want you to have this." He handed her the wooden box he'd been cradling on his lap.

Puzzled, Anya took the box and lifted the lid. Under a sheet of tissue paper, she found a layer of soft red wool with a tartan plaid of broad green stripes and a thin gold stripe.

"It's, um…lovely." She stroked a hand over it, savoring the softness. "But I don't understand. It's kinda early for Christmas things, isn't it?"

"It's not a Christmas decoration. It's a shawl." His expression was way more expectant and hopeful than fit a basic gift. Something else was afoot, she realized, and set the box on her legs as she examined his offering more closely. With trembling hands, she lifted the edge of the wooly wrap from the box, and discovered a worn tag that read, *McNabb Tartans Company—Clan Cameron.*

Without asking, she knew. This wasn't a new shawl. It was an heirloom. Her breath caught as she scrambled to recall her British history, or more specifically Scottish history. Tartans were more than pretty plaids worn by Scots. They identified the many clans through the centuries. Tartans were a mark of familial belonging. Of inclusion, protection, loyalty. And Brody was giving her one from his clan, his family…

"Brody, I—" As she lifted the soft wool to her cheek, her heart thundering, she heard the clink of metal. Attached to the shawl was an elaborate brass pin, like a giant safety pin, but far more decorative, bejeweled and bearing a few tarnished silver charms.

And one shiny ruby solitaire ring.

She raised a stunned glance to Brody.

"I know these days a diamond is more common," he said, "but you said you like red. And I figured it would match your earrings…and my family's tartan."

She swallowed hard trying to find words.

"With me being her oldest Cameron grandson, Nanna gave me this tartan and that kilt pin brooch to pass on the family name and a bit of our history. I want you to have it. I want you to be a Cameron, Anya."

The knot of emotion that silenced her squeezed tighter.

"Be my wife, Anya. Be part of my clan, my family, my life. And let me be part of yours. I want to know your family, your Patel traditions, and blend them with mine to build our own unique traditions and history together."

The surprise and poignancy that had clogged her throat gave way to a joy and love that stole her breath. But she nodded. And tears puddled and spilled from her eyes. And she flung her arms around Brody's neck and clung to him.

"All right, listen." He pulled back and flashed a lop-sided grin as he dashed at her tears with his palms. "I've proposed too many times and been told 'no' too often to be denied the benefit of *hearing* you say 'yes.'"

She scowled as she laughed and struggled for a breath.

He raised his eyebrows and tipped his head slightly, waiting.

After one more cleansing breath she managed a strangled, "Yes."

As if someone had turned on the sun behind his eyes, his blue gaze filled with light and his smile beamed at her. "Finally!"

Anya filled her lungs, as the pressure of years of doubt and her childhood need for acceptance lifted like the morning mist from the mountains. "Yes!" she said more clearly, laughter ringing in her voice. "Oh, definitely yes! I love you, Blue Eyes."

He kissed her deeply, lingering, unhurried as they savored the moment. Finally, he touched his forehead to hers and whispered breathlessly, "And I, being of sound mind and free of all inebriants, love you, too."

* * * * *

Don't miss other thrilling books by Beth Cornelison:

Kidnapping in Cameron Glen
Mountain Retreat Murder
In the Rancher's Protection
Rancher's Hostage Rescue
Rancher's Covert Christmas
Rancher's Deadly Reunion
Rancher's High-Stakes Rescue

Available now wherever
Harlequin Romantic Suspense
books and ebooks are sold!

#2235 UNDER COLTON'S WATCH
The Coltons of New York
by Addison Fox
US Marshal Aidan Colton is sworn to protect those in his custody. But he's never had a more tempting—or challenging—assignment than pregnant marine biology professor Ciara Kelly, who's become the target of a killer. Can he keep his professional distance, or is it already too late?

#2236 PLAYING WITH DANGER
The Sorority Detectives
by Deborah Fletcher Mello
When New Orleans police detective King Randolph starts on the murder investigation of a young woman found in the Louisiana swamps, he discovers private investigator Lenore Martin is also on the case. Forced to team up, both find that working together has its own challenges because the attraction between them cannot be denied.

#2237 SECRETS OF LOST HOPE CANYON
Lost Legacy
by Colleen Thompson
With an abusive marriage and damaged reputation behind her, real estate agent Amanda Greenville does not want any entanglement with her roguish cowboy client. But handsome Ryan Hale-Walker may be her last chance to fight off a dangerous land grab—and heal her wounded heart as well.

#2238 DRIVEN TO KILL
by Danielle M. Haas
When the driver of a car-sharing service attacks Lauren Mueller, she barely escapes with her life. Now she must trust the one man she never wanted to see again— Nolan Clayman, the detective responsible for the death of her brother—to keep her alive.

HARLEQUIN
PLUS

Try the best multimedia subscription service for romance readers like you!

Read, Watch and Play.

Experience the easiest way to get the romance content you crave.

Start your **FREE TRIAL** at
<u>www.harlequinplus.com/freetrial</u>.